THE COLLECTIVE

R. S. WILLIAMS

Copyright © 2017 R S Williams

All rights reserved. No part of this publication may be reproduced in any form, except for reasonable quotations for review purposes, without prior written permission from the author.

This book is a work of fiction. Any references to historical events, real people or real people are used fictitiously. Locales and public names are sometimes used for atmospheric purposes. Other names, characters, places and events are products of the authors imagination, and any resemblance to actual events, places, or persons, living or dead, is entirely coincidental.

ISBN: 1539948390

ISBN-13: 978-1539948391

Cover Design by Victoria Cooper Art

Edited by Utopia Editing & Ghost writing Services, LLC

Formatted by R S Williams

❀ Created with Vellum

*to my parents
who always stood behind me and allowed me
to follow my dreams, no matter how many
times they changed*

*

"Not all treasure is silver and gold mate" -
Jack Sparrow, *Pirates of the Caribbean*

1

TILLY

Matilda Gregson took a step back from the stack of books she had been looking through and cringed as they came crashing down. Standing with one in hand, she peeked through her fingers to see if anyone had noticed the commotion she had created. Thankfully, the librarian was still tapping away at her keyboard. Although, she imagined the woman's expression turning sour as she continued hitting the keys. The students on the table to Tilly's left were all wearing headphones, completely oblivious to her accident.

This dissertation will be the end of me, she thought as her eyes rolled at the mess she made. Since her father died she'd had a keen interest in History as he used to read her bedtime stories about historic adventures. Her father was an archaeologist, always amid history, and a storyteller. It led her to the decision to study History at university; she wanted to teach it to other children as her father had done with her, although unknowingly through made-up tales.

During her studies, she'd found that one of her main interests was pirates, a keen feature in most of her father's stories. But writing her dissertation around them didn't make it any easier. It meant long nights of research and takeout food sessions in the library. Even if food technically wasn't allowed in the library. Tilly had gotten good at smuggling in coffee and energy drinks too, to keep from falling asleep.

The librarian's keyboard tapping stopped. Tilly supposed the librarian was just waiting to finish her sentence before coming to see the commotion. The dreaded sound of the woman's heels hit the wooden floor. Shit. Tilly tried to pull herself together before the librarian got closer. Taking a few steps back, she stumbled into another stack of dangerously misplaced books and toppled them over.

"Miss Gregson, I've asked you before not to make a commotion, I'm afraid I'm going to have to restrict your access for the week." Her voice sounded like it was coming from her nose, like Roz from Monsters Inc.

"But I'm doing my dissertation! Please, Elaine, I can't afford to not be in here," Tilly pleaded. "I'll clean everything up right now. I didn't mean to—"

"Just like you didn't mean to spill your second cup of coffee this morning? Which by the way nearly ruined my shoes."

Tilly attempted to make a puppy dog eye face at Elaine, in the hopes it might make her punishment less harsh. Getting kicked out of the library was not an option for her at this point. Her dissertation was due in a few weeks.

The librarian sighed. "You'll just have to take a collection of books and go for today. Last chance, if I catch you again -" The woman pointed at her and Elaine's face went a shade of red as she turned and walked away mumbling.

Tilly knew there was nothing Elaine could do to keep her out of the library. It was integral to every student for study and research, but that doesn't mean she couldn't kick Tilly out for the day. Tilly watched Elaine sit back at her desk and then bent down to start clearing up the books. She didn't see the point in stacking them up again but she couldn't just leave the sea of literature she had created in the centre of the aisle.

From her crouched position on the floor, Tilly could see the librarian's desk, and the librarian herself continued to peer around a teetering stack of Harry Potter books to glare at her. Tilly flushed and quickened her pace. Another person came around the corner and stepped on her hand, causing Tilly to cry out.

"Oh shit, sorry, I didn't see you there." The girl's voice was quiet. She seemed just as shy as Tilly was.

"That's all right," Tilly replied, shaking the pain away. "I hadn't intended to be on the floor, but for some reason, students are lazy and can't seem to put books back on the shelf properly."

"Ah, so what actually did you do? I did hear some sort of crash and she doesn't seem very happy," said the girl with a smile, pointing in the direction of the librarian who'd returned to shooting Tilly random glares in between her work.

"I tried to get some books from the middle and they ended up toppling over. You'd think I'd ripped all the pages out of her precious books the way she stormed over here," said Tilly gesturing to the librarian. The girl laughed as Tilly turned back to her re-stacking. When Tilly looked up the girl had gone, so she grabbed the three books she needed before hurrying back to her desk, where her friend, James Bennett, was sitting.

"Are you all right?" asked James, who was sitting at the desk looking up from his book. "You're looking a bit red-faced."

"I may have been the cause of that horrible crash of books you just heard," Tilly whispered, a strand of her brunette hair falling in front of her face.

James just sniggered. He was Tilly's oldest friend at university. They'd met during fresher's week when they were assigned to live in the same flat, and though James' studies were in the scientific field and Tilly found herself absently nodding along when he talked about his work, they'd always been happy with each other's company. When they were together, she always felt warm; he made it easier for her to calm down if she was stressing out.

"Well, look who it is," came a voice from around the corner. "How are we both today? Working hard, I see."

Tilly looked up to see Chris standing behind James. His hands were on his hips, blonde hair styled into a quiff. Neither of them said anything to him, almost ignoring his presence except Tilly couldn't help but laugh at the face James was making. "Not talking to me, then?" Chris carried on, as Tilly put her hand to her mouth to hide her laughter.

"Coxy, are you coming to help us," James asked, "or distract us like you do every other time you're in here? " He seemed more than a little annoyed. Chris Cox had been friends with James since primary school, but Tilly had a feeling their friendship had grown strong enough to include more than the average number of irritations.

"I just came to get you to leave but, I'd love to help," he exclaimed as he took the seat beside Tilly and picked up one of the books she had brought to the table. "I'm not sure I know too much on your subject matter."

"Pirates," Tilly said immediately.

"Pirates... do the films count?" asked Chris teasingly.

"No Chris, Pirates of the Caribbean doesn't count, even if I am including it in my dissertation." Tilly laughed, taking the book out of his hands and hitting him with it. Chris threw his arms up in defence of her attack but they both just grinned and giggled a little too loudly. James did not find it amusing, even when Chris threw a book at him.

"Oi! Watch it, you. Do you really want Miss Gloomy over there to come over and kick you out again? I'm pretty sure you won't be allowed in soon, T."

Their short interaction was followed by a loud shushing noise coming from the front desk. 'Miss Gloomy' was the boys' official nickname for the librarian because she always looked either unhappy or unimpressed with everything; they'd had never once seen her smile.

"Sorry, mum," chimed Chris. They all chuckled and went back to their studying. It wouldn't be long before Miss Gloomy came to throw Tilly out for causing a commotion; there was only so much she could get away with before her exclusion from the library became permanent for the whole term.

With the time she still had, Tilly employed Chris to help her sort through several of the books on the table. There were a few on the most notorious pirates, like Blackbeard and Captain Kidd, along with some lesser-knowns like the Irish pirate Grace O'Malley. Tilly took the most interest in the great Bartholomew Roberts, though. As the most successful pirate during the Golden Age, he would be a prime focus of comparison for her dissertation.

"God, this stuff takes forever," James complained as he put his head in his hands and leant forward on the table. "Dissertations are so hard."

"Stop complaining. How many words have you written today?" asked Tilly. She was all about word counts, it made her feel like she achieved something. It's much easier to not get stressed when you know you only have to reach a certain amount. They had set 500 words as a minimum daily limit, an attempt to reach 10,000 without losing their minds. Plus, the limited time spent in the library allowed their stress levels to stay relatively balanced.

"I don't know, probably about four hundred or so." James gave her a cheeky look. "Does this mean we can go and get some food? I'm starving." As if on cue, his stomach grumbled, and Tilly and Chris laughed at him as he closed his laptop down and started picking up his books.

"You know I'm always up for food," Chris said, helping Tilly stack her books ready to check out. "I'll text Claire to meet us. Where shall we go?"

"Yeah, we know you're up for it, you eat like a pig," retorted James. "Let me go see Gloomy and take these out, then we can decide where to eat."

After James had gone, Tilly and Chris went to put the books she wasn't taking home back on the shelves. It was a surprise to Tilly to see the girl from earlier again, the girl's golden hair and pretty features easily spotted, now that she got a good look at her.

The girl inspected the books as if she was looking for something. Not like a student searching for information, though, almost like someone searching for something lost. Frantically turning the pages, of each book she picked up, scanning for missing information. Tilly watched her as Chris wandered off to grab more books from the table. Tilly couldn't understand what the girl was doing, or why she was in the library.

Of course, there were many students she hadn't seen before, but most students went up to the shelves, grabbed a couple books, and sat down. This girl was picking them up, going through them, and then replacing them, one at a time. If anyone looked hard enough, she made it obvious she wasn't a student, had anyone been looking at her.

Chris came around the corner with the last of Tilly's books and added them to the pile on the end of the aisle. He bumped into her as he stopped, knocking her vision from the girl back to Chris.

"Come on, we better go," he said. "James has checked out his books and Miss Gloomy was asking about you." Tilly turned back to see if she could grab the girl's attention before she left, but the girl had already gone.

James turned the corner. "You look confused," he said.

"No, not confused, just...it doesn't matter," replied Tilly. "Come on then, let's get some food."

"I am totally confused, but food is a much better idea," interjected Chris before James could say any more. "I'll check and see where Claire is."

They'd barely left the library when Claire ran to Chris and locked her arms around his neck. Tilly still found it amusing that she was the only girl who could knock him off his feet, considering she was nearly 6ft tall. Three inches taller than Chris and she never let him forget it. Claire entwined her fingers with his and they carried on, walking hand-in-hand beside Tilly and James. The Little Pizza Cafe was close to campus and away from the hustle and bustle of the city centre, and since it was where they always went for lunch there was no discussion over which direction to go.

"How's student life treating you all?" asked Claire as they wandered down the steps to the main road.

"Pretty good, I mean I get to see you every day," Chris replied, bringing a smile to Claire's face. Sometimes Tilly thought these two were sickly sweet with each other. Claire wasn't technically a student at Laguna Bay University, although she did take a photography class on Thursday evenings. She lived in the city and had been a stranger to them until she worked late one evening at a local shop on the same street as the cafe, as the three of them decided to get pizza. Chris acted like a fool and asked her to join them for food, and to everyone's surprise, she actually said yes.

"Dissertations are hard," James whined, prodding Tilly in the side. She swatted his hand away with a smile. "I mean, why do they make the last year so hard?"

"Because they think that's how we learn," replied Tilly.

"You guys are so funny," Claire pushed her cheek up against Chris' arm. "You two make such a cute couple."

Tilly scrunched up her nose in response. She hated it when Claire brought this up, there was no way James liked her, and even if he did, they were friends. It would be weird.

"Come on, stop talking and let's get eating I am hungry," said James changing the subject as he opened the café door.

Tilly and James grabbed their usual table while Claire and Chris ordered the food. James slouched down into the corner while Tilly sat directly opposite him.

"Right, I got two mighty meaty and one mozzarella for us to share," declared Chris as he took his seat next to Tilly. He looked around. "They'll bring them over in a bit," he said looking around. "A bit quiet today, isn't it?"

They all looked around at the empty café; it was only them and the staff. Tilly noticed a homeless guy outside, though. At least, she assumed he was homeless, his grey jumper looked tattered and worn along with his washed out brown trousers, and he'd paced the windows a couple of times already.

Tilly turned her attention back to her friends as the pizza was brought out, and as they dug in Claire boasted about how her modelling career was going to take off: "I'm having my second shoot tomorrow. I'll be in all these vintage costumes from the 1700s."

Surprised, Tilly asked, "The 1700s?" What were the odds it was the same era she was basing her dissertation on? There was no way she could imagine Claire, the most modern dresser of them all, in a dress with a corset.

"Yeah. Hey, that's the same as your dissertation, isn't it? D'you want to come?"

Tilly choked on her drink. "Is that allowed?"

"I guess. I'll have to ask permission, though. It's like an interview. If I do well, they'll hire me for more campaigns."

"So, why are you taking a photography class if you want to be a model?" James asked through a mouthful of pizza. Tilly grabbed another slice.

"Eventually, I'd like to get behind the camera. Modelling pays the bills, but photography can build a career," she said. Instead of grabbing from the tray, she stole a slice of pizza out of Chris's hands.

Tilly shook her head at James, who was clearly not impressed with Claire's ambitions. He hadn't liked her when they met her, and he'd tried to turn Chris away from her but Tilly thought that deep down it was just because he didn't want her to take away his oldest friend. The four of them passed the afternoon away into evening with idle chat until it was dark outside. Chris and Claire were the first to leave; the boys always walked Claire home, and since Tilly lived with them she always joined because it was better than walking the streets alone.

When it was time to go, Tilly struggled to untangle her bag from the chair leg while James looked on. "Stupid straps," she mumbled, cursing. "Get stuck on everything, I swear."

James just laughed and grabbed her arm. The momentum from James's tug along with the release from the chair made Tilly stumble and fall into his arms. They exchanged a few glances and smiles before returning to their own personal spaces. He opened the door and gestured for her to leave. What a gent.

As Tilly got outside she noticed the girl from the library was sitting at the bus stop. Before Tilly could begin crossing the road, someone grabbed hold of her.

"Please, some food," the homeless man said, latching even more roughly onto her forearm, his gaze deepening. This was extreme begging, she'd never seen this happen to anyone before. Dumfounded, she just stood there staring at him listening to the beat of her heart quickening in her ears.

"Hey! Let go of her," demanded James as he closed the cafe door behind him. Her wrist felt instantly lighter as the homeless man let her go.

"Do we have any leftover pizza, James?" she asked in a daze.

"We aren't giving him anything T, there's a shelter around the corner."

Tilly pouted at him, and she turned away from the homeless man, who still stood near them but with his head bowed towards the floor. As Tilly went to walk forward to cross the road James caught her arm and led her in the direction Chris and Claire were walking. They only took a few steps when she heard the homeless man mumble something about the girl.

"What was that?" she asked him, trying to avoid James's arm keeping her from him.

"Nothing, nothing, never mind, girl bad," replied the homeless man. He scurried off down the road.

"Are you okay?" asked James. "I don't really..." Tilly stopped mid-sentence. She was so interested in hearing the homeless man's comment that she lost sight of the girl across the road. She was gone now, and Tilly was extremely confused. Did the homeless man purposely try to distract her?

"Hey, don't let that freak worry you. People are crazy." James placed his hand on her arm before tilting his head in the direction of her house. "Let's get you home before he decides he wants to come back. You really shouldn't have offered him food, T."

She stuck her tongue out at him and they started to walk home.

2
JENNY

Jenny was new to the world of The Collective. The older members all had books that told them everything about history, the future and the present and if something went off course, they would have to get the situation fixed. Being part of this society was a great honour for Jenny, especially as her mother had been in it but sometimes she just wanted to have a bigger part within the system.

Yesterday in the library, that girl had interrupted her while she was flicking through the history of Salem. She was tasked with trying to find out if it matched the version of events she had been given by Regent Lance. If it didn't, she would have to report it to the Regents and then one of the Collectors would go and change the timeline back to how it was supposed to be.

The recruits didn't get to do a lot of the missions. They read books and reported strange events. Spending their first years in the libraries of the world while the higher ranks got to use portals to go back in time, and sort out the past without causing rifts and ruining the course of history. Of course, this had to be sanctioned by a Regent.

She didn't know how it worked but the Regents of The Collective had a book which held the history of the world. It changed or glowed or whatever it did, Jenny didn't know, but once it had changed and told them the problem they would send out the Collectors to set it right. The recruits, however, stayed behind and wished they could go to check that nothing in the past had gone awry.

Jenny frequently brought up problems hoping that one day they would finally take her with them, to shadow a collector and see what happens.

She was ready for the chance to change history back to its correct course but they wouldn't give it to her. Always telling her to be patient, her time will come. She had been in The Collective for just over a year and they still wouldn't promote her to Collector.

Although, she had gotten her chip implant, which meant things were looking up. New recruits had to wait at least a year for theirs, it only took Jenny 8 months. Jenny slammed her book shut in frustration. Thinking about how she wanted to do her parents proud by moving up in the ranks as fast as her mum had was frustrating, which is why she hadn't been reading through a history book like she was supposed to. Instead, she was sitting in a coffee shop reading her current favourite fantasy novel. She looked at her cold coffee and decided it was time to go home.

As she stuffed her book in her back, the door opened and Jenny looked up to see Charlotte, one of the senior Collectors, walk in. Jenny looked up to Charlotte like an older sister since she had no siblings it was nice to have someone to care about. Behind her was a girl Jenny had never seen before.

"This is the coffee shop most of us come to when we want some downtime," she heard Charlotte explain to the girl. "As you can see there's never many of us in here, except Jenny. How are you doing Jen?" Charlotte waived.

"Not too bad Char, is this your new recruit?" she asked offering them a seat with a wave of her hand.

"Yeah, just giving her a tour of the area. Jenny this is Natasha, she's just joined and starts her training tomorrow." Charlotte sat down and motioned for Natasha to join them.

"Nice to meet you, Natasha, when did you join?" asked Jenny trying to make conversation.

"Only about a week ago, I think I'm going to get the hang of it. Especially with Charlottes guidance." Jenny didn't like her tone, and couldn't help feeling the pang of jealousy. Her confidence was something Jenny would never have and it made her dislike Natasha. However, showing that would not be a good thing.

"I've already seen the library I'll be researching in," Natasha continued, "it's a public one so Charlotte says I'll need to be extra careful." She laughed and Jenny forced a smile at her.

"Nice, I patrol the university library. Hopefully, I'll get promoted soon, I can't wait to be a Collector Trainee. My mum would've wanted this for me," Jenny looked to the floor at the mention of her mother and Charlotte placed a hand on top of hers.

"She would already be proud of you Jen, just remember that," her comforting words always made Jenny feel better. "Are you coming to the ceremony tomorrow? It'll be the last time I get to see you for a while. I've got an assignment and I leave after it, so I have to make arrangements for Natasha."

"Oh, well I wasn't planning on it but sure, I'll come to see you off." Jenny hated ceremonies. They were for the Recruits who were becoming Collectors, a bit like a graduation ceremony, and watching someone else get her dream was not something Jenny wanted to watch. She hated it when Charlotte went away, she was left alone again.

"Are the new recruits allowed in?" asked Natasha.

"No, chipped personnel only," replied Charlotte taking her hand off Jenny's. "You'll make it there one day. It's a stupid rule but one that's been around since the beginning of The Collective." Natasha's eyes were filled with determination. Jenny hadn't seen that kind of recruit for a while, the last few had been recruited out of need because they'd seen things they shouldn't not because they wanted to join, so it was nice to see.

"That's a shame," said Natasha. "I'm going to get a coffee; do you want one?"

"No, thank you, I actually need to go before Harvey comes and finds me," replied Jenny, grabbing hold of her bag as she stood up.

"Still trying to avoid him I see," laughed Charlotte as Natasha walked off to the counter. Jenny scowled at her. "You know you can't avoid him forever, he is a Collector and your supervisor when he's not on assignment he's supposed to teach you and prepare you for your own graduation."

"Yes, except I don't like him and I want you to be my supervisor," said Jenny as she walked around the table. Walking back towards the door she pointed and smiled at Charlotte. As she turned away the door opened and she walked straight into someone's chest.

"Oh, shit I'm so—" she stopped her sentence when she looked up and realised Harvey was standing in front of her. "Oh, it's you. Regents send you?"

"No need for the snappy tone love, I've come to collect you," his very posh British accent always annoyed her. "Nice to see you, Char."

Jenny frowned at his use of her nickname for Charlotte. He knew exactly how to get her frustrated, no matter how many times she tried not to get annoyed at him.

"Nice to see you too Harvey," Charlotte said with a smile. "How did your assignment go?"

"It went well, someone decided that the Romanian Diamond wasn't worth stealing so I had to become a master thief and steal it myself," his tone was slightly flirtatious, which only angered Jenny, but Charlotte didn't react. "If I hadn't who knows if the train robbery would've even happened."

"Well at least everyone is on the right track, excuse the pun," said Charlotte. "Oh, thank you, Natasha. This is Harvey, Harvey this is my new recruit, Natasha."

"Nice to meet you, love," Harvey extended his arm out towards Natasha for a handshake and Jenny sighed loudly. Harvey turned around and smiled at her with a hint of defiance in his eyes. A black car pulled up outside and Harvey clapped his hands together. "Time to go, that's our ride, Jenny." He spun back around to Charlotte and Natasha. "See you girls at the meeting."

Turning back to Jenny he walked back and put his arm around her back, using his other hand to indicate Jenny should leave. She scowled at him again and walked out of the coffee shop. Her back still warm from his touch.

A meeting? Jenny wondered what that could be about. Harvey had come to get her, did that mean she was invited to the meeting too? Recruits don't normally go to meetings unless it's necessary, like being paired with a Collector or the graduating ceremonies or getting chips implanted. He held out his hand, indicating for her to get into the black car waiting on the side of the street.

"Are you going to tell me what this meeting is about?" asked Jenny getting into the car. She had to scoot over to the other side as Harvey nearly sat on her as he got in.

"Jenny, I know as much as you do, and even if I did you know I can't tell you," he replied.

"Can you at least tell me where it is being held?"

"No, I thought we would just sit in silence in the car," he replied tapping away at his phone. Jenny just rolled her eyes, his whole 'better than you' demeanour really annoyed her and that was another reason she sat silently in the back looking out the window. "We are going to the church."

She could feel him sitting there next to her. He'd almost stopped moving entirely if she didn't know any better she'd think that he wasn't breathing. Oh, to live in one of her favourite books. She would have been a vampire, but she didn't, she lived in the world where time travel was possible and it was a secret to most employees of every government organisation in the world. Knowledge was shared on a need to know basis, for example, those in power like the prime minister or the president would have full knowledge.

The Collective had a vast amount of power where the heads of state were concerned, but Jenny had a deep nagging feeling that she would never get that far in. She didn't think The Collective Regents believed in her enough.

"The Church? But isn't that headquarters? I thought official meetings there were only for Collector ranks and above?" she asked, a little confused as to why she was being allowed access to a meeting.

"Yes, however they require all chipped personnel to attend. I don't know more than that," he replied not looking up.

They didn't journey very far, in fact, there was no reason they needed to go in the car in the first place. She could have walked there faster.

After pulling up outside, Jenny was surprised that Harvey did the gentlemanly thing of opening the door for her. She frowned at him with distrust whilst he closed it behind her. Jenny had never been to an official meeting before, or one that included the Regents, Collectors and Recruits.

The church was typical in its appearance. Its stone exterior weathered with age and moss growing around the wooden doors. They walked up towards the church and entered through the front door, Jenny admired the gargoyles above as she walked through.

Inside there were minimal decorations, only the stained-glass window at the far end above the altar in the apse and the decorative colour drapes over the tables. Jenny shivered, ever since her parent's funeral she hated churches, the only reason she became part of The Collective was because she wanted to make them proud of her. Little did she know that would mean spending time in churches.

Harvey was holding onto her elbow with a tight grip that was making her arm hurt as he pulled her through the pews to the right. In front of them was a tapestry which Harvey moved to one side to reveal a door. They both went through, and inside the room was another door to a lift. From what she saw from the outside she knew they couldn't be going up either. Harvey took out a card and swiped it across the panel to the right and the doors opened. He pushed her in and then swiped the card again as if the lift would know where to take them.

The lift hadn't felt like it moved but the doors closed and opened again to reveal another hall. In front of her was an archway along with a round table – it reminded her of the story of King Arthur and his Knights of the Round Table. She smiled to herself at the thought that it could have been true, to a certain extent. Maybe she would take an unauthorised trip and see if it was.

"Harvey," one of the Collectors called. "How've you been?"

"Not too bad Emily. Haven't you just come back from the twenties? What was that like?" He asked her as they embraced. Jenny crumpled up her nose at their contact.

"Yes, I drank a little too much champagne with Josephine Baker she nearly didn't get on stage. That would have caused me no end of clean ups," she laughed and batted her eyelashes. Jenny pushed past them and stood with her back to them.

Harvey, noticing her movement said his goodbyes and tapped her on the shoulder to get her attention. He pointed to a seat and they moved over to the far side of the room. She sat and he took his place next to her. She hated that he was always there, but all recruits were paired with someone in the beginning. As she looked around she noticed that a few of the recruits weren't there yet and even some of the Regents were not in attendance—it must've been a spur of the moment meeting.

By the time everyone had arrived and seated themselves, the chatter in the room had disappeared. Jenny would've sworn it was so bad she could have heard a pin drop. She wondered if it was always like this before a meeting.

The Chair Regent stood up ready to address everyone and all heads turned to him. "You've all been asked here today because of a pressing matter," he said, voice deep and demanding. "Someone has used a time portal without authorisation," there were a few gasps, mainly from the recruits – trying to suck up probably, thought Jenny. The Chair Regent just ignored them and carried on, "We do not currently know where this person has gone or what they intend to do. We don't even know who they are. Therefore, I would ask that all Collectors investigate their current assignments and keep an eye out for any suspicious activity and the Recruits to be exceptionally vigilant with the books. I'm not sure what the impact will be yet but we all need to be extra careful. If they start changing history..." he trailed off not needing to say what everyone was thinking. If someone started changing things, especially big events everything could change. There might not be any Collective, there might not even be the world as we know it.

"If they start changing history, we might not be around to stop them. We need to gain control of the situation," he took a deep breath before finishing. "If you see anything out of the ordinary you must report it, anyone who doesn't and is found with the knowledge that can aid our search will end up Time Locked."

Jenny put her hand to her mouth to stop her gasp. Time Locked meant that whoever was found guilty would be sent to a random time zone with nothing and they would end up stuck there. Everyone looked around at each other with accusing glances as if everyone was suddenly a suspect. Although this person had accessed a portal they hadn't changed anything yet, which means the threat isn't imminent until they do. They would all need to be vigilant and report any suspicious activity.

I wonder what portal they used? Jenny turned her gaze to Harvey who had crossed his arms. She would ask him as soon as the meeting was over.

"All Regents," he continued, "will be subject to random pin checks. As you all know it takes two pins to make a complete emblem which will allow a portal to open or access to the circle. Anyone found in possession of more than one will be dealt with accordingly.

Recruits can continue with their research assignments but Collectors will no longer be allowed to travel alone. Regent's will accompany all active missions and all personnel will be subject to a search entering and leaving the building. No new missions will be given until this is resolved."

"Do you suspect it's a rogue agent?" called out Emily, starting others off shouting their theories and causing chaos.

"Settle down!" shouted the Regent. "I won't have you all accusing each other." People started to take their seats again. Jenny had never witnessed such distress before, she was rooted to her seat not knowing what to do. Worried about what might happen, scared at the outcome of finding out who used the portal, and yet she still wanted more information.

"Yes, we do suspect a rogue agent," the Regent finally clarified when everyone had settled down, "there have been a few people who have left The Collective on relatively bad terms it could be any one of them."

"I thought when you left you got your mind wiped and the broach took off you?" asked a male Collector Jenny didn't know.

"They do, but it always runs the risk that someone can trigger the memories, after all depending on which stage they were in they can technically still have implant residue. There's no way to remove everything we put in," explained the Regent.

"Just stay vigilant and report, that's all we can do for now." His voice stayed strong but his eyes betrayed him. He was worried about the potential ramifications of what had happened, at least that's what Jenny assumed from the conversation. Why else call everyone to warn them about it?

The Regents stood and left the room leaving everyone in an awkward silence. People still didn't know whether to start freaking out or not, Jenny just stayed in her seat searching the crowd for Charlotte. Upon spotting her Jenny noticed that Charlotte had already gotten up from her seat and was attempting to follow the Chair Regent, her face portraying concern. Before Jenny had the chance to get up and speak to her Harvey had grabbed hold of her arm again.

"Come on then love, let's get you home. I think this is more than enough excitement for one day," he said.

"Aren't you worried about what might happen?" Jenny asked as she manoeuvred herself around the chairs. "I mean what if whoever used the portal starts changing things?"

"They haven't though, have they treacle?" his use of pet names was starting to irritate her. "Until the Regents put an urgent tag on it there's nothing to worry about. It's just like when there was the threat of that guy who wanted to start a war..." he started clicking his hands, "what was his name?"

She had no idea who he was talking about so just shrugged her shoulders at him as they walked to the lift.

"Well anyway, that didn't happen and people got scared about nothing so until there is a threat that I can deal with, there isn't any point in freaking out about it."

Jenny was surprised by his logic but it didn't make her feel any better she would have to be extra vigilant when she was next in the library and try not to slack off so much.

"I'm going to be gone on assignment tomorrow so it looks like you get a couple days off to yourself and the university's history section," Harvey said a little too upbeat. He knew how much she hated being in the library. "I will meet up with you to discuss what you find next Friday." A week, Jenny had a week without her handler and she could not have been happier – not that she let Harvey know that. "Try not to do anything stupid while I'm away," he continued.

"Look I know you have to look after me, but I'm sure I can handle being in a library for five days by myself," she laughed at him.

"Seven. Seven days, Jenny."

"I'm a student Harvey – I have essays to write too!" she turned away from him and got in the car.

"I know you do," he said as he got in the car with her, "but just because I'm not worried about what the Regents said doesn't mean we shouldn't heed their words. We still need to be vigilant."

"I swear you're just here to annoy me," she retorted at him. "Why are you accompanying me home?"

"Just to make sure you get there safely," he smiled, his green eyes lighting up. Jenny scowled at him.

The ride back to her place wasn't far. The benefit of being in The Collective is that they want you close always, thankfully that was near the university campus too. Once they got outside her flat she said goodbye and watched the car disappear before turning to go inside.

Walking through her door Jenny had never felt so relieved to be home. After everything that had happened today she didn't know what to think, one minute she was all panic and the next Harvey is telling her to relax until it's more urgent. What was more urgent than unauthorised access to the portals? Thinking of Harvey, she could still see his face in her mind when she told him she wasn't going to be doing collective work over the weekend, it made her chuckle to herself. She did have essays to do, but they were nearly complete and wouldn't take her long, she just needed to get her head clear and out of books for a while. However, what she didn't expect was to come home, turn on her lights and find her ex-boyfriend sitting on her couch.

"I knew I should have taken that key off you," she said, silently cursing herself.

"Which is why I never offered to give it back."

"Well, here's your chance! Give it to me and get out," she said, her voice rising with anger. He always did know how to bait her. Noah looked so dashing too, with his hair arranged perfectly on his head, a slight quiff, light reflecting off the white shirt that clung to his biceps. He flashed that winning smile she'd missed for many, many months, and her insides almost melted.

"Come on little dove, come and sit with me," he cooed. Jenny felt heat rise in her cheeks.

"Seriously Noah, get out! I won't tell you again," she tried to keep her cool but her voice went up another octave.

"Not until you tell me who that guy was that dropped you home."

"What are you even talking about?" she asked him. Jenny was still standing by the light switch as she daren't go any closer, for fear of her old feelings returning. He couldn't just turn up here and expect everything to be okay.

"The guy in the black car that dropped you off, come on little dove, I'm not stupid. Is he my replacement?" he was goading her into an admission of still being single.

"You know exactly who he is Noah, stop trying to fish for information," she snapped. "Now will you please leave?"

Noah sat there and shook his head. She was going to get seriously angry in a minute. "If you don't leave now, I'm going to call the police."

"And say what Jen? I have a key, no doubt my name is still on the paperwork. I have every right to be here," he said.

"After what you did, I don't think you do Noah."

"Remind me what that was exactly."

"You went off gallivanting around Australia after you were dismissed from The Collective without so much as a goodbye, let alone a reason why," she said keeping her from him but moving towards the kitchen.

In her apartment, her lounge and kitchen were connected while her bedroom and bathroom had separate rooms. She stole a few quick glances before busying herself with making some food. She hadn't had time to eat in the coffee shop before Harvey whisked her off to that important meeting.

"Come on Jenny, I've missed you. It's been such a long time-"

"It's been almost two years," she interjected before he could finish his sentence. "Two years and you haven't once contacted me."

"Then don't you think it's time we caught up. I know you want to know why I kept your key all this time."

"It's time for you to leave Noah," she said sternly. Jenny refused to give into this kind of manipulation. Noah stood up and walked over to her breakfast counter, she tried her best not to look up at him.

"Jenny," he was leaning on the counter in front of her. "Let's be honest here. I've missed you, and you've missed me, just spend one evening in my company. If you still want me to leave in an hour then I'll go, I promise."

She didn't know if she could believe him or not but his winning smile made her insides go all mushy and she nodded her head.

"I take it you'll want food?" she said with a hint of a smile and poured more pasta into the saucepan.

3
TILLY

Tilly wasn't one hundred percent certain she wanted to go to this photo shoot with Claire, but she needed the research. Plus, seeing how people used to dress may help her dissertation feel more authentic. She had been struggling recently and was pretty sure the last five hundred or so words were not going to stay in her essay. Thankfully she had a lot of time before handing it in at the end of the year.

They had agreed to meet up outside the coffee shop as it was only around the corner from the photo shoot but after waiting for fifteen minutes, she'd begun to think Claire had ditched her. A girl could hope.

Fortunately, or unfortunately, Claire came bouncing down the road after a few more minutes, her hair blowing backwards from the speed of her brisk walk. She was definitely a model.

"So, sorry T, I had a nightmare in the hairdressers! She did my hair completely wrong but someone at the shoot is going to sort it out. Let's go," she breathed as she grabbed Tilly's hand and pulled her off down the street with her. Tilly was glad she had decided to wear her comfy boots as the studio was not 'around the corner' as Claire had originally told her. It was down the street, around three corners and across the main road.

As soon as they got inside the studio it was apparent how novice the shoot was. Although they had an authentic dress from the age, the photographer, other models, makeup and hair assistants were all around the same age as each other, at around twenty. The set was a green screen filled with a few props like lights and chairs to make for a living area. Claire was immediately swept away by the hair stylist, who introduced herself as Val and then plonked Claire down into a chair. Tilly felt as if she was watching a time lapse on YouTube of a behind the scenes clip. They were still setting up so there were people moving lights, setting the camera height, checking costumes and having their makeup done.

"Excuse me," exclaimed one of the assistants, whose hands were full of costumes. "You're obviously not one of the models, you can take a seat over there instead of standing in the way," he called as he ran away. Tilly rolled her eyes at the short man who was now out of sight, shook her head and made her way to the sofa that he had pointed at.

"Right, the first girl, please! I need to test the lighting," called the guy behind the camera. "Where is Claire?! She's up first." His voice was clearly agitated and they hadn't even started; this was going to be a long day.

Claire emerged from behind the racks of dresses from the 1700's in a light pale blue dress that had a greyish tint to it. The edging, underskirt and corset were done in a floral print which covered most of her middle and the arms cut off just above the elbow with some fabric hanging down the back of her arms. Her hair was up in a bun and her makeup accentuated her eyes. She reminded Tilly of Elizabeth from Pirates of the Caribbean—it was the perfect dress for a governor's daughter.

"Ah perfect, right come on," called the photographer waving his hand to her, "and where is the governor? After this shoot the pirates are next, so get them ready."

A few of the boys lounging in the back moved into hair and makeup at this announcement as if they were late, but Tilly's attention was on the set and the girls' dresses. She started frantically writing down their colours, patterns and even did some drawings. Tilly drew some of the male's costumes as well. There was only one thing that took Tilly's attention away from the photo shoot and that was Claire.

Her modelling skills, in Tilly's opinion, were not at as high a standard as she was expecting. Claire's facial features seemed dark and moody not neutral. She took some lovely photos but in half of them her facial expressions were laughable, in fact, Tilly did laugh to herself on a few occasions. Luckily none of the other models noticed.

"That'll do for this shoot. Claire, you were lovely. Next costumes please!" Dave's loud voice echoed around the room. Then as if someone had clicked their fingers and allowed everyone to move again the studio was filled with noise and movement. Claire came running off the set towards Tilly and flung herself down on the sofa beside her. Her skirt came up all around her and Tilly couldn't help but burst into laughter. She and Claire had never had a friendly sort of relationship but Tilly suspected that was because she was only around to be with Chris.

"So," said Claire after patting down her ruffles and stifling her laugh, "what did you think?"

"It was interesting, I'm looking forward to the pirate side of things."

"Oh, you took down notes, can I see?" Claire didn't wait for an answer before pulling the notebook from Tilly's hands and flicking through pages, "You have a very talented hand, you ever thought about designing?"

"Um, no," blushed Tilly, snatching her notebook back.

"Well I think you should, you're very good," said Claire as she folded her arms.

"Claire, you're needed for a costume change," called one of the assistants.

Tilly said a silent thank you to the girl who had called Claire away from her. She didn't think she had enough talent to do design, she was barely good at drawing. They had changed the setup a little so it now looked like the deck of the ship, or at least it did on the screen, it was still a green screen but there was now barrels and a mast on the platform. Her main focus though was the tall, dark-haired boy dressed as the captain of his ship, his cool green eyes captivated her and her palms immediately began to sweat a little.

He wasn't paying much attention to her but she still felt that he looked familiar. She'd seen him somewhere before, maybe not in this life, but a dream...or something. Tilly blinked; she was being ridiculous. When she finally managed to tear herself away she started to draw the entire set down on her notepad along with a couple of outfits. He seemed to be a natural at modelling and it wasn't just Tilly who was staring in awe at the young man in the pirate outfit. She'd always had a thing for pirates, the bad boys of history.

"Harvey, just move slightly to the left, I want you to seem important, the centre focus of the photo."

The photographer was starting to get on Tilly's nerves. His voice was very loud and demanding, it sent a shiver through her every time he spoke. Luckily, it wasn't long till the shoot was over.

Most of the day had gone, and Claire came bouncing back over to where Tilly sat. "Did you get much down for your dissertation?"

"Yeah, actually I did. It was interesting to see what they actually wore during those times," replied Tilly with a smile.

"Glad you enjoyed it." Claire's smile was wide and her eyes had lit up. "I wasn't too sure about you coming, to begin with, but it was actually quite nice to have you around. Shall I text the boys?"

"What do you mean?" asked Tilly completely ignoring the comment about the boys, "why weren't you sure?"

"Well we've never really been close, we only hang out because of James and Chris," Claire looked down at the floor like she was a naughty child being told off. "I guess I just assumed you didn't like me intruding on your little threesome."

Tilly made a face at the reference but ended in a smile towards Claire. "Honestly, I always thought the same."

"Really? That's such a relief, so maybe we should try being friends now?" laughed Claire with a kind smile on her face.

"Yeah," Tilly wasn't quite sure how to feel about Claire's admission of friendship seeing as they never really talked before. It used to be Chris, James and Tilly then Chris met Claire and now their threesome was a foursome, but it wasn't bad. She was just used to only speaking to Claire when they were in a group, and in a way, she liked being friends with her too.

Claire linked her arm with Tilly as they got up off the sofa. "I really need to get out of this dress, wait for me and we can get some food?" Tilly nodded in response to Claire as she ran off. With nothing to do Tilly's eyes wandered back towards the male model. He had just walked off set and was starting to change shirts. Where had she seen him? "No." The words escaped her mouth before she could stop them.

"Are you talking to yourself now?" asked Claire, who had reappeared.

"Oh, uh, nothing," Tilly stuttered, her eyes glued to him. It was impossible. No way. No...way. Tilly looked down at her history book, thumbing to the last page she'd finished reading. And there he was, smiling that mischievous grin, straight from the pages of Blackbeard's Myths.

The model sensed her eyes on him, because he turned at that moment, giant green orbs glancing at the cover. One eyebrow quirked, he smiled at her, the modern version, and Tilly couldn't help but look down and compare the two. It was uncanny. It was impossible.

He laughed, and it was so self-satisfied—the laugh of a pirate.

"Go talk to him," Claire said, yanking Tilly from her inner turmoil with a shoulder bump. "He's hot. He's totally checking you out, too."

Tilly was sure she heard Claire mutter a "God knows why" under her breath, but let it slide.

"No. Let's go," Tilly said, grabbing Claire by the purse strap and pulling her toward the door. The boy raised a hand and lazily waved as they went by, and Tilly shuddered.

4
JENNY

JENNY HATED MONDAYS. Especially as she now had to spend the term break in the library, checking history books for The Collective. All her other classmates and the other students got to sleep until midday, go out and party at night, and watch countless re-runs of their favourite TV shows on Netflix, stuffing their faces with pizza, while she sat in the library at nine a.m. flicking through the pages of "Buccaneers and Pirates of Our Coasts". She wasn't really even paying attention to the book, just sitting idly on the bean bag flicking the pages one by one pausing in between to check if Harvey was going to appear. He wouldn't of course as he was on a mission with a Regent, but she really didn't want to be there.

There were only two good things about the library on term holidays – no staff members and barely any students. You had the odd few dotted around the different sections, usually, the ones who were doing science or law and needed the extra time to catch up or find out more information on their current subjects but other than that it was empty. Jenny knew there were seven students currently in the building, and three walking outside.

Jenny closed the book on her lap and pushed it to the ground, glancing up at a girl who'd just walked in through the library's front doors. Sitting where she was, Jenny was able to see every entrance to the library as well as having a full view of the lifts. She liked this area because it was right by the glass wall which let in a lot of natural light, and when she got bored she could people watch. Not that there were a lot of people to watch at 9 o'clock in the morning, considering on a normal day there can be up to 500 students in the building at peak times. It always allowed her to pretend she had a normal life, no knowledge of The Collective and no chip in her head.

The girl who had just walked in was easy to watch. She walked slowly as she frantically sent a text on her phone, then looked up towards the history section. As she turned towards Jenny's direction she could see that the girl was the one who had nearly knocked the pile of books onto her. Jenny continued to watch the girl until she disappeared from view behind some of the shelves, and her ex-boyfriend, Noah, had appeared next to her. She really hated it when she zoned out.

"Hello, earth to Jenny! You in there?" he said loudly causing a scene.

"Shut up," Jenny snapped with a quick look around to see if anyone had noticed their outburst. The only person she could actively see was the boy sitting with his book open taking notes, but he had earphones in and wasn't paying any attention. "I thought you were going to leave me alone?"

"When did I say that?" he smiled back at her. Jenny rolled her eyes at him and started to wriggle out of the bean bag to stand. Noah's hands pressed up against her stomach as he pushed her back down.

"Noah! Stop it I'm trying to work, I need to grab some more books."

"Trying to work? Are you kidding me? You were sitting there daydreaming. You forget I know you, Jenny, you probably haven't changed subjects which means you don't even have a proper subject of study anyway," he laughed at her. Angry at him she slapped away his hand and stood up.

"Just because it's not marine biology and it doesn't whisk me around the world to study fish, doesn't mean it's not a proper subject!" The emphasis on his subject matter along with his time away was important to her. She stormed off kicking the book she had left on the floor. How dare he come back after two years and pick apart her life. She hated how much she liked it – if only she was normal, or he was part of The Collective.

She wasn't sure what she was doing as she marched through the aisles of books. All Jenny knew was that she wanted to get away from Noah and make sure he was gone by the time she got back. Fate seemed to already have this planned for her and when she turned left at the end of the aisle to zig-zag her way through she was met with a face all too close to hers and a smack as their heads collided together. Jenny shut her eyes and brought her hand up to her forehead, as if that would alleviate some of the pain, and groaned. The person she had collided with was doing the same except they didn't even make a sound.

"Ow! God, I am so sorry," came the all too familiar voice of the person Jenny had just walked into.

"It's okay," replied Jenny opening her eyes and squinting at the girl in front of her. "Oh, it's you."

"You're the one I almost toppled the books onto! I am so sorry for that," said the girl in realisation, then held out her hand and said, "I'm Tilly. Nice to finally meet you properly." Her smile was a little timid, but her eyes had lit up a little.

"I'm Jenny," she said shaking her hand gently, "how come you are in the library this early?"

"Trying to figure out which pirate stories are true. Some books say different things."

Jenny froze. Different things? Normally such a statement wouldn't frighten her, but after the meeting with the Chair Regent, Jenny's senses were on high alert. Tilly smiled awkwardly. "Can I have my hand back now?" she asked, glancing down.

"Oh! Sorry," Jenny said, releasing Tilly's hand and wiping her sweaty palm on her jeans. "So, like, what sorts of 'different things?' Different pirates, right? Completely different times?"

Tilly shook her head. "No, same pirate. Just really different facts—or, I guess I shouldn't call them facts right now since they're all so different."

Jenny wiped at her jeans again; man, she was sweating like a pig! She needed to try and get some more information out of this girl, she could help her.

"Are you reading about different pirates?" asked Jenny, just to check before she internally freaked out.

"Nope, focusing on William Kidd. Probably just some fiction and non-fiction but I still need to read everything. Plus, my friends will be asleep until two so may as well make good use of my time," she said smiling as she got up and darted around the end of the aisle to look at more books.

Jenny was amazed at how placid her comments were for a few moments, of course as Tilly wasn't part of The Collective it probably wouldn't be obvious that someone was playing with time, and that was why the books were different. Jenny snatched one of the books out of Tilly's hands and began to flick through it, frantically turning the pages and hoping that nothing had changed.

When you are initiated into The Collective you undergo an operation in which a chip is inserted just behind the ear which alters your sight as you read books or watch people, one of the main reasons Jenny found it so fascinating. If it was blue you were seeing the future or watching someone on the correct path if it was white, it wasn't life changing or altering in any way but if it was red, then there was a problem. Red meant it wasn't on the course it was supposed to be or it had been tampered with. There are also orange and green. Orange meant it could be changed or influenced by anyone which could alter their life, or history a lot and be set on different paths, but green meant it could be changed or influenced by someone significant to the person or time. However, green events were usually pretty rare. Then there were the black lines that means the end. Death is inevitable at this point and there is nothing anyone can do to stop it.

The book Jenny had swiped from Tilly's hands was a multitude of colours. The words were swimming in red, white and orange. No blue. This was a massive problem which needed to be resolved as quickly as possible. Jenny couldn't believe that it was happening to her. Maybe after this, she could finally move up in the ranks.

"Sorry, I need to borrow this, catch you later?" she breathed. Not waiting for a reply from Tilly—who clearly protested—Jenny bolted down the aisle and ran for the door ignoring the shouts of Noah from the section she had been seated at. This was too important to stop for anyone.

While running she took out her phone and dialled, "I need to see you now, it's important!"

5

TILLY

TILLY STOOD there dumbfounded as Jenny disappeared into the distance away from the library. She stood completely still for a few seconds before actually closing her mouth and returning to her book shelf. Slightly confused and annoyed, she began searching for another book to study from. She ran her hand over the spines in the book trying to steady her mind but ultimately came up empty handed, she couldn't focus on the books. Instead, it drifted to the strange way Jenny had acted.

She decided that she needed to go after Jenny but when she turned the end of the aisle she saw that she was too late. Jenny had already disappeared from view and even if she had gone after her, there would be no guarantee that Tilly would find her. Forcing herself back to the books she reached up and grabbed the top of one, jumping when a hand touched the top of hers.

"Sorry," said the male voice next to her, "I didn't mean to make you jump."

"It's okay," Tilly replied automatically, "I wasn't really paying attention." Her eyes darted up to the man's face and her eyes widened when she realised who it was. The handsome young man crouched in front of her was none other than the boy who had captivated her attention at the photo shoot with Claire – Harvey.

His dark hair slicked back with a quiff at the front, but there was something different about him. Something she didn't quite trust in those ocean blue eyes. She gulped down hard trying to pull herself together.

"Sorry, better get going. Lots of work to do," she said, quickly and hurried off, not wanting to spend too much time with him worried that her palms might start sweating again.

"Hey, wait up!" he called.

The sound of pounding feet was behind her, she knew he was following her but she didn't know why. She slowed down as she came to a seating area in the library where the bean bags were and spotted a book on the floor. Not taking a chance to think that he would catch up to her she dropped down onto a bean bag picked up the book and covered her face with it. Praying that he wouldn't spot her. Which was stupid because she was out in the open.

No one approached her for a good five minutes before she lowered the book from her face, to be met with Harvey and his blue eyes sitting across from her.

"Why are you running off? Surely I'm not that scary?" he asked her.

"No," she blurted, "I mean, no you're not scary, it's just my dissertation isn't going to write itself," she replied.

"What are you working on?"

"It's based on the Golden Age of Piracy," she explained. " But recently all the books I've picked up are all telling different stories so I'm having to do a lot of research."

"Really?" he responded, almost too interested. His voice went a little high-pitched. "That's interesting, can you show me?"

"Just pick up some of the books, they're all on the shelf," she smiled. Tilly was terrible at speaking to people she found attractive, she cursed herself. He didn't move an inch just smiled at her showing off his white teeth. Unsure if he understood what she meant she pointed to the shelves.

Taking her hint, he stood up and walked away to the shelves, but he only got a few steps before turning back.

"I'd prefer not to go without getting your number. Would you be interested in giving it to me?" he smiled at her. She lowered the book further and closed it on her lap.

"Oh, um, sure." She said unsure of what was happening. He handed her his phone and she typed in the number. "Right, better be off now." She got up and started to walk away before turning around, "you're not going to follow me, again are you?"

"No. Not today," he said smiling at her again, "maybe I'll find you another day though."

"What's that supposed to mean?" she asked him, a little worried about his answer.

"Just that we might bump into each other again, you're interesting," he replied getting up and walking away. For the second time today, Tilly was left in awe of the people walking away from her.

☙❧

Lunchtime saw the arrival of the boys on campus, which Tilly was unprepared for. She had spent the afternoon shopping in the mall close by, to try and take her mind off of Jenny and Harvey, and ended up buying more than she had originally wanted. She was walking along the road that cuts through the middle of the university campus site with four bags in her hands from various stores, not one being a supermarket even though her fridge shelf was barely full. Not paying attention to her surroundings, she jumped when the boys snuck up behind her. Hitting them both playfully she made them carry her bags back to their house at the end of the road.

"I thought you were supposed to be buying food?" asked James as they closed the front door to their student accommodation. Tilly's cheeks flushed.

"I guess, I got a little distracted," she said as they dumped her bags by the stairs.

"Honestly girl you need to control your spending habits," laughed James.

"Shut up both of you. It's not like I spent my entire loan on apple products – is it Chris?!"

"Hey, I totally needed that iMac," he argued. "I'm just glad Student Finance doesn't take on board biological parents as well as adoptive ones otherwise I'd be in so much more debt." Chris lowered his eyes to the floor and laughed. He got the good end of an adoption case. His biological parents didn't want him to think they gave him up because they didn't want him so they try and compensate with money while he's studying.

"Claire is going to come over tonight – want to join us for a film?" he asked changing the topic of conversation.

"Yeah can do – I've got some books for more research, but I'll do that in the morning while you both get your beauty sleep," she said smiling and giving James a little wink.

"Actually, if we pop to the shops then she can meet us there and we can get some desserts, and you can get some food," said Chris, emphasising the emptiness of her fridge section.

"Come on T, let's go do your favourite thing and shop," James swung his arm around her neck and tickled her chin. All three of them grabbed a coat as it was getting quite cold and then they left en-route to the supermarket.

※

"I think I'm going to ask Claire to stay over tonight, you guys don't mind, right?" Chris asked as they turned the corner to enter the supermarket.

"Oh, so that's why you were going to buy the chocolate spread," laughed James. Tilly cringed at the comment made by James. She knew that fornication sometimes included the use of other things but she'd never heard of chocolate spread being used before. Of course, all she did know was what the boys had spoken about and the weirdness from Fifty Shades of Grey.

"Seriously guys?" she asked as she grabbed hold of a basket, "we are in public and no-one wants to hear what Chris is going to be doing with chocolate spread."

"Sorry T didn't realise you were so touchy today," James continued to laugh.

She scowled at him as she walked away to start her shop. Tilly had no idea what she wanted or needed for the fridge as her mind was still preoccupied with Jenny and Harvey. It was still playing on her how they had both just gotten up and left. Especially as it had left her with so many questions to ask. Why was she so interesting to Harvey? Why did Jenny need to take her book?

"I'm sorry T," James made her jump out her thoughts as he put his arm around her shoulders. "I know you're a sensitive flower, I didn't mean to upset you."

"You didn't," she said picking up some carrots. "I just don't like talking about those kinds of things."

"I'll hang back with Chris and let you shop. I'm pretty sure he just asked me about cream."

Tilly made a sickly face and turned away from him. Her stomach grumbled as she turned the corner to go down the next aisle. At the other end, she was sure she saw Jenny turn the end of the aisle and she moved to catch her in the next one. As Tilly got around the corner again she was disappointed. Jenny, the girl from the library, was not in the supermarket and she didn't know what to do about getting her answers. She just hoped that next time she saw Jenny there would be enough time to ask her all the questions.

6

JENNY

JENNY DIDN'T KNOW what came over her as she ran. Her lungs burned as she pounded down the road, book in hand, to meet Harvey. She hadn't told him what it was about, just that it was important. She had obviously freaked him out enough that he agreed to postpone his Collecting trip and meet her before he left with the Regent. Her heart was beating hard in her chest as she rounded the corner towards the church. She slowed down to a walking pace as she panted, trying to get more oxygen into her lungs and looked for Harvey.

He wasn't hard to spot at all. Standing outside the cafe, back straight, her handler was all professional in his suit and tie. The hat he was carrying looked like something out of the twenties era. Maybe that was a giveaway as to where he was going on his trip. Harvey looked as handsome as ever and from the smug look on his face every time a woman walked past him, he knew it. Which, for Jenny at least, took away some of his charm. No woman likes a man with a big ego.

There were a lot of people on the street, which Jenny noticed as she weaved her way between them. When she finally reached Harvey, he was looking at his watch.

"Sorry, I got here as fast as I could," she panted excessively. She knew he hated it when people were late but she hoped he might take pity on her if she seemed out of breath.

"It's fine, but I was just about to leave," he commented. "What is it that was so important I moved my trip till tomorrow?"

"This," Jenny replied lifting the book up into view. "Now let's get off the street." She looked around to see if there was anywhere to go inside but in all honesty, the only place would be Harvey's car. Harvey frowned and indicated that they both get into the car. With the speech from the Regents yesterday, they were unsure who would be listening to The Collective operatives. Jenny let him take the book off of her and they both got in the car before he could open it.

"See the colours are all wrong," she insisted.

He scanned through the pages, his face giving nothing away.

"I don't see anything," he said finally shutting the book.

"What do you mean?"

"I think you might need a new chip. Let's get to headquarters and get you one," he said calmly, moving his hand out so she would step forward. Once she had, Harvey placed his hand on the small of her back. "If you still see the same colours inside, we will take this further."

"But shouldn't you check your chip too? If we aren't seeing the same thing it could be either of us," asked Jenny, confused. A hint of fear had started to creep into her mind. She looked up into his green eyes and tried to read his mind – even though that was impossible without the correct artefact.

"We will check mine too, but we should really get to headquarters," he replied with a stern look in his eyes that said shut up and do as I say. Harvey tapped the window in the back of the car indicating to the driver that they should move now.

When they reached the church, he wrapped his arm around her back as they walked in and she snuggled in just a little. He was warm and, even though she would never admit it out loud, she kind of liked it.

Once they were safely inside the lift that took them down to the basement levels of the church, Harvey let her go. She felt a coldness where his hand had been but shivered it off and side stepped away from him so they weren't too close. The doors opened and they stepped out. Instead of going into the large meeting room directly in front of them, Harvey led Jenny to the right and through a door located at the end of the hallway. There were a few more doors inside and they entered through the last one on the right.

Inside, Jenny saw what looked like an alchemist set, along with some technological items and assumed this was where the chips were made. Behind the set, in the corner, was a small man, slightly aged, asleep and drooling on his apron.

"Gary, wake up," said Harvey at normal volume. The man in the corner did not stir. "Gary, I said WAKE UP." Harvey shouted in the man's ear. This time the man opened his eyes and sat up straight.

"You should know better than to wake a man whilst he's sleeping, Harvey." Gary's voice was strange to Jenny. "What do you want?"

"We need new chips, have you got any?"

"Yes, they're over on the shelf behind you. Which you knew and didn't need to wake me for."

"Well, you looked too comfortable on your stool. Where is Doug? Isn't it his shift today?"

"No, he's sick." Gary's voice was sharp and to the point. Jenny was almost offended for Harvey but just looked around the room trying not to.

The shelves were full of different boxes and labels for various tools The Collective used, the largest being a box marked CHIPS; they had extra as the technology was always malfunctioning. Even though The Collective had been around for years they've still had to grow with the times. Before they used amulets but they were lost too easily.

Harvey walked over to it, ignoring the sharp tone in Gary's voice and picked out two, handing one to Jenny as he turned back to a very annoyed Gary. "Can you make sure ours are working properly? We aren't seeing the same things," he said, handing over his chip and making a gesture for Jenny to do the same. Reluctantly she pressed the back of her ear and the sickness washed over her. Ejecting the chip felt like a wave of seasickness had descended over her before coming to a calm emptiness—it felt like she was handing over a piece of herself.

"Yes, I'll look into it. Now can you please get out and leave me alone?" snapped Gary taking the chip and inserting it into the computer. Jenny got the feeling he didn't like people, or maybe it was being caught sleeping on the job.

Jenny put the new chip in and instantly felt the change; having a chip inserted was a lot easier than taking one out. This chip had a little more information than her last one. It actually gave her a bit of a headache to see the colours brighter than before. She knew she would get used to it, but at that moment the sudden change hurt. She wouldn't let Harvey see that though, she hated letting him see how she felt. Something about Harvey enticed her, but also scared her. She scolded herself quickly for even thinking that.

"How does it feel?" asked Gary, a little more calmly. "It'll probably be a little brighter for a while, I upgraded a lot."

"Gary, how do these even work?" Jenny replied ignoring his earlier question. "How do you link them to The Time Codex?"

"That is not something I can discuss with a Recruit Jenny, you know that. Now how does the new chip feel?" said Gary. Jenny stuck her tongue out at Gary's omission, she really wanted to know how everything worked but she knew until she got up through the ranks she would learn all there was to learn and maybe even become a Regent. That was her dream.

They returned to the meeting room of The Collective's basement and sat down. Jenny took a quick glance at Harvey and noticed he was looking at her in a weird way. She scowled and looked away while he opened the book on his lap and flicked through the pages again.

"I'm still not seeing what you thought you saw Jen, look," he said, leaning the book in her direction; sure enough, there were no swirling colours just white and blue lines. Although she swore to herself there was black surrounding the last word, but she hadn't been taught anything about the colour black and it faded just as soon as she saw it.

"Yeah, maybe my chip was broken and in need of the new information," she said quietly, "but at least I got it checked out. If what I saw had been true it could have been a problem."

"It could have been, but the story is the same..." Harvey stopped mid-sentence and stared at his page. He flicked back and forth a few times. "Maybe you were right; I've never heard of a pirate called Laurie Munoz or a ship called The Solitaire. Isn't William Kidd supposed to be a famous pirate? In this, it says Munoz is important. Almost like Kidd is just another Pirate, not a famous one."

Jenny was worried. This was bad and she didn't think it could have gotten worse except he mentioned William Kidd: the pirate that girl who was always bumping into Jenny was writing her dissertation about. If she didn't believe in coincidences she was going to start soon because this was one too many not to be.

For the second time that day Jenny snatched the book from another's hands and stared at the pages. True enough, both the pirate names mentioned were there on the page stating they were regarded as the "lords of the pirates" and terrors of the Caribbean Sea. It was all wrong and dread settled into her bones. Someone wasn't just meddling in time—they were drastically changing it.

They stayed in the meeting room until the Chair arrived and then they both tried to hurriedly explain what had happened but with them, both speaking at once nothing could be comprehended from what they were saying.

"Will you both please be quiet? I can't understand when you talk at the same time. Harvey what is this all about?" asked the Chair. Jenny sat back into her chair, disappointed that she wouldn't get her chance to talk.

"Chair Matthews," Harvey said in what sounded to Jenny like his most professional voice, "The book was brought to my attention for having some misrepresentations in it. We were required to get new chips to see the extent of the change, nothing we can't handle but we thought we should report it."

Jenny couldn't believe what she was hearing. He sounded so official and making it out like it was just another problem to fix.

"I suggest we get someone to look into this and check it out before it turns into something we can't handle," finished Harvey.

"Right, what misrepresentations are there?" asked Chair Matthews. Jenny was growing more annoyed at the fact she wasn't allowed to speak. She was just waiting for the right moment then she could attempt to explain everything. Chair Matthews would see that she is worthy of promotion, she found the book, and she would fix this situation.

"There are new Pirate names in the book, different from the timeline in The Time Codex, it's throwing up all sorts of colours."

"New names? This is curious, and what colours are they? As long as they aren't too far we may be able to send someone in to check," said Chair Matthews, "where did you find this book?" That was Jenny's chance.

"I was in the library doing what I was asked, looking through the history books, when I noticed a girl who I had recently bumped into," she said cutting Harvey off before he could answer.

"Don't see what that has to do with anything," mumbled Harvey.

Rolling her eyes Jenny took a deep breath and continued, "I had just walked into her when I realised that her book was glowing all sorts of strange colours. I regret to admit that I just snatched the book and came straight to Harvey with what I had found as I wasn't sure what it meant – or how to handle the situation."

There was silence after Jenny had finished her speech. Although it wasn't in as posh a voice as Harvey had used, from the look on Chair Matthews' face something she said definitely bothered him. He took a step back and sat down in one of the chairs looking weary, and rubbed his temples.

"Chair Matthews?" asked Harvey, prompting for a response.

"Sorry, I was just thinking about what to do. This is a very interesting tale," Chair Matthews looked up from his hands at Harvey. "If it's not in The Time Codex then it's not how history was supposed to be." He turned towards Jenny, "now who is this girl that you keep seeing?"

"No one I've ever met properly, she's a student on campus," replied Jenny.

"Curious, and how many times have you seen her?"

"Almost every day since the big meeting."

Chair Matthews lifted his head more and widened his eyes. Apparently, he didn't believe in coincidences

"Did she seem like she knows anything?"

"No," replied Jenny, "she's a student doing a dissertation on Pirates, I don't really know much more about her." It suddenly struck Jenny that she had snatched a book out of a strangers hand and run away from them. Not really a first impression you want to make. No wonder she only had friends in The Collective.

"If she doesn't know anything that can help us then leave the civilian to her normal life. We don't need to interfere. Harvey, go on your assignment, then when you get back we will all deal with this mess together. I will confer with the other Regents and pass on any instructions upon your return. You are both dismissed, and Jenny, keep looking in those books. I fear this will not be the first strange thing you find during that timeline."

Chair Matthews stood from his seat and walked out of the room. Jenny would leave the girl to her normal life, but she would also ask a lot of questions and try to find out some more information. Maybe this girl could do her work for her? She would only know by asking. Without waiting for Harvey Jenny started to make her way back to the elevator. She didn't want him to ask too many questions, she hated lying to him but she would when it was required. Hearing his footsteps behind her she turned around on the spot in the elevator and moved backwards giving Harvey space. As the doors closed, the awkward silence was broken.

"What are you going to do now?" he asked.

"Not that it is any of your business but I'm going back to the library. After all, it's only early afternoon," she lied, her voice just a little too smug accompanied by a winning smile. "You're off on your assignment so I'll talk to you when you get back." As quick as she finished speaking, the doors opened and Harvey put an arm out to stop her from leaving.

"You're not going to do anything that will get you into trouble are you Jenny?" he asked her, his face indicating that he didn't believe a word she had just said to him.

"Harvey, you know me. I wouldn't do anything that could compromise my promotion," she lied again, her heartbeat speeding up. What if he could tell? He made another face at her and moved his arm.

"Please behave Jenny."

As he said his last words Jenny darted out of the lift as quickly as she could. It would take her a while to get back to the library so she started off in the direction, and when she felt she was out of Harvey's watchful eye she turned a corner and headed for her flat.

As she turned the corner she saw Tilly walking along with some shopping bags and her two friends sneaking up behind her. She wasn't going to be able to talk to her today with those two around. Jenny followed them for a while until they went into their house before she turned to go back to her own flat. Jenny cemented her decision there and then. She would use Tilly to do her research and find out everything she could about the timeline she had found. Continuing on towards her flat Jenny just hoped that Tilly would be in the library tomorrow morning.

7
TILLY

THEY HAD SPENT SO LONG in the supermarket that when they left, it was dark and it had started to rain. Chris and James were carrying the bags and making jokes but Tilly's mind was, as they liked to say, away with the fairies. Her mind focused on Jenny and Harvey.

Tilly caught the tail-end of the conversation James and Chris were having about Claire as one of them accidentally knocked into her. She hadn't joined them yet and Tilly was glad, she was sure it would go straight to Claire's head. They had both been saying how amazing it was that she was getting more into the modelling career but Chris wasn't happy with that 'Harvey chap' hanging around from her last photo shoot. In fact, it was the mention of Harvey's name that caught Tilly's attention, especially after the weird situation in the library earlier that day.

"You alright T?" asked James, touching her shoulder.

"Yeah, I'm fine. Where's Claire?" she asked Chris, changing the subject. He got out his phone and checked it, shaking his head.

"She hasn't messaged me so I guess she'll just meet us back at the house."

"Oh, I see," she looked down at the floor. Her mind was all over the place and she wasn't really sure how to feel. Her curiosity was also scaring her. Maybe she'd ask Claire about that guy when she came over, she didn't even realise he had been looking at her until she had pointed it out. If Chris was annoyed about him hanging around her, Tilly wanted to know why. Secretly hoping she wasn't trying to set them up or anything.

"T, you seem a bit off. Are you sure you're okay?" asked James attempting to put his arm around her shoulder. He didn't make it through and was now standing awkwardly next to her.

"She's fine James," said Chris, grabbing his shoulders and moving him away. "Probably just doesn't want to be asked the same questions over and over again. Right, Tilly?"

She nodded her head in response, but she hadn't really been listening.

"Oi, you." Chris's hands grabbed her shoulders and she pulled herself out of her thoughts and smiled. "God you're annoying Tilly, I thought you were just ignoring us."

"No," she started. Both boys were in front of her with crossed arms not looking impressed at all. "Okay, I'm feeling a little out of sorts okay. You mentioned Harvey and I'm worried Claire's trying to set us up or something." She scrunched up her nose as she finished speaking. Chris burst out laughing and James just stood there. His eyes portraying sadness.

"That sounds like something she would do, thinking she's helping. Well, you've made me feel better about him hanging around, as long as he leaves my girl alone," Chris swung his arms around James' shoulder, "everything is fine."

⁂

Claire was waiting outside the house when they got home and although Tilly wasn't in her right mind for most of the night, she did take a few moments alone with her in the kitchen. Tilly was preparing a few bits for the evening, popcorn for the movie and fizzy drinks for everyone to drink when Claire walked into the kitchen and headed straight to the fridge.

"What are you getting?" she asked, wanting to start off the

conversation as normal as possible. Jumping right in with accusations was probably not the way to carry on this new-found friendship.

"The boys wanted some beers, you need any help? I can pop back in before they stick the film on?" Claire smiled before she left the room, Tilly nodded as her answer. She could feel her heartbeat starting to race. *Was it going to be that hard to ask her about Harvey?*

"What do you want me to take back in?" Tilly jumped at the sound of Claire's voice. "Oh sorry, didn't mean to make you jump," she giggled.

"I was lost in thought, grab the popcorn out of the cupboard?" Tilly pointed to one of the cupboards on the other side of the room. Taking a deep breath, she decided to ask the question that had been on her mind since Chris mentioned she'd been talking to him. "Claire, what have you been speaking to Harvey about?"

"Chris told you, didn't he?" she said sounding a little cross. "I swear that boy can't keep his mouth closed at all."

Tilly stood there waiting for her answer. Claire rolled her eyes. "I was trying to get you a date alright. You and James need someone, then we can be a group!"

"Aren't we already a group?" asked Tilly, quickly adding, "I don't need or want a date Claire. You should have asked me first."

"Sorry, didn't realise it was a touchy subject, I just wanted to do something nice."

"Well it wasn't nice, and next time just ask beforehand. Seriously the guy is creepy," she tried to sound convincing. He had creeped her out in the library but there was something underlying that made her want to see him again.

"Noted, shall we get back to the film now?" Claire picked up the popcorn and left the kitchen. Somehow Tilly knew this wouldn't be the first conversation where Claire over stepped boundaries.

She wasn't in her right mind for most of the night, drifting in and out of the conversations throughout the film. The boys didn't notice that Claire and Tilly avoided talking to each other, but then a petty girl's fallout wouldn't concern them. An explosion from the film brought Tilly out of her doze and to the conversation that was being had without her.

"Are you sure you didn't say anything else to her?" asked Chris. "She seemed pretty upset when she came back in and she hasn't spoken since the film went on."

"Maybe she just wanted to watch the film?" retorted Claire. "Seriously, I was just trying to do something nice for her, he seems like a nice enough guy."

"Maybe she doesn't like him?" said James. "She might have her eye on someone else, there could be hundreds of reasons she's upset about what you did. I agree with her, you should've asked."

"Of course, you agree you're in love with her."

Tilly wriggled on the sofa trying to get a better ear, eaves dropping on her friends isn't something she liked doing but this was a conversation she'd never heard them have before.

"I am not," replied James, quieter than usual. "Not that this has anything to do with this conversation."

"Okay, let's just stop a second." Chris was being his usual dominant self and taking control of the situation. "Claire, no more meddling in Tilly's love life without asking her first and James no more blaming Claire. She tried to do a nice thing and it back fired. You've learnt your lesson haven't you love?"

Tilly assumed Claire nodded her head because then they were making noises like they were play fighting. Having your eyes closed made it hard to know exactly what was going on without the talking. Another explosion and she decided to, for all intents and purpose, wake up and announce she was going to bed. Hoping some sleep would make this evening go away she went upstairs and crashed out before her head even hit the pillow.

❦

Tilly woke up from a strange dream she couldn't fully remember, in a cold sweat. Unable to get back to sleep, she was in the library within the hour. Some days she hated being the early bird in the library, when she was younger she used to get teased for being the one who wanted to study and do well. If her bullies could see her now they wouldn't have any more words to say. She was top of her class with her final year in university almost over, ready to go on to do work experience and become an archaeologist.

Inside the library, Tilly didn't see anyone else until around 8:30 a.m., when a couple of girls came in and went upstairs to the computer suite.

Not long after that, while Tilly was browsing through the shelves of books on history searching for some more information on pirates, she felt a tap on her shoulder. Turning around, she was met with Harvey's blue eyes.

"Didn't realise you were such an early bird," he said grinning at her.

"It's the only time I have to come here, means I get everything done," she said turning back to her books hoping he would leave her alone. Instead, he moved to her side and leaned against the bookshelf.

"Come on, that's not true, is it? You like it in here," he said, looking at her very intensely.

"Yes, I suppose I do. Reading is a nice escape from the harsh reality that is adulthood," moving her head back to the shelves she laughed slightly. Was she blushing? She definitely shouldn't be feeling like that! Tilly side-stepped down the shelf to look for another book, and also put some distance between her and Harvey. Even though she didn't suffer from it, she was beginning to feel claustrophobic with him being so close to her.

"What are you looking for, maybe I can help?"

"Anything with facts about pirates in the 1700's."

"Pirates?" he asked, a hint of surprise in his voice. She still refused to look at him though. Her hands were starting to sweat again.

"Yes, pirates." She spotted a book up on one of the higher shelves but before she could reach up and grab it another pair of hands did.

"Fancy seeing you here at this unreasonable hour again, and here I thought I was the only one crazy enough to come to a library before anyone else," said the girl from the day before. What was it with these people just popping up?

Tilly forced a grin. "Jenny, right?"

"That's right. Here." Jenny handed the book to Tilly, before glancing over at Harvey where he still stood, leant against the bookshelf. She frowned at him as she folded her arms, "didn't I just leave you to go on your trip?"

"Yes. Yes, you did, I just had to say goodbye first," Harvey's voice stuttered a bit and almost sounded as if it wasn't his own as he moved past them. "I – I'll speak to you both later!" With that Harvey exited the shelves and left.

Things just kept getting weirder around Tilly. What was his problem? Does he know Jenny?

"So, what are you looking for today?" asked Jenny breaking the silence between them.

"Do you know him?" asked Tilly ignoring Jenny's questions and acting on random instinct. The nagging in her mind needed to be silenced and that was only going to come by asking Jenny and Harvey questions.

"Yeah, we work together. He's sort of my partner," replied Jenny.

"Oh, sorry I didn't realise he was involved," her cheeks flushed with embarrassment. How could he be flirting with her when he has a girlfriend?

Jenny lifted up her finger and pointed at her. "Bad choice of words. Work partner not romantically," she clarified. "Didn't mean to make you uncomfortable." Tilly's cheeks flared with heat again.

"So, he's single," asked Tilly, unsure why she needed to know the answer to that.

"Yep. Free as a bird that one, he's not the type to settle down though." Jenny seemed a little annoyed to Tilly. It only made her more curious. "Need some help with the books?"

"Sure," responded Tilly handing her a couple of them. "I'm sitting just over here."

"So, what are you trying to discover?" Jenny tried another line of questioning.

"I'm not sure anymore, all these books are saying different things to what I remember. I feel like I have been reading fiction for the past three weeks. I really don't want to start my dissertation over, it's difficult enough as it is!" Tilly moaned. "Then there is your work guy hanging around and not leaving me alone, didn't you say he was going away?"

"Yeah, he has a work assignment to do."

"What kind of work do you guys do?" asked Tilly, unable to control the urge to know more about the guy who had made it apparent he wasn't going to leave her alone.

Jenny was looking at her intently as if she had words on her tongue that she couldn't say out loud. "You okay?" asked Tilly.

"Me? Oh yeah, sorry I zone out when I think," she laughed. "We actually aren't allowed to discuss our work."

"Really? You working for the government or something? You seem a little young." Tilly wasn't sure Jenny was telling the truth, what job can't you talk about?

"No, I-I work in a bank, so not allowed to discuss things. Signed a non-disclosure agreement when I started." Jenny grabbed a book and started looking through it again. Tilly liked that this was an easy conversation, normally she wouldn't get on so well with girls. That's why she lived with Chris and James. Maybe that was the issue with Claire too? "Want me to help and then we could get lunch?"

"Yeah, that sounds great!" Tilly beamed.

They both took half the shelf of history books that had information about pirates and carried them over to one of the large tables. Spreading the books out over one side of the table, they got started looking through them all. Tilly flicked through the pages of the book and looked up at Jenny. She had stopped looking through and was just staring at the book. "Find something interesting?"

"Yeah...have you ever heard of a pirate ship called The Solitaire?" asked Jenny not looking up from her book.

"Um... No, I don't think so, not in depth anyway. I think there was something mentioning that name in one of these books,"

Tilly replied picking up two of the books she had just passed over. She handed one to Jenny and they both went back to reading.

"Yeah, here," Tilly said turning the book around to show Jenny.

"The pirate ship known as The Solitaire was one of the most feared but never seen. Their flag put fear into the hearts of any man who saw them. Rumours would circle about how the Captain persuaded men to come aboard and join the crew, many were never seen again after."

"Creepy, right?" said Tilly cheerfully, "I never heard of it before so put it to the side."

"Can I see it?" said Jenny reaching for the book.

"Not going to run off with it again are you?" laughed Tilly trying to make a joke.

"No," chuckled Jenny. Tilly was glad she hadn't made a fool of herself. Usually, her jokes don't go down so well. "You know I'm beat, it's lunchtime want some food? We can leave them here right?"

"No actually we need to put them back – but one of us could get food and bring it back in here?" Tilly was smiling. "So, are you gonna get something for us to eat or not? What the hell…"

Tilly looked up to see Jenny running off. Tilly turned the book back around and began to read the rest of the passage when someone sat down next to her making her jump.

"When do I get to have a one-on-one study date with you?"

Tilly looked up from the book and saw that it was Harvey. "I thought," she started to say as she gestured in the same direction as to where Jenny had just disappeared. If she didn't know better Tilly could have sworn she saw Jenny's blonde hair disappear behind the library's doors. She was going outside and Tilly hoped she was getting food. Her stomach made a small noise as she thought about it. "Aren't you supposed to be on a trip somewhere?" she asked him, getting her mind off of food. He smiled at her.

"Yes, but don't tell anyone I didn't go," he said putting his finger up to his lip and fluttering his blue eyes at Tilly. She scoffed and turned herself away from him back to her books. She wasn't going to let him flirt with her.

"What's the matter, don't want to talk to me?" he said taking a seat next to her.

"Why are you here?" she asked, unable to stop herself from speaking to him.

"Because I wanted to ask you something."

"Oh really? And what's that?" Tilly made a face at him. Why on earth was he here? Was he really that keen on her?

"Do you ever think about just getting away from here and going on an adventure?" he mused.

"An adventure? Like what?" this had Tilly's attention. He was sounding like a crazy dreamer.

"Yes, you know, like in the movies, an adventure. Two strangers meet—that would be you and I—and they go on an adventure and become the best of friends," he laughed as he spoke.

"Have you been reading too many children's books or something? Things like that don't just happen. That's why they are stories," she insisted.

"Do you trust me?" he held his hand out.

"I don't even know you," she stood up and headed towards the door.

"Come on Tilly, live a little. Let me show you an adventure."

"You know you sound really creepy, right? Honestly, we aren't in a movie."

"No, we aren't but that doesn't mean we can't have some fun either," Harvey explained. "Why don't you trust me?"

"Because like I have already said, I don't know you, and now you want me to run away with you?"

"Tell you what," he started as he stood up, putting his arm down. "Meet me outside in an hour and I'll show you something incredible. Deal?"

Tilly rolled her eyes, this guy just wasn't giving up. She knew she should say no. A stranger asking to whisk her away on an adventure wasn't exactly something that happened every day and screamed danger, but then he looked so innocent. He wasn't going to leave so really her only options were to continue the argument of her saying no, or agreeing and giving herself an hour to get out of it.

Standing there looking at him she made her decision to give herself an hour to find Jenny and make a proper decision.

"Fine, an hour," she said turning around in the direction Jenny had just gone.

As she reached the door Jenny jumped out and scared her half to death. Holding her hands up indicating that Tilly shouldn't speak they moved away from the library.

"That is not Harvey," she declared, pointing.

"What do you mean?"

"His eyes. Harvey's eyes are green, and I just rang him while you were speaking to that fake. I don't know who that is – or why he looks like Harvey but he is bad news," she explained.

"Maybe he has a twin?" offered Tilly thinking that could be the only logical solution.

"He doesn't have a twin."

"Okay, well I'm supposed to meet him in an hour, what do we do?" asked Tilly.

"What do you mean you're meeting him in an hour?"

"I kind of agreed to some elaborate adventure to get him to stop talking and allow me to leave," said Tilly. "Honestly, he's very persistent."

"What kind of adventure? You just agreed?" Jenny's voice was pretty high and Tilly didn't really know how to react. "This makes absolutely no sense, like none at all."

"You're telling me," responded Tilly. "What else was I supposed to do?"

"Oh, this is not good," Jenny had started pacing, it was making Tilly nervous.

"What do you mean it's not good? I'm so confused, how did I get myself into this?" Tilly threw her arms up.

"First of all, this is not good because there is an imposter saying he's going to take a random girl on an adventure, and second, you didn't get yourself into anything," replied Jenny, "it's just a mess and I don't know how to fix it."

Tilly pouted at her, she didn't like this but they were between a rock and a hard place. Either she met up with Fake Harvey and end up god knows where, or she ignores it and he comes back tomorrow when she's in the library and they start over again.

"Okay," Tilly looked at her, confused. "What would be the next logical step before we both freak out."

"I should make a call and report this, but then it isn't really anything to do with the books." Jenny was still pacing as she spoke, changing direction with each sentence. "I mean we could just continue this and get you to meet him, but that could be dangerous."

"You don't really work in a Bank, do you?" asked Tilly. Something about Jenny's anxiety made her nervous. Things weren't adding up. Jenny turned to look at her.

"Why do you ask?"

"You just said you needed to make a call and that this didn't have anything to do with the books. Banks don't really need information on pirates from the 1700's," said Tilly. Jenny didn't look shocked.

"Damn my terrible lying abilities," Jenny clenched her fists and shook them as she spoke. "No, I don't work for a Bank."

"Well, are you going to tell me? I mean now's a pretty good time to fill me in, isn't it? There's an imposter impersonating your partner and planning to whisk me away," Tilly was starting to get a little hysterical.

"I'm going to need to ask you to come with me. You're going to meet the Regents."

"The who?" exclaimed Tilly. "Why can't you tell me what you do, but these Regents can?"

"It's not within my authority," said Jenny sighing, "If I tell you and they find out I'll get in a lot of trouble."

"What about meeting Fake Harvey?" Tilly protested. She knew it wasn't a good enough reason, she could see it in Jenny's eyes, but she didn't really know either of these people and now both of them wanted to whisk her away to god knows where.

Tilly wasn't sure what kind of things Harvey, Fake Harvey and Jenny were involved in but she didn't want anything to do with it. She was feeling pressured. Jenny was moving away from her, urging Tilly to follow.

"So where are we going?" asked Tilly, she wasn't going anywhere until that question was answered.

"The church," replied Jenny. "You coming, or not?"

Reluctantly Tilly followed. Tilly didn't really have a choice, it was either go back to Fake Harvey or go with Jenny. The library girl seemed like the safer option, at least that's what she told herself, as she blindly followed Jenny.

8
JENNY

JENNY HAD NEVER BEEN SO CONFUSED in her life. Harvey was supposed to be on a trip, whatever that trip was, which made sense as to why he would run away when she appeared. She was convinced it wasn't actually him though so it must have been a fake.

Of course, Harvey was unavailable which meant she had to try someone else. Charlotte thankfully answered her phone and Jenny's questions. In fact, she really only answered one, as Jenny wasn't allowed to know. First, Charlotte said that Harvey had gone on his trip and therefore couldn't possibly be in the library, and second that Jenny was probably crazy (and more than likely fancied him) if she was imagining him talking to her new friend.

Fake Harvey's eyes were all wrong. They were blue, which Jenny knew was wrong because she had always liked looking at his green eyes. They reminded her of emeralds. Smiling to herself she realised she was going into a daze.

She blinked hard to rip herself from her thoughts about Harvey's eyes and looked behind her to check that Tilly was following. Once they were far enough away from the library Jenny stopped walking and took out her phone. Tilly peered over at her, confused, but she wasn't going to explain out there, she would have to meet the Regents and they would decide whether to let her in or not. For now, all she could do was phone them and explain what had happened.

"Hello? Yes, I need to speak with Chair Regent Matthews. Now, it's urgent," said Jenny.

"Who's calling please?" answered the lady on the other end of the phone.

"It's Jennifer Monroe," said Jenny. "You know exactly who I am Julianne, put me through."

"Jenny, you know I cannot do that. Can I take a message?" Jenny rolled her eyes at Julianne's comment.

"I have already spoken with him on this matter and honestly, no, I don't want you to take a message. Put him on the phone." Jenny noticed Tilly's face after she finished her sentence so added, "please."

"Jenny, it can't be that urgent. I can offer a message that's all, please don't make this harder than it has to be." Jenny had to admit that although she didn't know much about Julianne, there was no reason for Jenny to dislike her. However, she was making it really hard not to shout down the phone at her.

"Julianne, if I don't speak to him he's not getting the message. So please, TRANSFER THE CALL." Tilly flinched as she raised her voice. Jenny mouthed a quick apology to her before Julianne answered on the phone.

"Okay, I'll put you through. Is that all?" Julianne's voice was timid and Jenny felt bad for her a little. Guilty almost, for shouting and making her feel like she had to transfer her call. She also felt relieved that she was getting her way. Was this how her mum did it?

"Yes, thank you."

"Erm, who are you ringing and why?" asked Tilly looking at her watch.

"Oh sorry," Jenny realised she hadn't actually explained anything to Tilly she just said, "come with me" and started dialling. "I'm calling the Ch-" she stalled before she accidentally revealed anything. "The Chief. He will know what to do."

"So, you work for the police?" Tilly said quietly as Jenny turned away from her.

"Hello?" said Chair Matthews as he answered the phone.

"Yes, Chief Matthews," Jenny winced at the use of the wrong title. "It's Jenny, there are two Harvey's and one of them is preying on Tilly."

"Who is that? What do you mean two Harvey's?"

"The girl I found the book on. There are more books and they are supposed to be meeting soon and I didn't know what else to do." There was a moment of silence as Jenny waited for an answer.

"Let her go, and follow her."

"Let her go? Are you sure?" Jenny cut in as the Chair started to speak again.

"Yes, follow her and I will send Charlotte as back up for you, she's with me now. Where are you?"

"Just down the road from the library, we will head back now." Jenny hung up. What the hell just happened? She did not like this plan even one little bit and it was still absolutely crazy to even allow someone like Tilly, with no knowledge of her world, near someone like this Fake Harvey. Tilly had turned herself away from Jenny so she poked her in the arm to get her attention. Tilly jumped at Jenny's touch.

"Sorry, you looked glazed staring at the road," she said when she noticed Tilly's annoyed expression.

"That's okay, I guess, so what are we doing?"

"You are going to meet this Harvey doppelgänger and I am going to follow you from afar," she said, trying not to allow her emotions to come out. Her idea would have been to take Tilly to headquarters and protect her while Fake Harvey was hunted down and brought in. Who knows what this guy was doing when no-one was around.

"Is that even safe? Whose decision was this? Do I even get a say?"

"I don't know, the Chief said so, and you do but it wouldn't make a difference. You'd probably meet him anyway," replied Jenny, looking at her watch. Thirty minutes.

"How do you know what I would do, you only just met me?" Tilly protested.

"I think we are slightly similar in some ways. Curiosity gets the better of us. We like to explore things that are different, even if that is slightly crazy and our inner voice is telling us not to do it."

"Yeah, I guess," Tilly looked to the floor.

"Tilly, look at me," Jenny stood in front of her. Something inside her wanted this girl to be her friend. Aside from Charlotte, Jenny didn't have many friends, another one, especially one not in The Collective would be different. "I promise you, nothing bad will happen because I'm going to be right behind you."

"I won't be meeting him alone?" Tilly sounded worried, scared almost. Jenny needed to reassure her that nothing would happen to her.

"No, of course not. The Chief might be a little eccentric sometimes but he's not crazy. You're not going to meet someone we suspect is." Jenny tried to think of the right words to not scare her even more. "Not who they say they are without me. Anything could happen otherwise."

"Can I ask you something?"

"Yeah, what is it?" replied Jenny.

"Would you go and meet him if our roles were reversed?"

Jenny didn't know how to respond. She didn't know how she would react if the roles were reversed. It was hard to comprehend as she knew Harvey and imagining that she didn't and then all of a sudden having him pursue her and trying to spend time with her was something she knew would never happen. If it did, she probably would be just curious enough to meet him.

"Yeah, I would," she said after a few moments of thinking about it. "Just not alone."

She watched Tilly's face as the recognition that they were similar in more ways than one came over her. She smiled and got one in return. She needed Tilly to trust her completely for this idea to even remotely work in their favour.

Jenny looked at her watch again, twenty minutes left, they had better get moving. She waved her hand in a motion that indicated

Tilly should follow her and they made their way back to the library.

Once there, Jenny got Tilly to stand outside and wait while she put herself into a position that meant she could watch but not be noticed by anyone who was looking. She stood by the shops' windows, watching Tilly in the reflection.

Tilly was sitting with her back to Jenny. There were only a few other people walking around, but seeing as it was nearly ten a.m. on a student campus there wouldn't be many of them around. They had arrived with five minutes to spare but the waiting was slow. Clock watching always made time feel slower.

Fake Harvey finally arrived and Jenny watched as he came out of the library and sat down next to Tilly. She couldn't quite hear what they were saying but it wasn't long before they both got up and started walking towards an exit that went off campus.

Jenny waited for a few moments before starting to make her way after the pair. He led Tilly down a few remote alleyways and streets, making it difficult for Jenny to keep up. But keep up she did. Down the streets and alley ways, her trail ended at an old, boarded-up shop with a lot of graffiti on the outside. They were gone, and Jenny felt incredibly guilty for letting Tilly down. She was too slow and didn't see where they had disappeared. It had to be down the alley's, it was the only place that would provide cover.

As if God was listening to her pleas Jenny heard a door slam and headed in that direction. Running down the alley way she noticed a back door that was open. Maybe the door that slammed didn't shut? Jenny opened the door enough for her to squeeze through, as quietly as she could and stepped inside.

There wasn't much inside but it didn't look like the kind of place that should be boarded up. Inside was an expensive interior complete with a built-in kitchen. It was a really nice place, but Jenny knew it wasn't something Harvey would live in and there weren't any pictures or other identifying factors to tell Jenny who lived there. There were only two other doors inside which meant they had to be behind one of them. Jenny wiped her finger along one of the kitchen counters as she walked past - no dust. That meant it had recently been cleaned. Suddenly, she heard a sound come from one of the rooms, and then the gap under the door lit up.

Everything happened too fast for Jenny after that. She ran to the door to find it locked and had to get her hair pin out to pick it. Once it clicked open she couldn't act quick enough to open the door. She could sense something was wrong and was becoming panicked that Tilly would be in danger. As the room came into view she saw the time tunnel. The time tunnel's light was illuminating the room with its blue and white lights. Jenny had never seen one before and to her, it looked like a doorway with a shimmering centre. Fake Harvey was stood there holding onto Tilly's arm.

"What is that?' said Tilly high-pitched and clearly worried. Her arm was outstretched as she pointed to the time tunnel. Jenny was frozen in fear watching the scene unfold.

"That my dear is a time tunnel. I told you we are going on an adventure," said Fake Harvey as he smiled at her. Jenny wanted to move forward, wanted to save her friend but she couldn't move.

"I changed my mind, I don't want to go, I don't want to go through that. This was such a bad idea," Tilly replied as she tried to un-grip his hand from her arm. "Let me go, Harvey!"

"Why have you changed your mind?" Fake Harvey took a few steps forward towards the time tunnel pulling on Tilly's arm. Jenny wouldn't forgive herself if she stayed rooted to the spot any longer. Taking a step forward the wooden floor creaked below her foot and both Fake Harvey and Tilly looked around at her.

"Jenny?!" they called in unison.

"Jenny help me!" called Tilly as Harvey dragged her closer to the portal.

"You can't stop this Jenny."

"Just watch me try!" Jenny shouted as she ran towards them. As she reached out her hand to grab Tilly's she stumbled as her hand didn't connect with anything. They were gone. Forcing herself backwards, before she fell into the time tunnel and ended up god knows where she landed on the floor staring at the shimmering light as it disappeared.

She wasn't sure how this had happened, but she was damned sure she was going to find out. A noise came from outside the room like a door shutting. Jenny slammed her fist into the floor in frustration and looked up as Charlotte walked in.

"What happened?" asked Charlotte as she moved to Jenny's side. Her facial expression showed concern and worry.

"Fake Harvey just opened a time tunnel and took Tilly through. I tried to stop them but I was too slow," explained Jenny as she squeezed Charlotte's hand. "I can't leave her there."

"You don't even know where there is." Jenny gave Charlotte a sour look as she stood up. "I'll make a phone call and see what can do done," continued Charlotte, "Stay here until I've finished." Charlotte went outside into the kitchen area and Jenny looked around the room they were currently in. Walking over to where the time tunnel had opened she noticed there was something on the floor. Bending down to pick it up she turned over the gold item in her hand. To her, it looked like some weird pin that was incomplete. A half circle with a gap and then another half circle.

"Okay, we got to go back to headquarters," said Charlotte as she walked back into the room. "What's that?"

"I don't know I found it on the floor. What did they say?" asked Jenny.

"I have to take you back to headquarters. That's all they told me."

Charlotte and Jenny left the building and made their way to the church. Without wanting to take longer than necessary they called a taxi, there wasn't a lot of traffic and so arrived within twenty minutes. They were greeted with the entirety of the Regents from the city, sitting around the table in the meeting room, all thirteen seats full. No other members of The Collective were around.

Jenny felt like she had all eyes on her as she followed the beckoning arm movement of the Chair to get her up to the front of the room. She felt overwhelmingly shy for a few moments as she stood directly in front of all the Regents. Looking at Charlotte she only nodded and smiled, maybe a hint of reassurance.

"Jenny, why don't you tell everyone exactly what you told me on the phone," Chair Matthews started, "if what you and Charlotte have described is true we have a huge problem on our hands."

"This is not something I would lie about," she replied directly to the Chair. It was easier to pretend she was just talking to him than a room full of the city's Regents. "You told me to follow and I did. Charlotte obviously followed me and came in after the commotion. We were inside this abandoned shop, on the inside this shop was more of a home with a fully functioning kitchen and lounge. I saw a light from under one of the doors and picked the lock. Upon gaining entry I saw a time tunnel and watched it close as Tilly and Harvey walked through it. Then Charlotte came in and we found this on the floor."

Jenny held out the pin she had picked up from the floor.

"That is a portal pin. Regents have them to travel between times. You need two of them to activate a time tunnel but it's a one-way door and closes after it's been used, leaving one-half behind," said one of the Regents who had a sour expression on her face.

"Do you have any inkling into where, or more exactly, when they went?" asked the angry Regent.

"No, there were no obvious signs," replied Jenny as she lowered her head.

"It's okay child, we have other ways," said a female Regent. She was slightly older than the others, less scary and her eyes told Jenny she wanted to help, along with her smile. "Is there anything of hers that you have?"

"No only the pin they used" Jenny held out the pin in the palm of her hand for them to see.

"I see, can I have it please?" said a male Regent who was next to the lady that just spoke. "It's not a complete pin so tracking them could be difficult, but it could possibly work. Follow us. We will need you to find them as you're the only one who has seen this girl."

He, along with the old female and two others, stood and went into the Regents Room in the back of the Sanctuary. This would be the first-time Jenny knew of that someone other than the Regents entered this room.

Inside, the room was extravagant, rectangular in shape, and the walls were a deep red with gold patterns covering them from floor to ceiling. There were sofas lining the left side of the room and a big screen on the right. The screen almost covered the entire wall. The female Regent who had spoken to Jenny first was at the far end of the room near a table with strange artefacts on it. She placed the pin inside a navy bag, splashed some water on it and dropped it into a golden goblet that was as big as a basin.

The bag caught fire and smoke filled the room. The smog the smoke had created was so dense Jenny could hardly see anyone.

"Don't be frightened by what you see," called out the male Regent, "it cannot hurt you, nor can it see you. You are merely looking through a window into whenever they have arrived."

As his voice called through the smog all of a sudden, the smoke turned to a vision. It was night, and Jenny could see the moon reflecting off the sea's waves. There was no sound but she felt the motion of rocking, almost as if she were on a boat. Harvey swung around into her view and the scene changed. She almost felt sick from the motions. He was dancing, but not with Tilly, she couldn't figure out who this woman was but they seemed to be having fun. Jenny searched the scene with her eyes but she daren't move from her spot; she felt rooted.

Tilly was sitting off to the side, she had a mug in her hand and was laughing. She was wearing an old lady's dress from the early 18th century. She looked like a noblewoman. As Jenny turned her head she watched a barmaid scoot off. She knew exactly where they were.

"They're in the golden age of piracy," Jenny called out to them, "he took her to where she is studying for her dissertation."

"Okay," said the lady. "What I need you to do is focus on Tilly. If you think of anything else you could end up anywhere."

Jenny's eyes widened at the information she was being given.

"We can open the door to get you there, please stand back."

Jenny stood to the side as two of the Regents came together. They pulled out their pins and linked them together, placed it on the floor and stood back. The portal opened from the ground up making a doorway of swirling colour. She wasn't sure on what she needed to do but for now, she would just walk on through and hope she could focus on Tilly long enough to find her.

9
TILLY

FEAR CREPT over Tilly as she watched her friend disappear. Jenny had burst through the door and tried to stop Harvey from taking her through the swirling colours but she was too late, and now she was staring at the horizon. It was night time and the sea was calm but her heart was not.

Concern came for her friend but this was quickly replaced by concern for herself. Tilly wasn't entirely sure what had happened and stared into the darkness where Jenny had once been. Harvey was behind her hands on her shoulders rubbing them to keep her warm. There was a chill in the wind.

"Come on, let's have our adventure," he whispered into her ear. Tilly turned around as his hands slid down her arm to her hand and took it. He pulled gently to lead her away down the docks to a small fishing village. She wasn't sure if it was the beginning or the end of the night as there were barely any people around. Most of the buildings had no lights on and it was very quiet. Only faint sounds could be heard in the distance, along with the rush of the ocean.

He walked her through the street adjacent to the docks and stopped by a nearby tavern. He opened the door for her and waved her through. Inside she was met with music, drunken men and women, and laughter. She also noticed how everyone was dressed. All the ladies were in dresses along with their hair in bonnets or fancy up-dos. The men were in traditional dress for the 1700's. She thought she had arrived in a re-enactment of the time.

"Ah, Master Thomas you are back!" called the barman, "I have clothes all ready for you both in your rooms above, as requested."

"Perfect, thank you," said Fake Harvey. He turned and smiled at Tilly. "Let's go and sit down."

"Harvey, where are we?" asked Tilly refusing to move.

"Where do you think we are?" he asked her with a sly smile. "Take a look, and give me a guess."

It was then that it hit her, she was in the 1700's, but she couldn't be. Could she? She looked around at the tavern but she still didn't want to believe it. She shook her head and closed her eyes. This was not happening. Tilly opened her eyes again in the hopes that she was back in the weird flat like building he had taken her to and her imagination was just going wild, but it wasn't. Her hands went up to her head, it was starting to hurt.

"I think we should get you upstairs now before you make a scene." Harvey put his hand behind her back and moved her through the tavern to some stairs near the rear of the building. Upstairs, a door opened to reveal a small room with a bed inside it. On the bed was a royal blue dress and there was a girl sitting in the chair by the window. She stood up, nodded and left without another word. Weird? When she looked towards Harvey, who she assumed was still stood behind her, she saw he was closing the door and leaving her in the room.

Tilly sat on the bed and put her head in her hands. It was pounding with thoughts about how she was here, what was really going on and more importantly what did Fake Harvey want with her? Why was she so important? Trying to keep her thoughts and questions at bay she laid down and fell into a slumber.

෴

When she awoke, her head was still pounding. Outside it was

slightly lighter but the sky was dark and the stars were shining. Lying on the bed next to the dress, she jumped when a handmaiden walked into the room.

"Sorry, miss, I was asked to wake and dress you," she said lowering her head.

"Um, that's okay... sorry, could you just tell me where I am?" Tilly asked her, "and what's your name?"

"My name's Sarah miss, and you're in the Three Roses Tavern," the handmaiden said.

"Right, but where is that, exactly?" Tilly tried to get some more information out of Sarah.

"America miss," replied Sarah. Tilly rolled her eyes.

"Okay, let's get this over with. I'll put this stupid thing on, I'll play your little game, but then I'm calling the police."

"The police?" Sarah looked at her all confused.

"Yes, you know, the people who enforce the law?"

Sarah just nodded at her and helped her into the dress. Her breath was a little too short when the corset was pulled tightly around her rib cage. She was given a pair of shoes which were pointed at the front with a square buckle. Tilly noticed that the dress covered her feet and so after the handmaiden had left the room she switched them for the ballet pump shoes she came in. Once she felt comfortable enough she opened the door and headed downstairs.

The main hall with the bar was still booming with people. There were people dancing, drinking and laughing. Tilly watched in awe as the barmaids lifted their full trays above flailing arms and beneath others. She spotted Harvey and walked over to him. As she passed one of the drunken men drinking with his arms around a lady, he slapped Tilly on the backside. Tilly stopped dead and turned around.

"Don't touch me," she said.

"What did you say to me?" said the man.

"I said, don't touch me," she crossed her arms. The man laughed at her and reached forward again.

"And just who do you think you are, missy?" said the man,

readying himself to stand. Tilly was about to get ready to slap him when Harvey appeared at her side and stopped her.

"That, my good sir, is my lady and if you touch her again I'll cut off your hand," Harvey said as he slipped his arm around her waist. He grabbed the top of his hat and tipped it towards the man.

"You should keep a better leash on her tongue," the man grumbled as he sat down. Fake Harvey scowled at him.

"And you should watch who you are speaking to."

Before anything more could be spoken a boy ran up to the man and whispered something in his ear, causing the man's eyes to go wide. Whatever this boy had said clearly disturbed the man enough for him to nod his head.

"Apologies, I will endeavour to keep my hands to myself," said the drunken man lowering his head away from Harvey's gaze. Tilly didn't understand what had just happened but she was pulled away by Harvey and seated at a table in the far corner of the tavern near the bar.

Tilly hated the way her dress puffed up when she sat down and constantly pushed it down for the next few minutes until she got it to settle. She felt ridiculous. When she looked up Harvey was looking at her, smiling.

"Like the dress?" he asked her.

"It's lovely," she said sarcastically giving him a scowl.

"Don't worry, it's only for tonight. Tomorrow the adventure starts," his eyes lit up, putting the feeling of dread in the pit of her stomach. She didn't know where she was, or why he had basically dragged her here but this was not going to be a fun adventure for her.

"Are you hungry? I've heard some girls get angry when they're hungry. I'll get someone to bring you over some food."

Fake Harvey trundled off to the bar and Tilly watched as he spoke to the barman. He was handed two tankards and given a nod as they both looked in her direction. Feeling slightly exposed with both of them looking at her she moved her gaze from them to the others in the tavern. It wasn't long before her gaze fell upon

Fake Harvey, and she watched him as he went over to a smaller table near the bar. He placed the two drinks there and slapped one of the men on the back as he started laughing.

Before long Fake Harvey had interacted with most of the people in the tavern and as she continued followed him around her vision was blocked by someone standing in front of her with a plate of steaming food.

"Broth for you dear," said the barmaid as Tilly looked up at her. "Nice fresh bread too, that should fill you up." The plate was put in front of her and Tilly couldn't stop her hands from reaching for the food. Her belly made a noise that she hoped no one else heard.

"Not from around here are you," commented the barmaid. Tilly looked at her after taking a bite of bread and shook her head in response. "So, what are you doing here in our tavern? He doesn't normally stay this long."

"You know him?" asked Tilly as she swallowed her mouthful.

"Aye, he comes here often. Only ever stays two nights though and then disappears for a bit." Tilly was curious, how did he come here often if Harvey was from 2015?

"What does he do?"

"Don't you know love?" asked the barmaid, "he's a pirate. We only let him in because he pays so well. Always drinking and eating us out of our stock. Here," she waved her hand and ushered Tilly along the bench a little bit so she could sit down. "Name's Martha, I'm the barman's wife."

"Nice to meet you," replied Tilly. "Can you tell me more about him?"

"A nice girl like you, sure, just don't go repeating it. There's too many stories about him and the crew of The Solitaire. They ain't nice people missy, and if you can you ought to get away from him."

"Martha, get up woman we got work to do!" called the barman. "I need three more broths!"

"Sorry dear, duty calls. If you're still here I'll come back and tell you." Martha got up and scurried off back through the door, to what Tilly assumed was the kitchen.

She wasn't sure what Martha could tell her but if there was time she wanted to talk to her more. Before long the barman was calling for last orders and Martha had not returned. Everyone she was with seemed to be having a good time but all Tilly could think about was what she was doing here. What was the purpose? As people started to wander to the street Sarah reappeared and told Tilly she was supposed to take her to her room. Upstairs, after Sarah had helped her undress and get into bed, Tilly led down and pretended to be asleep until Sarah left the room. As the door closed she started to feel the tears running down her face. Sniffing and wiping them away she tossed and turned until she finally fell asleep from exhaustion.

When Tilly awoke the next morning, she was not prepared. Her handmaiden from the previous night was standing at the foot of her bed facing her. She sat up as she jumped and shuffled herself to lean back on the head board. The girl just smiled, moved her arm out and pointed to a set of clothes on the chair in the corner by the window to the right of her.

She swung her legs out of bed and went over to them. She was happy to see they weren't another form of dress but more suited to her taste, although still very classic. In fact, they were what Tilly would call "pirate-like." Although she liked what Sarah had in her hands Tilly still felt uneasy. Frowning she moved forwards and tried to grab the clothes but Sarah took a step back away from her.

"Um..." Tilly started saying as she turned around. "Sarah, would you mind leaving the room while I change. I feel I won't need your help with dressing this time."

"Of course, miss, but I'll be back in a few to do your hair. Master Thomas says you're not to look like a lady today."

At first, after Sarah had left, Tilly was confused by Sarah's comment, but after more thought, she remembered that in this time women were only supposed to wear dresses, not trousers. She dressed in the trousers, shirt and jacket as quickly as she could, in the hope that Sarah would not return until she had, and sat down at the table in front of the mirror to wait for her. She wasn't a fan of the way she was dressed; the shirt was made of cotton and was very loose. She would much prefer to put her jeans back on before gallivanting off with Harvey on some unknown adventure. She pulled off the jacket and hung it on the chair behind her as Sarah re-entered her room.

"Miss, you need this too," said Sarah who had returned with a hat so large Tilly wasn't even sure it would fit on her head. "You should be wearing the jacket."

"I was hot," replied Tilly with a pout. "I don't want to wear it."

"Master Thomas says you must, I'll not have you leave this room without it. Now let me do your hair."

God, she's pushy, thought Tilly as Sarah yanked her hair back and pulled it into a tight bun. As Tilly sat uncomfortably in her seat Sarah lowered the hat onto her head. It did fit her. Almost perfectly, the feather attached to it stood atop, only bending slightly over. As extravagant as a pirate captain's hat, thought Tilly. Her thoughts wandered to her playing as a captain on a boat. Something she used to imagine herself doing when her father told her stories. She giggled at her overactive mind but stopped when she felt Sarah remove the hat. If it wasn't for Tilly knowing she was female she would definitely think at a first glance she was male. Blessed with a small chest, which didn't show through the shirt, along with her deep brown eyes and no makeup, she did, in fact, think she could pass as a pirate captain.

With hope in her eyes and a sense of adventure in her heart she stood up from the table and marched out the room. When Tilly entered the tavern's main room she was surprised by the reaction she got – which was none at all. She thought someone would have recognised her from last night, even if she was dressed up like a man.

She made her way back to the table they sat at the night before, and it wasn't long until Harvey appeared next to her and his eyes were gleaming along with his smile. He was looking exceptionally handsome. From what she could see, he had on a dark grey coat that came down to his knees and was open at the front; a white shirt with a red belt and gold buckle, and black trousers with matching boots. What she didn't expect was the pistols strapped to his side.

"I've got you a few gifts before we set off on our adventure," he said, still smiling. As she didn't know how to respond, she just smiled sweetly back at him. Maybe if she pretended to go along with this craziness she could find a way home soon.

The gifts were not the type she was expecting. In her mind, she was thinking authentic jewellery and fine dresses, what she got was an extremely well-made sword, two pistols, and a compass. Now she really was beginning to look like a pirate.

"Where did you get all of this?" she asked him.

"My secret, but I had them made for you. For our adventure," he was doing that smile again. His happiness shone out of him but it actually creeped her out a little. It was almost as if he adored her but they had only met twice.

"Come on then," he said, leaping from his chair and heading for the door. Tilly struggled to hold both pistols in holsters and her sword but she scrabbled them together and headed out the door to follow Harvey. He hadn't gone far, as it turned out, he had turned down the path back to the docks. In the sunlight, it was easier to see the ships that were docked there as most of them were dark colours that merged with the darkness of the night.

There were currently three docked in the port that she could see. The two closest that she could read the names of were The Fear of Atlantis, which she thought must have been a pirate ship, and Serenity, which Tilly didn't think looked like a pirate ship but that was the one she saw Harvey boarding. The third ship she only saw the name of when she approached the gangway to board the Solitaire – The Serenity.

It was a magnificent vessel. Larger than the Serenity and captivating with its colours.

"Come," said Harvey as he grabbed her by the arm and pulled her towards The Solitaire. Her eyes never left the man from The Serenity, he looked familiar to her although placing his face was something of a mystery, but as she was pulled further into the ships centre he disappeared from her view.

"We need to speak privately before the rest of the crew come aboard."

"What? Why aren't they already aboard?" asked Tilly.

"Because I needed to speak with you privately and they all had a rather late night. They'll be here when it's time to set sail, don't worry," he was smiling again, his blue eyes shining like the ocean behind him.

He opened up the doors to the captain's quarters and gestured for her to go in. Leaving the doors open, he joined her inside and sat down in the chair she was aiming for.

"First, you are the captain of this ship, another gift to you."

"What?!"

"Go ahead, take a seat, Captain," he was pointing to the seat across from him. This was weird, she had never captained a ship before. She didn't even know what to say to make the crew do what she wanted. Her mind was spinning again and that chair was looking more and more friendly.

"So, it's time for an adventure," he said producing a map.

"I don't understand what's going on Harvey," Tilly said sitting down on the other side of the desk.

"We are going on an adventure, and you are going to help me with something," he started to explain, before being distracted.

"Help with what? I'm a university student, not an adventurer," she countered.

"But you have the contacts."

Tilly frowned at him in confusion but he refused to say more. Nothing made her miss home more, or want her new friend Jenny. Maybe she would be able to shed some light on what was happening, she was involved after all. Harvey pulled out another piece of cloth with a picture of a telescope on it. Tilly had seen it before in one of the books she was using for her research. A strange feeling washed over her, she needed to find that telescope.

10

JENNY

Jenny had never been through a time tunnel before, normally it was only used for Collectors who have a mission. It was an honour for Jenny to experience this before Graduation. The Regents who had offered to help had made her dress in men's attire as it was easier to get about in the time period she was going to if you were a man. Her unruly blonde hair was braided underneath the hat she was wearing, some of it was hanging down the front of her face.

Her outfit of choice, as they had given her a few, was that of a soldier in the army. They had also strapped her chest up so that if anyone grabbed hold of her they wouldn't notice her breasts. Of course, they had to be careful which one they chose and so they mixed pieces from them all. At the very least she could pass as a rogue privateer if anyone speculated. Her knowledge of the era was almost perfect.

The Regents had moved her from the back room into another smaller room. It had nothing in it except for a giant circle. Jenny wasn't sure what it was used for, it seemed pretty random to have a circle painted on the floor though. The Regent obviously saw her confused face as she tried to work out what it was used for and answered the question.

"It's used for creating the time tunnel. You don't need it but this is more stable. Less likely to lose you in the void," he explained.

"Remember," said the female Regent, who Jenny now knew as Celia. "You need to be careful. This is your mess and you need to sort it out. Some of the Regents think you aren't ready to be tested for a promotion due to your need to prove yourself. You aren't your mother Jennifer." That hurt. Jenny looked at the floor as she continued to speak. "We are aiming to send you through to this location," Celia handed her a map and some paper. "Then you're going to want to go to this armoury and ask for a woman called Jaclyn. She has short brown hair, or she did last time I saw her, she will help you with the next steps. You'll need to find a Regent with a broach so that you can get home."

Jenny looked over the piece of paper and broach, they both had The Collective's symbol on. The paper itself was a set of instructions on where she was landing, how far it was to the armoury. In case I forget, thought Jenny.

"Remember Jennifer, we will be watching you if you weren't the only one who had seen the girl we wouldn't be sending you. Consider this a test," Celia looked hard at her and Jenny could do nothing but nod her head. Her heart was pumping already.

The Regents moved together and started to open the time tunnel. She wasn't sure what they did to it, Jenny assumed she would learn it one day when she became a Regent herself but for now she just watched as the tunnel came to life. With a deep breath, she took her first steps through.

The wind whirled around her ears, a light flashed in her eyes and her limbs were stretched as she glided through. Her feet hit the ground unevenly and her ankles buckled as her body weight shifted. She fell down and grazed her hands on the dirt as she skidded along the ground.

She cursed to herself as she stood up and wiped the dirt from her hands and knees. It had left a light scuff mark on her trousers but she wasn't worried, the mark brushed right off. Looking around she could tell she was behind a butchery from the smell of rotten meat but from where she was standing she didn't have a clue where to go.

Before she started moving she quickly checked her pockets for the note, broach and pistol that she had been given. Without them, this mission might not go too well. She hoped that some of The Collective's personnel in this time period would help her out. The hard part was finding them. Satisfied with having all three she made her way to the armoury, not knowing what she was going to face she needed weapons. Now she understood why her father had made her take fencing lessons for so many years.

From what she could tell when she looked up it was just past the middle of the day and there were a lot of people in the town. Children were running around and some merchants had set up shop selling foreign wares. Jenny wasn't interested, she was here for Tilly so fended off the merchants trying to grab her attention as she went past.

As one of the children ran past she looked up and saw a group of women perched on the benches by the fountain. She walked up to them and bowed her head.

"Ladies, apologies for the intrusion but would you be able to answer a quick question for me?" she asked them. A few of them giggled before one of them answered her.

"Depends on what the question is, young man."

"Nothing too impersonal, I am looking for a young lady who would have been new around here. Possibly arrived the night before, would you have seen her?"

The women looked between themselves as if having a secret conversation with their eyes. Then all but one of them lifted their fans to their faces.

"No, I am afraid we have not," the woman said, her tone cool and distant. Jenny instantly knew she was lying. How annoying.

"Thank you for your help, ladies," she said, turning away from them thinking about where she needed to go next.

The armoury wasn't that far away from where she had come through the time tunnel and fairly easy to find down the secluded road. The sword rack outside gave the place away, she remembered one that she had seen in the books she'd been studying.

Unsure if this was the place she was supposed to be at, Jenny thought of a way to be able to get the inhabitants to trust her before the sun set. Asking questions earlier hadn't gotten her very far. What was she to do? Waltz in asking for Jaclyn and spill her guts about The Collective? No, she needed to be clever. Unable think of anything else, Jenny picked up a rock and a twig from outside and turned her back to the building. She put the twig in her mouth and bit down as she dug the sharp edge of the rock into her skin creating cuts along her arms. Next, she ripped the corner of her jacket and wiped her graze along her knees to put a smear of blood on the fabric before going inside.

Creating a limp, which wasn't hard as her ankle still hurt from falling over, she entered the premises. Hobbling over to the desk she slammed her hands down on the counter to alert the owner's attention.

"Coming, coming," called a voice from the back room.

"Excuse me, could you help?" she said calling out in a hoarse voice.

"Of course," said the man appearing from the back. His eyes widening when he looked at her. "Good God man, what happened to you?"

"I was attacked on the way back to the barracks sir. My companions fought valiantly, I should have gone down with them. Blasted pirates saw to it that I be left alive and shamed just off the coast."

"You are not shamed, young sir. Come with me I'll get you looked at and cleaned up and then a hot meal. That should do it," he said rushing around the counter to grab hold of her so she could use him as support.

"What's your name son?" he asked. She hesitated, they hadn't thought of names before she came. Being put on the spot wasn't usually something she worried about but in this situation, she needed time to think. She let her head fall to look like she was losing consciousness.

"Son!" he said louder, "Stay with me, tell me yer name?"

"Uh, Wyatt, uh, Franklin," she blurted out and then looking at the man's face, put her hand up to her head and groaned. While he may have thought, she didn't know her own name, in the beginning, he wasn't going to question it now.

"Not the sort of name you hear around here often son."

Of course, it wasn't, she plucked two names out of the air. Wyatt the son of one of the Halliwell sisters in her favourite television show, Charmed, and Franklin because she had been reading about Benjamin Franklin before she started on the pirate books. He didn't seem too concerned about her stutter and carried on allowing her to lean on him for support.

He took her into the back room and laid her down on a straw bed.

"I'll just call the wife in from out the back and get her to see to yer wounds and then make you a nice meal. You stay awake son and we'll fix you right up."

He was a sweet man and everything happened just as he said it would. His wife came in and introduced herself as Katrina. She bandaged up Jenny's self-made cuts after putting cream on them to aid healing, and then made a broth for them all to eat. Over dinner, Jenny told them the story about how her travelling group got separated when they were attacked and she didn't know if any of them had survived. They had come to the town looking for a lady who was new.

From the look on their faces, they didn't know much about her but suggested trying the docks as two ships had set sail recently and a third was leaving tomorrow. She helped Katrina and her husband clean up, all the while keeping up with the limp, but they made such a fuss she went to the back room of the armoury and laid down.

Jenny felt bad for what she was about to do. These were good people but she had no money and needed a sword. She was going to steal from them and she wasn't happy about it. When night fell, she snuck up to the door, pressed her ear against it and listened.

She heard no footsteps and concluded that they were both asleep upstairs.

She turned around and went to the small window of the room she was in and saw a bush just below the ledge, perfect for hiding a sword in. Guilt set in, along with nerves, and she returned to the door of the armoury. She removed a pin from her hair and began to pick the lock, stopping a few times to check her generous hosts were still asleep.

When she heard the click of the lock, she slowly opened the door; it creaked loudly. Jenny cursed under her breath and stopped dead in the hopes that she hadn't woken them. The night was silent. Inside the armoury, there were a lot of swords to choose from but she chose one of good making - although probably not the most attractive.

The sword was thin and light, easy to spin around in her hand. The hilt was well made with a small circular design around the grip. It felt right in her hands. She stuck it in her jacket and snuck out of the room to where her bed for the night was. As she was coming through the door she heard movement from upstairs, she dived for the bed.

The owner of the armoury entered the room. Jenny sat up on the bed and tried to look startled.

"Is everything alright? I heard noises down here?" he whispered to her.

"I haven't heard anything, but I am a deep sleeper. What do you think you heard?" she asked him.

"Don't worry son, probably just an old man's paranoia," he laughed slightly and went to turn around.

"Do you want me to check the shop with you just in case?" Jenny was trying to sound like she was grateful for his help and kindness, but she wasn't sure it went down like that at all.

"No, that's alright. I'll go back to sleep but let me know if you hear anything, okay," he smiled weakly and headed back out to his living quarters.

Guilt ran through her again as she removed the sword from

her jacket and dropped it out the window ready for her to come back and take it.

In the morning things were very normal. The shop owner got up and went about his daily business in the shop while Katrina asked Jenny for a lot of her help.

"Wyatt, would you mind chopping up some wood for us before you go to the docks? The ship isn't leaving until lunch and my husband needs to look after the store."

Jenny almost hadn't responded, not used to being called by the name she had made up but did so just in the nick of time by appearing in the kitchen and accepting. There wasn't much wood to cut up just two logs that they wanted into three's and then split in half for their fire. Winter was coming and it would be a god send for Katrina and her husband to already have some wood cut.

The axe was already outside the back of the house by a tree stump, to cut the wood on, and the two logs that they wanted cut. She couldn't refuse Katrina as she had been so kind to her, and her food was amazing even if it was basic.

Jenny grumbled as she walked out to the yard; her back was sore from sleeping on that straw mattress. Her hosts were incredibly kind, and she knew it wasn't their fault, but still straw... as a mattress.

"Okay Jenny; think like a man, swing like a man, chop wood like a man—" Her voice cut off as she nearly dropped the heavy iron axe straight down on her boot. "Christ! How does anyone even lift this thing?! Can't they just throw the whole log on the fireplace or something?"

She went to lift the axe again but paused as a voice came from behind her.

"Well, well. It's not every day that you see a woman posing as a man," he said. Jenny spun around in shock to see who had spoken. She was pleasantly surprised. Stood before her was an actual soldier, although he looked more like a ship captain from the way he was dressed and he was very easy on the eyes. His dark hair and eyes combination was always a weakness of hers, which is why she didn't understand her attraction to Harvey.

"I don't know what you mean sir," Jenny replied after mentally scolding herself for thinking about Harvey.

"Really? You're shorter than any of my soldiers, you can't lift that axe and weren't you just mumbling about thinking like a man?" he cocked his head as he finished speaking. Jenny furrowed her brow, was this guy for real? "It's alright I won't tell anyone, and I'll even help you chop up this wood."

"That's not necessary," she insisted. Who was this guy? What a creep!

"I think you'll let me help."

"And why is that sir?"

"Because I saw you throw that sword out of the window and it's currently being taken to my ship, of which I want you to accompany me on."

"Because that's not creepy, why were you watching me through the window?" asked Jenny, growing more concerned with every word he said.

"A few of my men were talking about some ladies they had met, they were very fascinated with the young man who had just arrived and started asking questions about the two people that arrived into town last night," he smiled at her. Why did he have to be cute? "I can only assume one of them was this man," he held up a wanted poster with Harvey's face on it. "And I'd quite like to catch him. You obviously know him."

"That still doesn't explain how you saw me through the window. Do you always stalk your prey?" Jenny said batting her eyes. *Why am I flirting with him?* she thought scolding herself. *It probably won't get me very far.* "I mean, it's not like you'd know I was in there?"

"My swords were getting sharpened here, I came down from up there," he was pointing to behind the armoury, "and I saw it being flung out of the window. The one which you were trying to steal is mine, I think you owe me considering you were stealing from me."

Jenny refused to say anything.

"I'll take your silence as an admission of the crime, so how about I make it easier for you. You come with me and help me find these people, or I tell the owner, you get arrested and punished for your crimes," he was still smiling at her, but his eyes said he was deadly serious.

In anger at his proposal, she lifted the axe and brought it down on one of the logs. She didn't quite split it as she wanted but she did more damage to the log than she imagined she would. Jenny swung again bringing the axe down with a little more force and went all the way through.

"You need my help, I know where they've gone and you know them, they will trust you. We can help each other," he insisted.

"And if I don't help you, you'll turn me in?" asked Jenny already knowing his answer. He nodded. She was in a catch-22 situation and her only option was to go with him.

"Fine but you can chop up the rest of the logs," she said walking off to the bench that was by the door to Katrina's kitchen. As she turned around to sit down she noticed him smiling again as he went over to the axe and started to chop the rest of the log up.

Once all the log chopping had been done Jenny called inside and said goodbye to Katrina. Her husband had gone out so Jenny was unable to thank him in person, but Katrina said she would pass on her regards. The captain had waited outside for Jenny and he escorted her to his ship.

The Serenity was unlike any ship Jenny had ever seen. None of the pictures she had seen in books or films could ever do something like that justice. She stopped walking halfway down the docks and the Captain turned to her.

"If I'm going to come with you I need to know your name," she said crossing her arms.

"Captain Joseph Lawson, at your service," he said bowing his head.

"Okay stop that right now or I am not getting on your ship," she said laughing. "Seriously, stand up."

He stood up straight and smiled.

"Thank you. So what's the deal, how is this going to work?" she asked him.

"You are going to come on board as your male alter-ego. You'll be my guest which means you won't be bothered by the crew when you are in your cabin and you will join in with our meetings as we discuss how to track Harvey and your friend."

"You're not going to tell them my secret?"

"I think that is one best kept between us. Shall we?" he put one arm behind his back and the other he held out indicating for her to go in front of him.

The boat wasn't too far away from them and she was even more amazed when she got on board. From the aroma surrounding her, she could tell the ship was freshly painted. All the crew were busy working away with ropes and sails to make sure it was ready to go as soon as Joseph gave the order.

She was looking around and holding up the gang plank which she didn't realise until Joseph cleared his throat behind her. She scurried onto the deck with her head slightly down as she realised that she was being really girly. Although she did like the fact she had caught Joseph smiling at her.

As Joseph came on deck he instantly started barking orders at his crew. They all rushed to do as he commanded. They were setting sail and were one step closer to Tilly.

11
TILLY

TILLY'S HEAD was spinning as she tried to focus on the map in front of her. Half of her was still trying to compute what was happening and the other half was trying to play along so Fake Harvey didn't suspect anything. She wanted to know why he wanted her here but she wouldn't be able to ask him out right. Fake Harvey seemed like the type of man who doesn't take kindly to people not doing what he wants.

"So, we are sailing in this direction," Harvey continued. "You're not listening, are you?"

"I'm sorry it's just all a little bit overwhelming. Can you not explain it to me like I know what you're saying? Because I don't. Describe this like you would to a five-year-old."

He lifted an eyebrow and then spread the map out properly putting weights on all the corners to keep it down.

"So, we have sailed from this little town here and we are on our way across this section of the sea to an island in the Bermuda Triangle," he said pointing at the map in correspondence with what he said.

"The Bermuda Triangle? There isn't an island there..." Tilly said, trying not to sound condescending.

"No one knows what is in the Bermuda Triangle, that's why we are going."

"Well, that's because there isn't anything there. But whatever."

"Just trust me, okay? And shush."

"'Trust you?' Trust you? After you literally hijacked me through some crazy time warp thing and dressed me like a sailor and refuse to let me go home?! Okay, sure, I'll definitely 'just trust you.' Maybe if I had the memory of a goldfish."

Fake Harvey stood back and stared as Tilly ranted. "You done?" he said when she was finally out of breath, thankful that she wasn't still wearing that horrid corset from the night before.

Tilly glared. "Yes."

"Good." He continued to explain the route they were taking, and that before they went on their journey they would be stopping on the island of Tortuga to pick up a couple extra crew members and allow the men one last night before a long journey of work.

"Are you kidding me?" she said, disgusted with his 'boys will be boy's speech'.

"What?" he said shrugging his shoulders like what he'd suggested was completely normal. "You've read numerous books about Pirates, you should know they'd want to do this."

"It's still absolutely disgusting. Let's just not mention the fact that your crew are cretins again okay? I don't need to know anything about that," she said screwing up her nose at him. Tilly leant back and crossed her arms expecting Harvey to react.

Harvey smiled at her and shook his head, "you know, I thought you'd have a stronger stomach for a girl into history."

"How long are we staying there?" she fired back ignoring his comment.

"Only one night," he answered snatching the map from her hands. "We go, the crew have a bit of fun, I pick up the rest of our crew, we get food and in the morning, we leave again."

As it was only a one night's journey to Tortuga there wasn't a reason she could think of to avoid it. Tilly rolled her eyes. The Tortuga she had read about was not the place for a woman, yet

Harvey had absolutely no qualms about taking her there. It made her curious but Tilly also knew she would have to be cautious.

"And what do you need the telescope for? I mean, it's a telescope, can't you just buy one?" Her curiosity was getting the better of her. She should just go to bed and play along.

"Buy a telescope? Yes, I could just buy one, but this one is special. It's imbued with magic," Harvey said making the emphasis on the fact it was magical. Who did he think she was, an imbecile?

"You really expect me to believe this telescope you want to find is magical? What does it do, see into the future?" Tilly waved her arms, doing Jazz Hands as she said her last sentence, then laughed at her own sarcasm as she sat back into the chair and folded her arms.

"Actually yes, it can show when people are going to die." His sudden facial expression was so serious Tilly wasn't sure how to react.

"I think I need to sleep," she announced, standing up. Playing to his game she continued, "I take it this is my room, as I am Captain?"

"Of course. I shall take my leave," he said, standing up just as abruptly as she did. "I apologise if this was too much, but we don't really have the time to wait around, I need that telescope."

Before she could respond to his words Harvey left. Feeling an overwhelming sense of fear, she ran to the door and locked it. There was no way anyone was coming in here while she slept. As she got changed she realised she should strap her chest so that if one of them ever grabbed her… Her mind trailed off to thoughts of female pirates. She could be one of them if she got some training. She would ask Harvey in the morning for a trainer, at least then if this ever went bad she could defend herself.

Tilly walked back to the table with the map and the picture of the telescope. All through Harvey's explanation, she kept thinking it couldn't be true, but then again, she had just been transported back in time. Could it be that impossible? How could a telescope show you how someone is going to die? Knowing that much into the future is wrong. It also wasn't normal. Any mystical object that she had read about in stories, fiction and non-fiction, were infused with the elements or connected to various gods, not the ability to see someone's death.

She looked at that map all night until she finally succumbed to fatigue. Unable to stop her eyes from closing she fell asleep on the desk planning her next move.

※

Tilly was jolted awake as she felt herself move. The ship rocking was a weird sensation which she wasn't used to. Lifting her head from her arm and wiping the drool from the corner of her mouth, she put her hand to her head. She was slightly confused. Waking up in a different setting to her usual room was odd, especially on a moving ship. The term 'sea legs' came to mind.

As her vision came into focus she realised she was in the captain's room on The Solitaire. Which was where she was last night but her dream had been so realistic she was confused. Tilly shook her head as if that would wake herself up a little more and looked down. She grimaced at her own saliva which had managed to get itself over the map. As she wiped it off with her sleeve she noticed the tiniest dot within the area of sea that Harvey had said was where they were heading. It was very easy to miss and it was no wonder most modern day maps said there was nothing there.

She scrabbled around the desk looking for a magnifying glass. It was still dark and the only illumination was coming through the glass doors of her room. The moon lit it up wonderfully but it was easier to see once she found a lantern, the fire bathed the room in a warm glow of light. It definitely made her appreciate her modern-day technology, but there was something magical about seeing through the past's light.

Tilly wasn't sure on the time but the only sounds that could be heard were the waves, and possibly some footsteps up above but that would only be one of the crew members at the helm. She thought they were sailing pretty steadily and the steps above her were not that frequent. Unsure of why she was trying to keep so silent, she went about searching the cabin.

Over on one of the chests to the right of her were some tools, one of them being a magnifying glass, which was exactly what she was looking for. Bringing it back over to the map she started looking at the island. Even though the magnifying glass it was still just a minute dot. Tilly wanted to draw the triangle out on the map but she didn't have anything to write with. She slammed her hands onto the table; if only this was modern day.

Trying to avoid the risk of her growing frustration giving her intentions away, she decided to leave her cabin on the ship and go out on deck. She unlocked the doors and opened them, allowing the moonlight to bathe her and the room. Walking out on deck was slightly eerie as there was no one around, except for the boatswain at the helm. They looked at each other but neither one made any motion towards the other. Tilly turned around and walked over to the port side of the ship. She leaned against the ledge and looked out to sea.

Their journey to Tortuga wasn't long and she could already see the land coming into view. This made her wonder why no one had called out that fact.

"You alright, Captain?"

Tilly jumped at the sudden appearance of one of the crew members. She had seen him before around Harvey but had never spoken to him. He was wearing a hat, which was what made Tilly recognise him, but it cast a shadow across his face to obscure his features in the waning moonlight.

"Yes. Can't sleep, first time on a ship in a while," it wasn't the truth but it wasn't a lie either.

"Ah yes, the first night can be daunting. I'm Bill, your second officer; obviously, Master Thomas is first," he smiled weakly at her. Tilly got the feeling he didn't like her all that much.

"Are you okay?" she asked him, feeding her curiosity about his feelings towards her.

"I'm fine, just trying to feel out the new Captain. God knows what Master Thomas is thinking."

Ouch. Tilly knew this wouldn't have been taken lightly but she didn't know what else to do, it's not like Fake Harvey gave her a choice.

"I will have to meet everyone properly when they are awake before they have their fill of Tortuga," she laughed trying to lighten the mood with a joke. He gave her another weak smile and leaned next to her.

"Be careful pretty lady, other members of the crew might not take kindly to you being on board," he frowned at her. Tilly's eyes widened in surprise at his knowledge she was a woman. "Don't worry," he continued, "I'm his second, he tells me things but I won't say anything if you won't."

Tilly literally couldn't speak, she didn't know what to say to him. Fear crept over her as Bill kept on staring at her, something about him was familiar but she couldn't place it.

"Do you know where we are going afterwards? He didn't tell us," he asked her, changing the subject.

Tilly thought this was strange. Surely if Harvey wanted to go off chasing after some mystical artefact he would have at least told his crew. She scowled to herself. Goosebumps trickled up her arms and along her neck. She shivered. "I believe he was waiting for me. We will be announcing our journey tomorrow."

From the look on Bill's face, that seemed to have satisfied his curiosity for now. She did wonder how she was going to make searching for the telescope sound like an adventure that everyone would want to take part in. At least, Tilly thought to herself, I have time to think about the words to say.

Bill walked away leaving her to her thoughts. She was grateful although she would have preferred company, or the ability to sleep. She didn't stay for much longer after Bill left her, only a few more moments looking at the calmness of the sea and feeling the light breeze on her face. Tilly closed her eyes for a few moments and thought about being back home. How she was going to get back there she didn't know. She choked back a few tears before pushing from the railings and walked back to her cabin.

This time, after locking the door, instead of falling asleep at the desk Tilly actually went to the makeshift bed to the right-hand side. Sitting down she was surprised to find the bed was a lot more comfortable than expected. She thought she would be sleeping on an uncomfortable bed of straw, but it was a well-made mattress, probably of duck feathers which would have been expensive around this time and curled up.

☙❧

The next morning Tilly was woken by Harvey. He was sitting at the desk looking over something, the only conclusion Tilly could come to was that he had a key. He didn't even apologise for it, but he did blow out the lantern – which she had also forgotten to do. As she got herself up from the bed her hair fell around her face. Tilly didn't notice but Harvey cleared his throat and moved his hands around to try and make her aware. It was too early in the morning for her to care. She needed her coffee and that was something she just couldn't get here.

In her cabin, there were three people besides Harvey. Bill and the boatswain stood on either side of him, but there was also a small lad with them.

"Who is that?" she demanded.

"Powder Monkey," replied the boatswain. "Captain." He added the last word and bowed his head when he saw how angry her face was.

"If he isn't related to anyone on this ship he is being taken back as soon as you are all finished in Tortuga. He is not to leave the ship," she said with arm movements to accommodate. She couldn't stand the thought of a boy being on this ship. He was so young, and it felt good for her to have some control, considering her situation.

"Captain, I believe we have some business to discuss," said Harvey, trying to change the subject and cool the atmosphere. "Shall we begin?" Harvey didn't wait for Tilly to respond but she didn't mind.

"Now I'm sure you're all aware that I am the captain, so I have some amendments to what my First Mate has in mind for our journey," Tilly stated. She was testing how these people were going to react to her authority. "You have one night where you are free to do whatever you like on land, but anyone not back by the time we set sail tomorrow will be left and therefore no longer part of the crew." Everyone was quiet as she laid out the rules, and no one argued. "Right, you can all leave. First Mate, deal with the rest of the crew."

Once they docked in Tortuga and the crew took their leave Tilly was surprised that she had a desire to go on land too. She didn't know what she would find but she hoped she would find someone who could train her how to fight. It was the only way she was going to get herself away from this madness. She had decided against asking Harvey for permission because, well, she was captain and she could do whatever she wanted. She would play that role until she could go home.

Tortuga was definitely the exact same as it was portrayed in any pirate film she had seen. Drunk men everywhere, and women in dresses that were very revealing for that time period. As she walked down the docks she noticed a small tavern with not many people in and she decided she would start her search in there.

Inside it was warm. There was a roaring fire and no more than about seven people seated at various tables.

"Drink?" asked the barmaid.

"No, actually I'm looking for someone to train me, um..." she paused on that thought. "I'll just take an ale thanks."

The barmaid nodded her head and dropped a tankard on the table in front of her. Tentatively she reached for the ale. *Well, when in Rome,* she thought to herself as her fingers closed round the handle. Bringing the drink to her lips the strong smell reached her nose and she almost gagged. It definitely wasn't something that she could drink. Looking up she noticed a man staring at her. She took a sip of the ale and swallowed it before she slammed the tankard down on the table. The surrounding men cheered in response and then went back to whatever they were doing to those women. Tilly looked away.

"Train yer in what?" came a man's voice. As she turned she saw the man who had been staring at her was now leaning against the wall by the fire.

"To fight," was all she could muster out.

"Aye, I can do that laddy. For a price," he crossed his arms and lifted his legs up to rest them on the small table in front of him.

"Well I'll need to see how good you are and I'll need your name."

"Names Roger Morgan, privateer and an excellent swordsman," he stood to his feet in one swift movement and bowed his head. Men sure did like to do that around here.

"Well, so far I know you can boast about yourself, but I need to see what you can do with that metal stick you call a sword before I offer you anything." Tilly crossed her own arms and waited.

What he did next surprised her. He walked over to one of the other men and punched him in the face. This caused a ruckus and two other men pulled out swords ready to attack. Roger pulled out his own sword but was almost too slow to dodge the oncoming attack. He swerved to the left, spinning and pulling out his sword as he went. Tilly wasn't sure how to feel. Sure, she was impressed with his skills but she was also very aware that this man could teach her to fight like this too. That made her nervous.

He moved with such a finesse that she thought he could be a decent teacher. Against two men he was managing to hold his ground and attack them before they got to him. He defended, blocked their attacks, tripped one of them up and then shoved his sword under one of their necks.

"Gentlemen, I thank thee for the demonstration but I believe my potential client has seen enough. Let me get you both a drink," he gestured to them to go to the bar and he turned around and winked at Tilly. Something she was not expecting.

He stalked over to the bar and dropped a couple of coins for both the men to have a drink and then came back over to her. She could tell he was drunk but even so he fought well.

"So, did I pass yer test?" his rugged voice sent shivers down her spine. Tilly took a deep breath and put on her act of a confident captain of a ship.

"Indeed, although you'll need to sober up before we start. There are only a few rules you'll need to follow," she said, crossing her arms and moving closer to the fire. Turning back to him she tried to give him her best pirate face. Tilly hoped her glare seemed cruel enough for a pirate; she imagined the time when Chris spilt spaghetti sauce on her new H&M dress. Yes...that should do it. She hoped.

"I don't do rules, mate," he scoffed.

"Then I guess you don't want bed, food and a place on my crew."

"Yer a captain? And yer don't know how to fight?"

"Hence why I need you. You in?"

"Aye, but I 'av one more question," he said raising his eyebrows.

"Ask away," she said with a flick of her hand.

"Are ye tryin' t' keep the fact you're a lass hidden or does everyone know?"

"How?" Tilly's eyes widened with her response.

"Ye not exactly built like a lad, and t'e flick, ye definitely a lass," he said. She knew she wasn't fooling anyone but hearing a complete stranger tell her was not what she expected.

"It's that obvious?"

"Aye, lass." He said. Okay, this needs to be nipped in the bud.

"First, stop mentioning I am a woman so much. It's infuriating. Second, sober up. Third—follow me."

He did as she said. He necked back his drink, put the tankard on the table, stopped talking altogether and he kept right behind her.

Tilly checked below deck once they had gotten on board. She wanted to have at least one lesson without everyone watching how rubbish she was going to be. Not that a lesson with a drunk privateer would prove to be informative. There weren't many spaces on board to practice, so she mentally decided she would only practice during the evenings. If it came to it, she wanted to be sure she knew how to defend herself from Harvey, maybe even kill him. She shuddered at the thought. Could I really do that?

"So, first lesson: You usually need a sword to learn how to fight with them," Roger slurred, stumbling a little on the deck.

Tilly narrowed her eyes. "No duh, Privateer—I'm about to go get it. I'm not a complete imbecile." She darted inside her cabin, took off her coat and emerged with a sword in hand. He gasped at the sight of her. "What?" she asked him, confused.

"You know you really do look like a man sometimes, that sword is beautiful!" he exclaimed. She laughed and pulled it from its sheath.

"Are you right or left-handed?"

"Right."

"Okay, put the sword in your left hand; it will be beneficial for you to learn with both. We will swap each lesson."

Tilly was impressed, again, she never thought he would be a good teacher but he would certainly be better than Harvey. All she could be think about was how to keep up her charade with the fear seeping out of her.

"One thing before we start," she said. He nodded to her to show he was listening. "You are under my command and are loyal to me. One mistake and I'll have you thrown overboard." Tilly couldn't help the need to feel in control. If her charade was going to be convincing she needed someone on her side.

"Now you're starting to sound like a real pirate, love," he said, laughing. "Hold it loosely in your hand," he said grabbing hold of her arm. "If it's too tight someone will knock it out of your hand and it will hurt, but don't let it get too loose otherwise you won't be able to attack."

He showed her how loosely he held his and she tried to mimic him by spinning the sword around in her hands. Roger showed her some simple defence moves, which she practised by herself and then he would slowly attack and she would defend. This carried on for most of the night until her crew decided to return.

"What happened to your accent?" Tilly asked him as they stopped for a break.

"What happened to my what?" She could tell by his face he was playing dumb.

"Your accent, what happened to all the 'yer wee lass' and the slur you had while intoxicated?"

"I'm not from around here, I didn't want to miss the chance to be on your crew. I wasn't intoxicated either," he didn't wait for her to respond. "I lied."

"Why?" she asked him. "Why would you need to lie?"

"It's hard to explain, so let's just say I am looking for someone and I think your crew might be able to help me."

"That makes absolutely no sense," she said throwing her hands up in the air. "I'm not comfortable with it either, who are you looking for?"

"Oh, just someone from another crew, who left and I've been tasked with finding him," replied Roger, he looked at her holding the sword and Tilly could just sense what was coming next. "I suggest we retire for the night, Captain. It seems your crew are on their way back and you have learned a lot tonight. A quick study."

"Yes, that's a good idea. Did you want food?"

"No, thank you. I'll find a bunk downstairs," Roger bowed his head and went into her cabin closing the door behind him. Tilly walked to the gangplank and watched as her drunken crew returned for their beds. She had to stop a few of them as they tried to bring women on board, telling them if they wanted company they would have to go elsewhere for the night.

12

JENNY

JENNY WASN'T ENTIRELY sure she could trust this Joseph Lawson. He had followed her, tricked her and given her no choice but to come with him. She kind of hated him for it but at the same time, it was her best option to find Tilly. How else was she supposed to navigate through the 1700's with no ship? There was something that was bothering her about Joseph though, his face was oddly familiar. She'd seen his face before, in a photo maybe?

He had allowed her to walk first onto the ship and followed closely behind her but he didn't expect her to stop as she got on and walked straight into the back of her and then they both fumbled and apologised to each other. Jenny was in awe. She'd been on a ship before but the more modern ones, it was nothing compared to this. She found herself wondering why ships were never made like this anymore. She also thought that his ship hadn't been very important as she didn't know any reference to a ship called The Serenity in any of the history books she had read. However, not all of history was recorded.

"All hands to weigh anchor!" shouted Joseph as the crew scrambled to carry out his orders. "Set sail for Tortuga!" He turned his attention to Jenny and smiled. "Care to join me for dinner?"

"Of course," Jenny said smiling back at him. She didn't exactly want to refuse and the mention of food made her stomach grumble. Instinctively her hand went over her belly and she followed Joseph into his cabin.

"I figured you'd be hungry," he said. Unable to find words for fear of her belly crying out for food again she nodded her head and gave him another sweet smile. Inside his cabin was extremely decorative, there were lots of light colours on the walls and lots of paintings of ships.

"Were any of these yours?" she asked, curious as to their use.

"Only two of them, the others were ones that my father captained. He was killed at sea."

"Oh, I'm sorry," said Jenny, cursing herself. "You take after him then?"

"Yes, he wanted me to be a Privateer and so my brother and I made it happen for me," he replied as the doors opened again and trays of food started to be brought in.

She had never seen so much food before, Jenny felt spoilt for choice. There were several different types of meat and fish, apples, bread, vegetables; she thought he must be part of something big to be able to have a chef on board to cook a meal so extravagant. Unless they had it pre-made and just warmed it up on the ship. The food was truly divine, and Jenny couldn't stop herself from digging in.

"So, now that you are more settled I have a few questions to ask you," he said as she took a mouthful of meat. She held her hand up to her mouth as she tried to chew it quickly.

"Go ahead," she replied after swallowing her food loudly and reluctantly putting her fork down. She hadn't eaten since that morning, and her stomach growled in protest.

"How do you know Harvey?" he asked stabbing some meat with his fork.

"I work with him, I've known him for years," she said wondering where his line of questioning was going. He pressed his lips together and nodded his head in acknowledgement of her answer. Jenny took a deep breath, he obviously doesn't believe me.

"What do you know about the ring he wears?"

"He doesn't wear a ring," she said instinctively. Harvey didn't like jewellery on his hands; he had told her once that the only ring he would ever wear would be a wedding band.

"Yes, he does," he said standing up. He walked over to a cabinet and pulled out what looked like a file before returning to his seat. He opened it up and looked inside. He pulled out a drawing of a hand and a ring and passed it to Jenny.

"How am I meant to tell if it is his? This is a picture of a hand," she said politely.

"You can trust me, it is his." He was looking at her blankly as if she should already trust him, but Jenny hardly knew him.

"Who drew it?"

"The last person to see him. My Second Mate is a member of his old crew, so I have it in good faith that it is his."

"The Harvey I know would never wear a ring that wasn't a wedding band," she said.

"Obviously, you don't know him that well," boasted Joseph.

"I know him well enough," she protested, frowning at him. Jenny didn't want to argue with him, after all he was helping her find her friend but she couldn't help feeling protective over Harvey, especially as this wasn't that Harvey.

"How well do you know him, exactly?" Jenny detected a twang of jealously from him.

"Excuse me?" she asked. "Why is that of any relevance to you?" she snapped.

"Of course, you're right. Well that's quite enough work talk for one night, don't you think? I'll show you to your cabin," he said smiling weakly. He obviously knew he had upset her with that comment. He wiped around his mouth with his napkin and threw it onto the table.

Her cabin wasn't far away from the captain's. There were a set of hidden stairs behind the ones up to the helm and these led to two cabins that were secluded and away from the rest of the crew. At a guess, Jenny assumed these were for the First Mate and a guest.

Joseph opened the door for her and stood outside as she

walked in. There were clothes laid out on the bed for her to sleep in and more in the wardrobe for the days ahead.

"Thank you," she said quietly still looking around. "What are these?" Jenny pointed to the clothes on her bed.

"They're clothes for you. I had a trusted advisor get them while we had dinner," explained Joseph. "I figured you didn't have anything else." His eyes were fixated on hers and she could see in them that he was sorry about earlier. "We will be in Tortuga by morning, get some rest."

Jenny smiled at him, trying to make him see that although she was mad she wouldn't be for long. After he finished talking, he shut the door behind him. Jenny could hear the sound of his boots echo down the hall.

She was alone on a ship in the ocean 300 years in the past. When she imagined the trips, she would go on as a Collector she did not imagine she would be there. Jenny had always hoped she'd get an assignment in the Victorian Era. Sherlock Holmes' time, he had to be real. She had read so much about The Collective Regents and their work there. She quickly got changed and settled into the bed. Tomorrow would be a long day.

❦

Jenny was jolted awake by the ship bumping into the dock. She realised she must have slept a long time as there was food on her side table and clothes laid out on the chair. It was creepy to think someone had come in while she was sleeping and done that. Even if it was a nice gesture. Tomorrow night she would have to double check she locked the door.

Another quick outfit change and she was soon on deck. The crew were stood in lines waiting for Joseph to give more orders, although from what Jenny could see he didn't seem to be around. She tried the door to his cabin and it was locked so she went up to the helm to see if he was looking at charts or something.

As she turned around, disappointment overcame her. Joseph wasn't at the helm; only his First Mate and the navigator were.

Neither of them took any notice of her. It was only when she turned around that she heard his instructions to his crew. She stayed on the upper level and leaned on the bannister to listen and watch.

"Your task, men, is to find out any information you can about our suspect and his assailants. I mean anything, we just need to know if he was here. Do not get swayed into the vile ways of the pirates. We may not be them but we need to act like it for one night without getting carried away. Clear?"

"Sir, yes, sir," said the crew in unison. As they finished speaking they turned and made their way to the gangplank to disembark the ship.

"Well aren't you a smooth talker," Jenny called out.

Joseph turned around and looked up at her. "Nice to see the sleeping princess has arisen, shall we go and find out some information or would you rather just stay here and sleep?"

"I hope it was you that entered my room while I was defenceless and not some other members of your crew," she scowled.

"It was your handmaiden. I brought one on board to help with the cooking, and to aid you. I thought you'd like it."

"Because everyone likes waking up to find their room has been entered while they were unaware," Jenny quipped as she walked down the stairs to join him.

"You, my dear, have a sense of humour about you. Come along or we will never find anything out," he called behind him as he descended to the docks below. Jenny scoffed and followed him.

The docks were filthy. The sunlight didn't do them any justice either, it just reflected the dirt and grime that has been left from the night before. Her boots were sticking to the wood, obviously, a lot of alcohol had been spilt last night - though no one was around to clean it. After walking by a few barrels that lined the docks, Jenny and Joseph passed a few unconscious men slumped in between them. No doubt they would be waking up with a nasty headache.

Not far down the docks, Jenny noticed a little back alley tavern with a lady outside cleaning. The only place that had someone cleaning it. She tapped Joseph on the shoulder and started to make her way down to the tavern's doors.

The tavern itself looked, from the outside, barely big enough for one crew let alone the numerous ones that docked there. It didn't even have a sign on the outside. Jenny was about to walk right up to the lady outside cleaning and bombard her with questions but Joseph put his arm out and shook his head. He stood slightly in front of her and cleared his throat so the lady looked up at both of them.

"Can I help yer, Cap'n?" she asked him with a disapproving look on her face.

"I was wondering if you would answer a few questions for us? We are investigating and wish to know if some people passed through here recently?" His voice had become all posh and Jenny had to stop herself from laughing by putting her hands to her mouth. The woman didn't respond, so Joseph continued. "Have you seen a man about this tall," he was making motions with his hands but she was continuing to sweep the floor, "lightly coloured hair, dressed like a privateer. He'll have a few companions with him?"

"Nope, not seen no one like that."

"Have you seen anything strange around here, or do you know the names of any recent ships that have docked here?" asked Jenny, getting straight to the point. Patience was never one of her strong points.

"There was a lass who came in last night, took one of the privateers with her, and there was a ship docked here last night—different from the usual ones. Might've been called the Solitaire or something like that. I don't know, my lad likes to sit by the docks and watch the ships."

"That's wonderful. Didn't perhaps say where they were going, did they?"

"No, sorry."

"Very well, thank you for your help," Jenny tugged on Joseph's sleeve to get him to come with her. He didn't seem annoyed that she had basically taken over his investigation; in fact, he seemed satisfied.

"You were good," he said, almost admiringly.

"The Solitaire, that's their ship," she said sticking to the point. There was no time for niceties; she needed to find Tilly. "We should ask the boys at the docks, see if they know the direction the Solitaire was going."

"You are good," he said, still acting as if she was a miracle worker. "We had better get to it then."

Jenny couldn't quite understand the way the captain was acting. He should have known what questions to ask and yet he was acting like he was dumbfounded and didn't know what to say. Or maybe he did that to test her and see if she was willing to aid this investigation and wasn't just along for the ride because she had no choice. She still hadn't gotten her sword back yet.

It was a short trip to the docks and easy to locate someone who might be able to help them. There was a sailor sitting at the end of the dock with his legs dangling over the edge. From his black trousers and dirty white shirt Jenny assumed this guy had to be from the pirate ship. As they got closer to him she realised he had a tankard of ale in his hand.

The drunken men who were slumped against the barrels were still there, they hadn't even moved a muscle. She scoffed as she walked ahead of Joseph and sat down next to the young lad.

"Hey, why so glum?" she asked him.

"They left me," he said without looking up.

"Who left you?"

The pirate looked up at her, studying her. For a second she thought he wasn't going to speak but he took another swig of his ale and grinned, bearing his blackening teeth at her.

"My crew," he said. "They're sailing to Bermuda." It amazed Jenny that men still bared their souls as soon as they got a drink inside them.

"Who's your crew?" Joseph asked him to place his hand on Jenny's shoulder trying to pull her away from him. Jenny took a few steps back obliging his guidance.

"You won't leave me here like they did?" said the pirate.

"No of course not!" Jenny tried to sound sincere, of course, they wouldn't be allowing a pirate on a privateer's ship.

"The Solitaire," grinned the pirate. "Captain talked about it. He brought a new Capitan on board and told me if I didn't like it to stay behind because they were goin' to the Ilsa de Rosa then on to Bermuda to find something."

Jenny's eyes widened in the truth that spilt from the pirate's lips. Her friend was on a ship sailing to Bermuda. She turned her head to look at Joseph, he was looking at her intently, but nothing could have prepared her for what happened next.

"Thanks for the help," he said quietly and stood up. Joseph kicked the pirate in the back and knocked him off the end of the dock.

"Are you insane?!" shouted Jenny as she rushed towards the edge, Joseph's arms caught her as she struggled to pass him. "He's going to drown!"

"Good then he won't be able to tell anyone else where we are going," Joseph's voice was still very matter of fact even though he was fighting her. Jenny stopped struggling as the pirate sank beneath the surface.

"We can't let anything get in our way," he said, his arms still around her. She looked into his eyes and knew he was right. Tilly was out there, with someone parading around with Harvey's face, who knows what was happening to her. Knowing it was for the best, Jenny went with Joseph back to The Serenity. Back to her chance at finding her friend.

13
TILLY

TILLY KNEW there must be something inside that cabin. Another map, some more drawings of artefacts…she didn't trust Harvey, not anymore. She had listened to the crew below decks as they gossiped between themselves after they had climbed into their hammocks. It was like listening to a bunch of girls. Most of it was just that, gossip; they had said how no captain should be as strict as she was, but they knew why.

"I don't get why we got her on board," said the last one to enter, his voice sounded well educated for someone who was supposed to be part of a pirate crew and he was louder than the rest of them. Tilly had taken to giving them all nick names, so he was now Loud Mouth.

"You kno' wha' Harvey said," replied another, "Harvey said she had te be 'ere because he needed what was comin'."

Tilly's ears pricked with curiosity, what was coming? How did it involve her? How did they know she was a woman? She moved closer to them, staying behind the barrels of gunpowder she had taken to hiding behind. Tilly was in a good position, easy to get in and out from behind without being seen.

"Who cares what Harvey wants," said Loud Mouth. "It's still a stupid idea!" From the tone of his voice, Tilly imagined he was throwing his arms up in the air as he said that.

Her eyes were growing heavy as the conversation continued but Tilly learned that some of the crew didn't know she was a woman, and that Harvey wanted her here because of what would come after her. Which made no sense to her. Moving her position a little so her back was against the barrel her eyes closed.

"Captain," came a whisper. "Captain, wake up." Tilly's eyes fluttered open and crouched in front of her was Roger. "Come on, let's get you back to your cabin."

Once back in her cabin Tilly felt a lot more awake and she had immediately started going through the drawers and cabinets.

"What are you looking for?" Roger had asked her. Although Tilly wasn't sure she could trust him she needed someone on her side.

"Something to prove my First Mate's disloyalty. The crew have been talking about his intentions and if what they say is true, it's not something I am going to tolerate. He thinks he can bring me here and then treat me like an idiot? I don't think so." She knew she was ranting but she didn't care. Roger's hands clamped down on her shoulder and he forcibly sat her down in one of the chairs.

"Stop for a second," he had said as he made her sit. "What do you mean he brought you here."

"Surely you must have noticed?"

"That you have no idea what you are doing, yes, actually I have," he said as he took a seat across from her.

"I'm not from here, I shouldn't tell you; he told me not to. It might mess up history if it's not already." She put her head in her hands and leaned her elbow on the desk. Tilly had a funny feeling if Jenny found her she would not be happy with this.

"Right, so Harvey, your First Mate stole you through time and told you that you couldn't say anything to anyone or you would ruin time?" Roger raised his eyebrows at her. "Sorry, but you know how far-fetched that sounds right?"

"You don't believe me, do you?" Tilly said looking up at him, "I'm being serious."

"Okay," Roger took a seat at the desk, "I'm not saying I don't believe you, I truly believe you believe what you are saying, but I'm not sure I believe you can't tell anyone about it." Tilly looked at him, tears beginning to form in her eyes. Roger sighed and tilted his head to the left. "Look you've already said a lot, so why not just tell me the rest."

"I can't" she sobbed, sniffing back the tears. "What if it ruins everything back home?"

"But what if it doesn't? You can trust me, I'm here to help you," he sounded genuinely interested in helping her, and Tilly's gut told her she could trust him. Even if they had just met, he had been nicer to her than anyone else. She took a deep breath and decided she would only share some of the information with him.

"I'm from the year 2015," she said, pausing to look at him. Roger blinked hard at her and then sat back into his chair and ran his hand through his hair. "I was brought here by my First Mate, he said we were going on an adventure but then he showed me a picture of a telescope he said he needed."

Roger was silent. He didn't seem shocked or confused by anything Tilly had just told him. In fact, he was actually quite calm about everything. Tilly thought this was strange so she prepared herself for an outburst of laughter at her madness.

"This is why you want my help with learning to fight?" he asked her.

"Yes, and he made me captain so I thought a captain should know how to use a sword. The pistol I am alright with," she answered.

"The pistol?"

"My father has a shooting range, he taught me how to shoot a gun," she clarified. "Oh—a shooting range is a place where you can practice shooting at wooden targets."

"Thank you - but I do know what one of those is, we have them here," he laughed.

She stood up and started going through the drawers again. Picking up the journal she had disregarded the first time she went through the drawers she opened it and started to read the first page;

Objects to Acquire:
    Future Sight Telescope
    Truth Candle
    Scarab of Madness
    Ring of Deception

Another line had been started but it wasn't finished. Tilly wasn't sure what this meant but she knew it wasn't a good sign. She handed the book to Roger and returned to searching. Both their efforts were halted when a knock came at her cabin door.

"Captain, are you in there?" It was Harvey. "I've updated the crew and we are about to enter the triangle, we thought you'd like to look at the map?"

Tilly walked over and opened the door.

"Apologies, Captain. We did not realise you were entertaining a guest. Who is he?" he asked forcefully.

"As you said—he's my guest, and you are to treat him as such. Let's go up on deck, shall we?"

Harvey nodded his head. Stepping outside, Tilly realised it was very light out, it must have been about mid-morning. Looking at Harvey's second, Bill, she realised she did know him. It wasn't just his face that was familiar.

"Bill, what is wrong with you? You're acting strange," scolded Harvey.

"Nothing, nothing," said Bill. As if in an instant, everything snapped together in her mind. He was the homeless man from outside the cafe. Tilly suddenly felt very unsettled and beckoned behind her in the hopes Roger would come with them to the helm.

All hands were on deck carrying out various tasks that ensured the smooth sailing of the ship, anyone not working was playing a game of cards. It was harmless fun and so Tilly said nothing about it. If she was too strict she would not last long as captain. The thought of a mutiny made a shiver run down her spine; *what would happen if I died here?*

There were not many men at the helm of the ship. The boatswain was checking the map every now and then as he steered the ship on the right course.

"We just wanted to update you on our course," Harvey explained. "Boatswain, if you would."

"We are only making two stops. The last one is the most important as we won't be able to stop again until we reach the invisible island," the Boatswains' voice was deep and he was one man you wouldn't mistake as anything other than a pirate.

"Invisible island?" Tilly asked.

"It's what we are calling the island, and as no one has actually seen it or given it a name, it fits," Harvey waved his hand as if to command her to shut up. Tilly looked around and noticed the other members around her. Bill was sniggering to himself like a child, he was obviously loyal to Harvey, if anything happened she would have to get rid of both of them. The boatswain had a neutral expression but his eyes portrayed a different story, but Tilly couldn't tell what that was. Roger looked like he was about to pounce on him for speaking to her like that but Tilly knew exactly how to handle this situation.

"Well, I know what it's called," she said, giving him a sarcastic smile. "Didn't you see it on the map in my cabin?"

Fake Harvey stared blankly at her, his thick brown eyebrows coming together on his forehead. "You…saw it?"

Tilly shrugged. "Of course, I did. All it took was a magnifying glass and a bit of intelligence. It's called Wyph Island."

There was silence from all on deck at the helm. Tilly wasn't sure how long they were all going to stay like that before someone spoke.

"So," Roger said pointing at the map and breaking the silence, "We are stopping there to wait. That port isn't free; are you sure we can stop there?"

"We aren't pirates, Master...?" Harvey started.

"Morgan," Roger supplied.

"Morgan. We are privateers. CHANGE THE COLOURS!" Harvey shouted to the crew on deck. Tilly watched as the black and white pirate flag was taken down and replaced with one of more colours and stature.

"That doesn't even relate to anything," she noticed.

"The people at this port won't know any different," Fake Harvey snapped back at her. "We will pay to dock, collect our supplies and be gone before they notice."

The Boatswain went on to explain their route and tell them how long it would take to get between each stop. Tilly took her leave, she wasn't sure how much more macho-man display she could take. Roger stayed with them. She expected he would come back and tell her how long this journey was but that wouldn't be for a while. Back in her cabin she laid down on the bed and prayed that Jenny would find her soon. She wasn't sure how long she could keep up the charade of playing along with Harvey's game.

A small tapping sound on the cabin door pulled her from her thoughts. She wasn't sure how much time had passed or how long she had been led there but it was still light out. As she sat up she could see someone at the door. From their build, she assumed it was Roger or Harvey. She called out to let them know she was coming and got up. Although slightly dazed she did manage to wake herself up from her daydream enough to get to the door.

"Yes?" she said as she swung the frosted glass door open. It revealed that it was, in fact, Harvey stood in front of her.

"Um, I'm sorry for the way I acted. Final decisions should come from you, I was out of line," he sounded very apologetic. This was the Harvey she originally met, the one who had whisked her away on an adventure to help her with writing her dissertation.

"Yes, you were out of line," she responded.

"It's a little before midday. We will be docking in an hour, you can already see the docks port-side," he said gesturing for her to look outside her cabin.

Tilly took two steps back and leant back on the desk. She wasn't sure she was cut out for sailing but she had to be strong. Harvey was stood in front of her smiling. He took a step inside and shut the door, blocking out the curious eyes of the crew.

"I really am sorry, are you sure you are okay?"

"Yes Harvey, I am fine," she replied a bit too sharply as she noticed he was playing with the ring on his right hand. He was twisting it around as if he was screwing it onto his finger.

"Good, we should be at the second location this time in two days."

"Two days? Are we staying here for a night?"

"Yes," Harvey clarified, "the second location is just for supplies."

"Second location? Another stop gap?" she said raising her eyebrows. Harvey smiled at her, "So it's a booty island where you've stashed all your plunder?" she asked him in her best pirate voice, then laughed at how silly she sounded.

"In as many words, yes. It's called Isle de Rosa."

Tilly nodded. They were going to be sailing into the middle of the ocean looking for an island that was hidden on a map that looked like it was drawn by a madman, they would need all the supplies they could get. Especially if it transpired that they couldn't find it and sailed all the way to Bermuda.

Tilly peered out across the sea to the small town they were docking at; it looked the same as all the others, but Tilly knew it was taking her one step closer to finding that telescope—and one step closer to seeing her friends and going home.

14

JENNY

STILL IN SHOCK, Jenny wasn't sure how she was supposed to act on the voyage anymore. They just pushed a drunk man off the end of the dock and left him. She was an accessory to murder, even if he was a pirate he didn't deserve to go that way. The handmaiden assigned to look after her had brought some food to her chambers, but she couldn't eat. A knock at the door pulled her from the vision of a drowning pirate.

"It's me, can I come in?" asked Joseph through the door. "I need to explain something."

"Come in," agreed Jenny. The door opened and Joseph stepped inside, closing the door behind him. "Are we near the Bermuda triangle?"

"No, we will be there soon, and there have been no sightings of The Solitaire."

"Oh," Jenny was a little disappointed. She desperately wanted to see Tilly and make sure she was okay. "What did you need to explain then?"

"I brought you something to help with this explanation," Joseph produced a flyer from behind his back. "This is the gentleman that you're upset about."

He was holding the flyer out for her to look at. It was an old wanted poster that had clearly seen better days. Jenny took it from his hands and studied it. The face was familiar, the scene from the docks flashed in her mind again, then she read the below;

MURDERER WANTED

"He was a murderer?" she asked, her voice but a whisper as she let out the breath she didn't realise she was holding.

"Yes, I could see you were still feeling guilty for what I did, but you shouldn't," he said to her. "It was me that did everything. He was a bad man who now can't hurt anyone."

Unsure what to say, she stayed silent. Staring at the face of the man who was no more. His name had been Marty but that didn't matter now that he was gone.

"We should get to Isla De Rosa soon; will you join me for an evening meal?"

"Yes," she replied scrunching up the paper with the man's face on. "I'll be there around sundown."

"Perfect," he said and took his leave, "I'll get the cook to start preparing food."

The sun started to set as Jenny got up off of her bed and looked out of her cabin window. Part of her was wishing Tilly was here so they could talk about history and Tilly could inadvertently help her out with her assignments. The other part was hoping Tilly was there, on the Isla De Rosa, so they could then find a Regent and get out of here. Something in her gut told her it wouldn't be that easy.

A knock came, and her hand maiden entered. "Miss, are you ready for dinner?" she asked after closing the door. Jenny turned around and smiled at her.

"Yes, I think so," she replied. "I'll go like this." Her handmaiden, Madeline, scowled at her and shook her head before leaving the same way she came in. Looking down at her attire she realised that having her waistcoat undone revealed her gender a little too much. Quickly she did them up and tied her hair in a low ponytail.

Satisfied she wouldn't look any better without Madeline's help, Jenny took her leave and went up on deck. There were a few members of the crew tying up the rigging and keeping an eye on the sails. She smiled at Gustav, Joseph's most loyal crew member, who looked up as she emerged from the stairs and then knocked on the door to Joseph's quarters. Without wanting to wait for him to answer her hand reached for the handle as a figure appeared behind the glass.

"Come in," Joseph says as he opens the door. He had changed into his less formal clothes. Now he wore a navy-blue jacket over an unbuttoned white shirt. They were both plain whereas his uniform had golden accents on. "The cook should bring us food in a few moments."

"Sounds good," Jenny's hands were starting to sweat. She smiled sweetly as she entered his cabin. "I'm sorry I freaked out earlier." Joseph pulled out her chair as she went to sit down. Unable to act like a normal human, Jenny nodded her head to the side in thanks and felt the overwhelming flush of embarrassment. Cursing internally, she hoped he hadn't noticed.

"I asked the cook to make something extravagant. Would you like some wine?" he asked her, picking up the jug. Smiling he poured her a goblet of wine and took his seat. After a few moments, the doors opened and the cook, Madeline and a crew member she couldn't remember the name of came in with the food and laid it out on the table.

"We have a dish of salted beef and a mango jus," exclaimed the cook as he placed her plate in front of her. His face showed that he loved to cook and wanted his food to be enjoyed.

"Thank you," she replied as the smell of the food hit her nostrils. "Madeline, will you wait for me in my room after dinner please?" Madeline nodded and smiled, her eyes lit up as she darted out of the Captain's Cabin. Then they were alone.

"Joseph, why did you want me to join you?" she asked him,

knowing she shouldn't question the man helping her. Curiosity usually got the better of her.

"Because I needed your help, we've been through this when I caught you stealing my sword. Plus, you know the man I am after, and I figured as you're after him too we could combine our efforts and find him faster." His answer made sense, but something about it still annoyed her. She shifted in her seat and felt a prick of something in her leg. Grabbing at it she felt the broach in her pocket.

"Are you part of any societies or are you just a privateer?" she asked, wondering if it was just a coincidence that the broach pricked her at that moment.

"No, just a privateer my lady," he replied stuffing his face with some bread. His eyes were elsewhere and she wasn't sure if he was listening to her.

"Oh," her hopes were dashed. She would need to keep looking for a Regent if she had any chance to get her and Tilly home safely. "Do we have a game plan for when we dock?"

"Yes," he said, clearing his throat, "We should do that."

"Are you okay? You seem distracted," Jenny said, annoyed he wasn't listening. He had started to play around with his food. Joseph didn't respond and continued prodding at his beef with his fork.

"Hello. Earth to Joe," said Jenny, waving her hand in front of his face.

"Don't call me Joe," he snapped. Then added, "Sorry, I was coming up with tactics for tomorrow. Scenarios we might run into." His face showed he hadn't meant to snap at her, but also that he didn't like the name, Joe. Jenny made a mental note not to call him that again.

"It's okay; let's call it a night and then we can start again when we get to Isle de Rosa," Jenny said, standing up

Jenny wouldn't exactly call it an easy sleep. The rocking of the ship out of time with the movement of her thoughts kept the fatigue at bay for most of the night. In the end, she only got three hours sleep before her handmaiden snuck in, the door creaking loudly from her entry. Jenny got up once she was alone in the room and dressed quickly. Upon leaving the room she was shocked to see Joseph standing outside, smiling with a sword in hand.

No words were exchanged as Jenny took her stolen sword back into her hands and clutched it to her chest. It was a weird comfort for her to have a weapon as a means to defend herself and a source of courage and confidence that she could pull from when needed. She felt safer with it in her possession. Her mind went to the pistol she had been given by the Regents. Hopefully, it's still under my pillow, she thought as she pulled the sword closer.

"Shall we go, or are you still having a moment with your sword?" asked Joseph. She stopped hugging her sword and smiled at him.

"Yes, let's go."

The ship was anchored on the northwest side of the island, which was covered in trees. They took one of the rowing boats to the shore and covered it with the overgrown shrubbery just off of the beach clearing.

Joseph had only asked four other members of the crew to come to shore with them—the rest were to stay and guard the ship with their lives. They would as well; his crew was very loyal. She'd seen their loyalty put to the test in Tortuga, one man even turned down the touch of a woman to stay on course to find out information. The crew also told stories about their other adventures when they took breaks about how they would do almost anything for Joseph. Once the boat was completely hidden by the shrubbery they all started to make their way into the forest to see what they could find.

Not long into the forest on their trek, the air around them started to get heavy. It was muggy, and mist started rolling in from all around. Jenny was starting to get worried about where they were; she had lost her bearings due to the fog that now surrounded them. She had subconsciously gotten closer to Joseph and her hand tightened around the hilt of her sword.

A scream came from one of the crew behind them, and as Joseph called out one of them shouted back.

"He's gone!" Douglas shouted.

"What do you mean, 'gone?'" Joseph called back. Fear took hold inside of Jenny as they edged closer together. Their group seemed significantly smaller even though they had only lost one person. Jenny waved her arm around to try and clear some of the fog that was in the way.

"Derek, he was right here and then he disappeared," called Douglas again.

"That doesn't make any sense," said a second member of the crew.

"Jenny, what are you doing?" asked Joseph frustratingly followed by the crew repeating her name.

"Jenny? Isn't that a girl's name?" asked Grant.

"Yes, I am a girl; time to get that out in the open and now you all need to forget about it. I was trying to clear the fog enough for us to see, because clearly whatever is on the ground swallowed up one of our friends!" Jenny spoke so fast she wasn't even sure if they understood one word she said.

"Uh," one of them started to say something but with one look from Jenny he shut his mouth and they all stared at the floor.

The one who had almost protested about Jenny being a woman took one step forward and disappeared. He plummeted down and all sound was gone after he was out of their eye sight. The men started to panic and Jenny knew she had to do something before she lost them all and was stuck on an island in the past.

"I vote we all take a step back before we all disappear into the ground and hope they are safe," Jenny shouted over the shrieks, taking her step backwards. "You two step around and come over here."

"Remember who is captain around here, Miss," said Joseph. "Boys, do as she says."

Even through her fear, she was happy as she watched her commands followed. They turned around and moved more carefully through the forest until they came to the edge of the fog. It stopped as if it was only meant to conceal the traps that had stolen some of their crew.

Jenny stumbled over a few rocks and grabbed hold of the mountain that had appeared next to them. The rock she had put her weight on moved down and a slab of it moved away, disappearing downwards to reveal a corridor to the inside. She looked back at the men in her group and they were all looking in wonder at what had just happened, but Jenny wasn't surprised after all the fantasy books she had read.

"So, what do you think we should do? Seeing as you want to run the show," asked Joseph.

"I thought I wasn't allowed to make decisions anymore, Captain."

"Okay maybe that was a little harsh, we are working together and so any insight is helpful," he said. "You are the one who knows the fugitive."

"I think we should hide around this area and wait. This could be an entrance to their loot, but we can't be sure."

"You two go scout the rest of the area. Don't go too far, be careful and be back within two hours. We will need to make camp or go back to the boat if they don't show," Joseph gave his orders and his crew members followed them without hesitation, even though Jenny could see the fear in their faces. A fate of disappearing into the ground wasn't one to strike courage in their hearts, but being loyal they did what was needed of them anyway.

"You know we don't need to return to the boats if they don't show," said Jenny after the two other crew members had gone out of view.

"Yes, but I don't want them to know we are staying out here all night. They get agitated easily."

"Then why did you bring them?"

"They're the two best fighters. As they are easily spooked they tend to defend themselves pretty well," replied Joseph as he leaned against the side of the opening and looked around.

Jenny peered into the doorway as well, but there wasn't much to see. The corridor was too long to see the end and it was only lit by small flames. Coming away from the door she tried to figure out how to close it again; if the pirates from the Solitaire showed up, it would be alarming for them to find it open.

"Isn't there a close switch for this thing?" Jenny whined as she felt the rocks around the opening.

"Did you think it would be easy to find?" said Joseph, stepping across the threshold into the corridor.

It all happened so fast after that. They were both feeling the rocks when Jenny heard a click and the door started to close. At first, it wasn't noticeable what was happening but with Joseph further inside the corridor, the door closed quicker.

"Joseph!" she called to him as the rock rose to her hips. He came running down the corridor too late.

"Hit that rock again, maybe it'll open!" he called as it reached his chest. Jenny frantically started pressing down on all the rocks she could but it didn't stop the door from closing. She was alone on a strange island and she had just lost her captain.

"Jenny?!"

She could hear his muffled voice from behind the door as she leant back against it and shut her eyes. She wasn't trying to block out his voice but he stopped calling her name after she didn't answer. Her breathing had become heavier and her heart was pounding in her chest, she could hear it in her ears. She was alone, and there was nothing she could do. What if they found her out here? She slid down the wall, feeling like she might vomit as she curled into a ball on the ground. Jenny was finding it hard to breathe and a dizziness came over her. *Get it together Jenny*, she thought to herself, *now is not the time to freak out. You need to move.*

Her chest was still tight but somehow, she managed to find the strength to get up from the floor. Not knowing where she could go, she started walking along the side of the mountain in the direction that the crew members went in.

It wasn't long before the scenery changed around her. Even with the mountain on her right, it was hard to tell it was taller on one side until she came to the edge of the forest. In front of her was a white sandy beach and the smell of the sea filled her nose. If

THE COLLECTIVE

she wasn't in the 1700's looking for a man pretending to be her mentor, who had abducted her friend, she could have seen herself enjoying some time there.

Her breathing had calmed down now that she had got herself moving. She wondered where her other crew members had gotten to, and only hoped they hadn't been consumed by the island. Going back to the ship alone would only get her questions she didn't have answers to and a possible mutiny. Jenny took one last gaze at the beach and turned around. Upon facing the mountain, she realised that it wasn't a mountain at all, it was, in fact, a dormant volcano with one side collapsed in on itself.

Knowing she couldn't be out in plain sight when the ship arrived, Jenny decided the best place to hide was up in one of the trees close to the beach. There were a few with lots of leaves and branches which would make a good base. It would give her a clear view of the entire beach which would allow her to see the sea and anyone coming towards them. Looking out to the sea from her position she saw the ship in the distance coming to shore. A small glimmer of hope filled her heart and she thought about seeing Tilly again. *I just need to get Joseph too.*

15
TILLY

HE WAS INFURIATING HER. Tilly wasn't sure how much longer she could put up with his nonsense. Here she was gallivanting around with a madman when all she wanted was to be home with her friends. Making a small prayer that Jenny was coming to get her, she got up from the bed and walked out onto the deck. *I can be strong until then,* she thought.

Their journey had taken far too long. Harvey was clearly agitated at leaving so late but it was his own fault for allowing the crew to take a full twenty-four hours on land. Now they were at the Isla De Rosa, collecting a few important items that Harvey said he needed for the journey. Whatever they were.

The deck of the ship was quiet, too quiet and looking around she noticed it was empty. Tilly knew they would reach Isla de Rosa tomorrow and so she assumed they would have been busy sorting out the ship but she was wrong. Going below in search of Roger she found a lot of the crew were in their hammocks and the rest were sitting around using one of the crates as a table playing a game of dice.

There wasn't much for them to wager with as they hadn't taken much loot since Tilly had arrived but they were still managing to play the game and better yet Harvey wasn't there. She kept to the shadows and just watched the game from afar; it was actually interesting to see how they played.

"Looking to have a go, Captain?" came Roger's voice from behind her.

"What? No, I was just watching. It's interesting to see what they say and how they react," said Tilly with a slight jump at his voice. "What game is it?"

"It's called Liars Dice, a simple betting game to pass the time. You've either got to make the same bid but higher or change the number on the dice. If someone thinks you're lying they call you out. Dice's are revealed and the loser gives up his bet," explained Roger.

"I think I'll just watch for now," replied Tilly, unsure of how this game worked.

"Ah," he said, "I think I'm going to join in." He stood up from the pole where he had been leaning against and walked over to the game.

Tilly watched as the crew grabbed one of the barrels and placed it on the empty side of the crate. A cup and five dice were handed to him and then the deck fell silent again. Tilly moved quietly to stand behind Roger and see if she could understand the game more.

"The wager?" asked Roger.

"Ten gold coins," replied the pirate, giving him his dice.

"I'm sure I'll have them by the end of this voyage. Shall we?"

All four of the pirates put their dice in the cups, shook them and slammed them down onto the table. As Roger lifted his cup up to see his numbers, Tilly peeked over his shoulder. On the table were three threes and two fives.

"You just joined, so you go first," said one of the crew members to his left with a wicked grin. Roger nodded in response and looked at his dice again.

"Four threes," he said in a monotone voice. Tilly noticed there was not a flicker of emotion in any of the men's faces. The guy on the right shifted on his barrel a little but made no other movements.

"Four, fours."

"Five, fives," the third man's voice was a little hoarse, Tilly couldn't decide if that was simply him or a tell that he was lying. Apparently neither could the last player of this round.

"Five, sixes," he took his hand off of his cup when he finally made his decision.

Roger was looking at all of his fellow players and then looked at his numbers again. Tilly hadn't seen any of the other players' dice so she didn't know what was going to happen when Roger made his final bet.

"Seven fives," he said sniffing and sitting back on his barrel as if he had just won the lottery.

There were a few moments of silence as the player to Roger's left lifted his cup and looked at his dice.

"Liar." The pirate who had spoken tipped up all the dices and put his hands on his head as he realised he had lost.

"You owe me ten gold coins, my friend. I'll claim them after the voyage." Roger stood up and stepped to the side. "Good game," he said slapping the man on the back.

Some of the men laughed, some of them didn't—it was hard to tell who was whose friend but as Tilly started to go after Roger, who was already making his way up on deck, someone called out to her.

"Playing, Captain?" asked Bill. Tilly hadn't seen him there, he must have been hiding in the shadows.

"Not tonight, you enjoy yourselves," she replied as she went to move.

"Oh, come on, Captain, let's have a round." He had a sly smile on his face and the rest of the crew had grown silent. Roger had stopped with one foot on the stairs.

"What are we playing for?" she asked as the crew cheered.

"One question."

"A question? I don't understand."

"If I win, I ask you a question. If you win, you can ask me one."

"And what makes you think I have a question to ask you?" He

definitely had her curiosity now, which she knew meant she would end up playing this stupid game.

"Your eyes," was his only reply.

That was it. She stepped aside and held her arm out waiting for him to pass then they both seated themselves at the makeshift table. Bill's face had a smile across it that made Tilly's skin crawl. She wasn't looking forward to his game.

"I'll join in," called Roger as he returned to the table. "I have a few questions to ask myself." He looked at her and winked before slamming his dice and cup onto the crate. Tilly followed with her own and Bill looked between them both before doing it with his own.

Lifting up her cup she was met with disappointment. Her hand contained only one number and it was two. She had 5 twos. Which was a bad hand unless they both had ones. Trying not to show her disappointment on her face she placed the cup back over and folded her arms.

"Ladies first," said Bill. His voice had a slight hiss to it, "I insist."

"Two twos," Roger said loudly, glaring at them both. Tilly wasn't impressed with his heroic acts and so before Bill could make his turn, basically shouted her answer.

"Four twos," she glared her smile towards Roger and then turned to Bill and fluttered her eyelashes. A feeble attempt to put him off.

Her attempt worked but not for long. Bill looked at his dice another two times before taking his turn.

"Two fives," he said giving her the same smile she had just given him.

Tilly sat back a little and tried to look like she wasn't worried she was going to lose.

"Twelve twos," called Roger

"You can't do that!" accused Bill. "You shouldn't even be in the game."

"Actually as there are no rules disallowing extra players joining in on a game of dice, I am well within my rights," Roger's voice was calm and he didn't even flinch when Bill smacked his hands down onto the crate in rage.

"Roger, you are a liar, so is our captain and I will ask you both one question."

"Yes, fine." Tilly put her hand on Rogers' arm before they decided to end this conversation with a fist in the others face.

"I'll start with you as you are so eager to answer, Captain. Were you planning on telling the crew you were a woman?" Bill's smirk had a darkness about it and there were a few gasps from the members of the crew who stood around. A few of the sleepers had awoken from Bill's shouts and were also listening to the conversation. Tilly gulped and looked to Roger, he gave her a sympathetic nod and she stood up. She played with her jacket and flattened it down at the ends.

"I have not once hidden that fact," she said looking Bill straight in the eyes.

"But you didn't come out and tell us either, plus you wear men's clothing," insisted Bill.

"You haven't come and told me you are a man, should I assume you are not one? And as for my clothes, these garments are easier to fight in," her voice shook as she spoke. It wasn't the strong vibe she wanted to give the crew.

Bill didn't say anything he just looked at her with a grin on his face. No-one said a word and she suspected if she dropped a pin they would all hear it. She thought he was going to start shouting again but Bill just turned around and stomped off up the stairs. Which, was a good thing as Tilly was starting to feel uncomfortable.

"LAND HOY!" called someone from the crow's nest. Tilly looked up to see him pointing to the starboard side. Land wasn't that far away and Tilly wanted to see where they kept their loot. The crew looked at her with harsh eyes and her stomach dropped. She would have to watch her back in case they decided to subject her to a mutiny.

Tilly let out the breath she was holding and walked up the stairs followed by Roger. When she reached the deck she saw Bill talking to Harvey at the helm and the crew going about their normal duties.

It didn't take long to get to the island, or at least that's how it seemed. The wind had picked up from behind them and sailing was quick and calm. Harvey and Bill gathered a few members of the crew, along with Tilly and Roger. There were ten of them in the small boat that they rowed to shore in. Harvey instructed the rest of the crew to stay with the boat. They weren't exactly ecstatic about it but with one look from him, they stopped whining.

She had never seen an island like the Isle de Rosa before; the beach was white sand; the sea was almost clear blue and the heat was sweat-inducing. Tilly felt her skin growing clammy the second they set foot on land. The heat that surrounded her was so intense her skin pricked and then tiny beads of sweat formed on her top lip and brow.

Harvey and Bill were leading the way towards the dormant volcano. She had overheard them talking about a couple of entrances and deciding on which one to use. They trudged over the sand in the clearing before they entered the trees and the ground became harder. There wasn't any breeze but Tilly swore she could hear the trees rustling.

Although curious about where she was going, she didn't pay much attention to where Harvey was leading them. The avalanched volcano ahead of them didn't look like it could be of any interest yet they were heading straight towards it. Tilly could still hear the trees rustle every so often—as if someone was following them.

"I think we should just go up this way, it'll be quicker," suggested Bill

"You can't walk up the volcano Bill, I've told you this," said Harvey. "As I explained to our Captain we have three entrances to the cave but only two are accessible."

"Yes, I remember," said Tilly, hoping that was the right answer. She hadn't paid much attention to their conversation.

"You didn't listen to our entire conversation, did you?"

"Sorry," admitted Tilly, "I was distracted by the beauty of this island." It was only a half lie but it got her the response she wanted.

"We need to enter through the North-East entrance which is around the back. It's also the closest one," Harvey winked at her as he said it. They skirted around the volcano until they came to a small clearing.

Harvey grabbed hold of Bill as he was getting too close to the weird fog that had appeared. Before Tilly could ask any questions, Harvey scolded Bill and made sure everyone heard what was said.

"Don't step into the mist unless you never want to be seen again." He turned to face them and added, "I don't know what's there but I have lost a few men to their curiosity. It killed the cat and all that, so stay away."

"What?! How?!" exclaimed Tilly, suddenly afraid to go any further. Someone walked into the back of her but she didn't move.

"Honestly, I don't know. I've never ventured far enough to see," replied Harvey. He didn't seem that bothered by it. "Just stick to the sides or we may not see you again."

"How did they disappear?" Tilly pressed on. She wasn't comfortable moving forward until she knew.

"They went down, and never came back up," Harvey was starting to sound annoyed. "I tried to find them, but I never found where they went. Now can we please move along?"

Tilly frowned at him but nodded her head anyway. Anything to get this ordeal over with was fine by her. Nobody said anything further as Harvey walked over to a section of the mountain's wall and pressed down on a rock. A section broke away and sunk into the ground to reveal a tunnel.

"It's like something from a movie," whispered Tilly to herself.

"What's a movie?" Roger whispered back. *Crap! He heard me*, she thought.

"Uh." Tilly didn't know how to respond but she didn't have to either. Roger winked at her and they followed the rest of the crew.

Inside was not what Tilly expected. Throughout the tunnel into the main room was plain stone and rock, but as soon as you stepped out into the internal cavern light filled every section of space. The golds reflection danced as Tilly walked past.

The room was filled with coveted treasures, some in overflowing chests, others stacked in piles—even the desks were covered. Although she tried to hide her amazement and adoration for the goods in her sights she knew her eyes betrayed her by the quick glances she took at the crew's faces. They were much the same as hers. Harvey strode forward into the middle of the cave's space and put his hands on his hips while he surveyed the room.

He beckoned her forward and took her hand in his. Leading her away from the crew, who had started rifling through their new-found hoard of treasures.

"I want you to come with me," Harvey whispered into her ear from behind. Tilly turned around to face him. His smile was shining in the dim light of the cave.

"Where are we going?" she asked hesitantly.

"It's a surprise, but I promise you'll like it," he held out his hand to her and she took it.

Switching places with her, he started to lead her up a set of stairs that were located at the back of the room. Although the stairs didn't go up for what felt like forever, Tilly was surprised by how far up they were when they reached the surface.

"I'm sorry about the way Bill acted towards you. He doesn't like taking orders from a woman."

"It seems the crew didn't take kindly to the news either," she said as she looked around at the view. They were standing on top of the volcano they had just entered. "They didn't say anything after I made my point."

Harvey smiled at her and the light from the sun hit his eyes perfectly. For a moment, Tilly forgot she was caught up in a world where she didn't belong. Harvey tucked a piece of hair behind her ear and produced a box.

"This is for you," he said pushing the box into her hand.

"What for?" she asked. The box was light and small.

"It's to say sorry," he insisted. "Please, open it."

Not needing any further instructions Tilly ripped open the box.

Inside was a medallion on a necklace. The small coin was stamped with a pirate emblem rather than the rulers head. Not that she knew who the ruler of this time was. For a moment, she was just a girl standing in a beautiful location in the Caribbean with a boy she might like. He took her hand in his and pulled her closer into an embrace. It would have been the perfect moment for him to kiss her but it was not meant to be.

"Captain, we found a stowaway," started one of her crew who had come upstairs after her. "Apologies; I didn't realise you were indisposed."

"Don't apologise, take me to this stowaway," she replied as she pushed Harvey away from her. It took all her strength, as it seemed he didn't want to let her go. Gathering her thoughts, she let go of any she had of kissing Harvey and continued down the stairs.

Controlling a hoard of angry men wasn't as hard as Tilly originally thought. She thought she would be ignored and none of the men from her ship would listen as they pushed the stowaway around in a circle. Although Tilly wasn't sure how to handle the situation, she didn't stand about and stare as long as she thought she might, but much to her amazement, there was no need for her to shout either. One flick of her hand, a few looks from crew members and all but Bill stopped talking.

"Bill, who is this?" she asked with a small bit of confidence in her voice.

"The stowaway we found amongst us."

"No—what is his *name*? Have you spoken to him or just simply pushed him around the room like a piece of meat?" she asked.

Bill's silence was as good a confirmation as any.

Tilly shook her head with a sigh. "So, stowaway, who are you?"

"Name's Joseph," he said after a few moments of looking around at the other people in the cave of wonders. He spent a few moments looking at Roger, a small look of recognition flickered over the stowaway's face which Tilly noticed easily.

"Why are you here Joseph?"

"I wanted to join your crew so I hid in the ship until you

docked and came in with you all," he lied so easily. He was wearing uniformed trousers, so she thought he must be a soldier.

"Really?" she questioned. "How did you get on the ship?"

He looked up at her. Tilly wasn't sure he had an answer to that question but he surprised her with a cheeky smile and a response.

"I snuck on while you were at Tortuga."

"I highly doubt that," she retaliated instantly. "You wouldn't have been able to go that long without food. So, unless someone was helping you," she indicated to the pirates around her. "I think you're lying." Joseph didn't respond to her and looked back down at the floor, his brown hair falling into his face.

"Are you alone?"

"Yes."

"Are you going to keep lying to me?"

"No."

Tilly smiled; this was the kind of conversation she needed to have. To show the crew she wasn't messing around as Captain. Even if it was just a ruse until she found a way home.

"Everyone back to the ship, and lock this one up in the brig. Find his companion."

16

JENNY

JENNY HAD BECOME BORED of sitting outside the damned volcano. She had seen Tilly and Fake Harvey, along with an entire ship crew walk by. Joseph was inside the cave they had all gone in. Worry was consuming her entire being for them both and she felt helpless sitting outside in a tree. She couldn't risk anyone seeing her. Who knows what Fake Harvey might do to her when they come face to face.

Unsure of whether they would be coming back she started to climb back down the tree she had perched in. Once on the ground, she made the decision to walk back to Joseph's ship. On the way, Jenny had to conceal herself behind a tree, as she passed by the cave opening the door started to slide down and she could hear voices coming closer. The tree she picked wasn't particularly wide but the shrubbery was enough to conceal her from passing eyes.

The first person she saw, and recognised, was Tilly. She was walking behind two people she assumed were members of the crew Tilly was now a part of, dressed in clothes fit for a captain. Although Tilly wasn't currently wearing a hat. Jenny moved a little to the left to get a better view of their lips as they weren't talking loudly. Not that it did much good, all Jenny could see was the look in Tilly's eyes. She was uncomfortable, but her facial expression was confusing. Jenny was unsure if Tilly liked her position or not.

Behind Tilly came four more members of the crew pushing and shoving a fifth person who seemed to have their hands shackled together. He had clearly been ruffed up a little but Jenny could see it was Joseph. Fighting the urge to run to them both, she caught a few words about going around the island past where they had docked. If she could get there and hide the boat while they passed she would be able to follow them.

Jenny had to wait for the rest of the crew to go past before she could begin to make her way back to her ship, and just when she was about to move from her crouching spot Fake Harvey and his companion emerged from the entrance. They were talking about coordinates, and although they weren't being overly quiet it was still hard to hear all the numbers as they passed her.

Unable to make out anything they were saying Jenny gave up straining her ears. She sat with her back to the tree, hoping they didn't hear the rustle of the shrubbery around her. Harvey and his companion were showing their intentions with hand movements, it looked like they would be going around the island past Joseph's boat. She needed to get back to it before that happened. She took a quick look over her shoulder and saw that there was no one left standing outside and the door to the cave had closed, leaving her free to run back to the ship. An inkling of dread filled her as she thought about what would happen when she got to the boat without Joseph and the other crew members, but it didn't stop her. Her only options were to return to Joseph's boat or try and smuggle herself onto Harvey's doppelgänger's ship. Neither were exactly an easy option.

Jenny made a quick decision and ran towards Joseph's boat as fast as her legs would carry her, avoiding the thick patches of mist that lay between the docked ship and the cave. Her heart was pounding at the thought she may not be able to convince the crew of Joseph's capture, resulting in Fake Harvey continuing without Jenny's pursuit. Being stuck in the 1700's would not be good for her career with The Collective.

Upon reaching the ship, Jenny noticed that the crew hadn't moved at all and were exactly where she left them. They hadn't moved an inch, almost like they had been frozen while Joseph, her and the others had gone to look for Tilly. The only thing that was different was that the two crew members who had gone back to the boat had returned at the same time as her with a look of fear on their faces.

"Back so soon? You only just left," said Derek, one of the crew members in front.

Ignoring his comment, Jenny turned to the right and spoke to Douglas, one of her companions into the forest. "Why do you look so scared?"

"Where's the captain?" replied Derek, before anyone else could speak.

"I-It's full of c-creatures," stammered Douglas as he collapsed to the floor. A couple of the deck hands helped him up and carried him off before Jenny turned back to Derek.

"What's full of creatures?" asked Jenny, not fully understanding what was happening.

"The mist."

"Where's the Captain, Jenny?" asked Derek again.

"They took him. He got stuck, they found him and now he's on their ship so we've gotta go get him, okay?" she snapped. "What creatures did you see in the mist Douglas?"

"I-I don't know. They had red eyes and chased us."

This island was weird and if it were up to her she would have never gotten into this mess to begin with. Harvey's look-a-like was a problem she could do without and when she found out who he was she was going to beat the living daylights out of him for kidnapping Tilly.

"Then where are we heading, Miss?" Derek asked her.

Jenny blinked hard. She was shocked by his response and could only answer with a question, "You're going to listen to me?"

"There's no one else capable of finding him, you saw them, you know them, so you'll lead us there," there was no pause in his words and she could see from his eyes that he was telling the truth.

Although it shocked Jenny, she was happy that it had been so easy to, effectively, take control of the ship. However, this did pose the problem of following Tilly without being spotted. Without wanting to have questions asked Jenny wandered into the Captain's quarters and sat down at the desk. She was going to have to use The Collective to get to Tilly.

Seeing the lines of time wasn't exactly the easiest thing to do, and controlling an implant inside your brain was hardly simple. It takes a while to get the hang of turning it on and off without needing to put her hand to her head in order to focus. Jenny still got a headache from all the colours running through her vision though.

Putting her head in her hands and closing her eyes she focused on Tilly and the doppelgänger and felt the change in her eyes. Upon opening, she could see all the lines of time around her. Jenny was happy to see most of the lines around her were orange or green however there was a line she had never seen before.

Purple light swirled in front of her as if it was trying to grab her attention. It danced in the dim light of the candles in the dark quarters of the captain's cabin. The light seemed to move back as she reached out to it, soaring towards the ceiling and then crashing back down onto the map laid out on the table, erupting like a firework show before calming down into the familiar lines she was used to. It flowed around a few islands and then out into the open waters, stopping in the middle of the Bermuda Triangle. Jenny didn't know what to make of it but she had a gut instinct to follow it. Before she had time to think about anything other than the path she had to take there was a knock on the door which made her jump.

"Miss, we are ready to set sail. Do you have the heading?" called Derek from outside.

Gathering herself together, Jenny made it to the door and opened it. Derek stood a few steps back from the door with the sun directly behind him, beginning to set.

"Yes, we have a heading," smiled Jenny as she tried to remember the direction she had seen on the map. She turned to walk back in and she heard the shuffle of feet behind her, indicating that Derek had followed her inside. "I believe we need to go north, then turn northwest and follow this path until we get to the Bermuda Triangle," she explained, tracing her finger along the purple lines in her vision.

"Right," said Derek with a frown. "I'll tell the crew." His tone of voice showed that he didn't understand how she knew an exact route.

Jenny didn't know if they would come across anything, but she just had to follow her instincts, and the route she was being shown by the implant. Giving him a sweet smile she touched behind her ear and turned the swirling lines off so she could see him clearly again. As Derek was the navigator it was his job to know where they were planning on going, however without an exact location it was anybody's guess as to where they'd end up. He picked up a bit of charcoal and drew in the lines Jenny had shown him on a map and she smiled again as he picked it up and left, slamming the door behind him.

Jenny returned to the chair behind the desk. Guilt was beginning to set in. She hadn't wanted to leave Joseph, and although she knew getting caught with him wouldn't have been the best position to be in, she felt guilty for leaving him. She slumped down into the chair and rested her head on the back.

☙❧

The banging of cannons jolted Jenny awake as the boat rocked from the impact. The explosions were quiet at first as she tried to shake away the sleep. The whistle in the air grew louder as she walked towards the doors. Hesitant to open them her hands hovered above the handles, but with a deep breath she grabbed them and opened to the deck.

The light from outside blinded her for a few seconds but Jenny couldn't believe what she saw when her sight finally came back.

Half of the crew were dead, blood and bodies scattering the deck. It was carnage. The shock came over her as she stood dumbfounded on the deck. Men were screaming as they laid there bleeding from wounds. One man had no legs. She stumbled back at the sight of him and covered her mouth with her hand. Mustering up the courage to move away from the dead bleeding men, she took a few steps forward. She ducked under some flying debris and tripped over a splintered plank landing in the middle of the deck.

On the starboard side of the ship loomed another. As crew members tangled together on the planks joining the two ships together she stared up at the colours flying high and two hands clamped down on her shoulders.

"She's the captain!" boomed a voice from behind her as she was thrust forward in front of many of the crew she had joined. Jenny imagined her face looked like a rabbit caught in headlights and Harvey's doppelgänger stood at the other end of the gang plank smirking at her. Jenny's first emotion was fear, which froze her to the spot as crew members from the other vessel climbed aboard the ship. A scream came from her left and she saw a man clutching his side leant up against the mast. Jenny scrambled over to him and grabbed his hand.

"You're going to be okay," she said to him. Knowing that he wasn't. Jenny wasn't a doctor but from the amount of blood gushing from behind his hand, it didn't look good. It was a good thing she wasn't squeamish. The man went to speak but his breath caught and the light faded from his eyes. She dropped her eyes to the floor and sobbed.

In her vulnerable state two men grabbed both of her arms and dragged her forward onto the other ship until she was face to face with Fake Harvey.

"Take her to the captain boys, and lock the rest of these low life's in the brig," he cooed.

Jenny was still being held by the two men who had grabbed her out on deck while she watched the crew being taken below to be locked up. She wanted to be like Elizabeth Swann from *Pirates of the Caribbean* and say she'd go with her crew but she had to know Tilly was okay.

Once the crew had been taken below deck Harvey knocked on the door to the ship's captain's quarters three times very loudly. The sound seemed to echo off the wooden doors. Footsteps were easily heard from the other side as nerves started to set in.

Standing in front of her was Tilly. Relief that she was okay allowed Jenny to relax slightly although her shoulders were still taut as the men's hands clenched her biceps.

"What is this?" demanded Tilly in an official voice. She glanced at Jenny, who thought Tilly winked and then shifted her gaze to Harvey.

"Are you kidding me right now?" Jenny said loudly. "What the hell are you doing?" Her next sentence didn't come as she was hit round the back of the head.

"They were following us, Captain. We decided to attack before they did and acquired their ship to add to your fleet," replied Harvey with a slur.

"Did you now? And when did I give that order?"

Harvey's face dropped with Tilly's words and Jenny tried hard not to smile. It wasn't very often she saw Harvey put in his place She was clearly doing well. In the dim light of the captain's quarters, Jenny caught sight of another person, but their face wasn't illuminated.

"Blow that pile of wood they call a ship up, feed the crew and put her in there. I'll deal with her in a moment." Tilly simply turned away from the boys, who were now staring with their mouths open and Jenny was promptly pushed inside after her.

She jumped at the sound of the doors slamming shut behind her but soon relaxed as Tilly gestured for her to take a seat. The figure Jenny had seen earlier was now visible and she could see it was a man. He had taken his place behind Tilly's seat with his arms behind his back, the stance of a guard. Jenny fiddled with her fingers, twisting the ring that was on her right middle finger.

She noticed the nervous feeling she was experiencing was the feeling she got when in the presence of someone high up in The

Collective. It was a feeling she knew well. The man was wearing a red coat that went down to his hips, and there was a sword hidden beneath the left side, revealed by the way he was standing. He turned his head to the right slightly as shouts came from outside followed by the sounds of numerous feet hitting the deck. Jenny didn't take her eyes of the man standing behind Tilly's chair, even as Tilly took her seat across the table from her. She moved a few items about on the desk and then sat still.

A few moments passed before the boom of an explosion filled the air followed by the sounds of splintering pieces falling onto the deck and into the ocean. Silence followed the splashes and then Tilly cleared her throat; Jenny finally looked away from the man standing behind her.

"I am so glad you actually found me," she said with relief as all sense of authority diminished from her posture. "He is scaring me, so I locked myself up in here with Roger, this is Roger by the way, and, yeah I just go out randomly to make threats. It seems to work." Tilly finished her nervous gibberish and blinked at her.

"What do we do?" asked Jenny, "I have no idea where to find the member of..." Jenny glanced up at Roger.

"It's okay; you can trust him, he's been very helpful to have around."

"The Collective," Jenny finished. "That's our ticket home so I guess we will just have to stick with Harvey until we can find this person, bring Harvey in and then go home."

They both stayed silent for a few moments while they contemplated their options. Jenny had never been in a situation where she wasn't in control and she didn't like it. She also knew there was something off with Harvey and it scared her to know he was the one calling the shots, but looking at Tilly gave her the impression there was something not being said. Her eyes darted up to Roger who was looking towards the doors, and it was then that she noticed a small incision like hers behind his ear. Taking a mental note to ask him about it when Tilly wasn't around she shifted in her seat.

"So, where's Joseph?" asked Jenny.

"He's in the brig. I'll have him out soon," replied Tilly. "I'm so glad you're here Jenny. I have no idea what I am doing. I can't blow my cover, they think I'm enjoying being here. I just want to go home, Jenny."

"I'll get you home," said Jenny as a knock came from out on deck.

"Captain?" called the voice. Tilly stood from her chair, put her coat on and opened the door.

"Yes?"

"One of the prisoners is requesting to speak to you. The one we found in the cave," said the crewman.

"Bring him up then. Why must I do everything myself?!" Tilly went to move past the guy in the doorway but he blocked her by waving his arms in the air.

"No, no, no. I'll bring him to you, Captain, please," he said and she slammed the doors in his face.

"That was a bit mean don't you think?" asked Jenny. Tilly turned around to her and laughed. It wasn't a laugh where she thought it was funny, it was scared, nervous laughter.

"If I don't act the part Harvey will take over as captain and he is a lot worse than me," her eyes went to the floor. She took a deep breath and wandered back over to the desk, "It's easier to play along and stay in here than to mess anything up."

Jenny wasn't sure what that meant, but she knew it wasn't anything good.

17
TILLY

TILLY KNEW she should have said more to Jenny but under the circumstances, and the watchful eye of Harvey, she thought it best to wait. The list of artefacts she found was burning a hole in her pocket but Tilly knew Harvey was up to something and she needed to find out more.

It took a few more days before they got to the Bermuda Triangle, and they did go through a pretty bad storm. It had lasted four days in total rocking the ship from side to side, the cold wind chilling everyone to the bones. Harvey just bellowed orders and forced them to continue working, Tilly had acted similar, to a certain extent. She had shouted at a few members of staff who were slacking but due to the cold, biting wind, so she tended to let Harvey deal with them instead. She wanted to be seen as a strong but fair captain - while keeping her authority. It didn't feel right forcing people to work in those conditions but Tilly knew if they didn't work through it they could end up lost or worse shipwrecked. Then there was the fact that if they didn't get to the island Fake Harvey might have heart palpitations.

The last few days had taken its toll on both her and Jenny. Tilly was tired and scared, not knowing what to expect when they finally opened the door to step outside. The storm had calmed down making movement around the ship easier on everyone.

"Tilly! Nice to be able to come outside, right?" asked Jenny as she descended the final steps.

"Definitely, the storm was terrible. Made my stomach flip too many times," replied Tilly and both girls laughed. "You'll be eating dinner with me in an hour or so."

Jenny smiled at her and then ran to Joseph, who was looking over the ships side. It warmed Tilly's heart to see them. Knowing she had friends here made it easier for her. Roger caught Tilly's eye as he crossed the deck.

"Captain," he called. "I think it's time for dinner."

"Jenny! Joseph!" Tilly called to them. Beckoning them into her quarters.

Once they were all seated with food Tilly asked the staff to leave them to their dinner. The food was very basic, easy finger food, no need to use a knife or fork and everyone started eating like it had been days since they'd had any form of substance. Tilly knew they had to devise a plan to keep Fake Harvey happy, Tilly in charge and get them in the right positions to thwart whatever it was he had planned with those artefacts.

"So, is there actually a plan to what we are doing?" asked Jenny, breaking the silence.

"Well, no."

"Brilliant," retorted Roger. "How are we supposed to play this?"

"I don't know," said Tilly. "All I do know is that we need to stop Harvey from getting this telescope he is searching for."

"What about if we just come out and ask him? You are supposed to be the Captain, right?" asked Joseph. Tilly smiled. *Yes, I am the Captain*, she thought, *but there is no way I can act that well.*

"Don't you just want to go home?" Tilly sighed. "That's all I want. I don't care about what's happening here."

"Do not let Harvey hear you say that," scolded Jenny. Tilly was hurt. She assumed Jenny was here to rescue her but maybe now seeing all this her priorities had changed. "It's not like he's going to let us walk off this ship and go home. Plus, where are we going to find someone to take us home Tilly?"

"Come on then," she said standing up, feeling a little defeated. "Let's find out what the plan is."

She led them out of the cabin onto the deck once the ship had stopped moving and went to find Harvey. Tilly was out of luck when she learned that he had already gone ashore to explore, telling the rest of the crew he would be back within the hour. Wondering how he would tell the time and if he was telling the truth she asked around about Bill to find that he was also missing. It wasn't until she decided to find the list she had seen in Harvey's handwriting that she found Bill snooping around in her quarters.

"What do you think you're doing?" she asked authoritatively with Jenny and the boys behind her. "Not only have you now made my cabin a mess, you're clearly looking for something so I suggest you take a seat and explain." Her voice didn't sound like the Captain she had tried to be; the truth was that Bill scared her as much as Harvey.

Bill looked up at her and Tilly felt her heart pump veraciously with fear, which was made worse by his laughter. Jenny pushed passed her looking like she was going to give him a punch but Joseph grabbed hold of her shoulders before she got too far.

"Leave the fighting to the boys, ay love?" said Joseph in Jenny's ear. Tilly liked the affection in his sentence but she wasn't sure it was the right time. Almost like he was whispering a secret; shame it was audible to her and Roger. The red coat moved her back a few steps and protectively stood off to the side in front of her, enough that she would be covered if someone was to shoot her but not enough to stop her from looking at Bill as he talked.

"Is that supposed to be a threat?" spat Bill, "You don't scare me. We've got two girls who are pretending they're men, a soldier and a mercenary for hire, not exactly the best team to stop this." He laughed again.

"Stop what, exactly?" demanded Jenny. Tilly wished her pistol wasn't locked away under the bed, it would be useful about now.

Guns usually were when you needed to threaten someone. "Is anyone going to answer me?"

"No, just shut up!" shouted Bill, his cheeks red with rage. "You," he pointed at Joseph "Think you can take me on, just try it?" He sprayed spit as he talked.

"Or not, Bill just explain what the hell you're are doing in my cabin," demanded Tilly. "What are you looking for?" She expected the same laughing reply as his eyes were wide with anger.

"Someone stole the list and one of the items on it. Master needs it back," he said. His expression changed from the amused look he had before to an almost robotic blank stare as he spoke. No one said anything for a few moments and then the glaze on his eyes cleared and the amused look returned. *That was weird,* thought Tilly.

"'Master?'" asked Tilly, although she knew the answer.

"Master Harvey."

"What does he need it for?" Jenny butted in.

"Jenny, please I can do this."

"Okay, jeez." Jenny rolled her eyes and took a step back. Tilly scowled at her. This was Tilly's fight and she would get it done. Joseph was still holding onto Jenny like she was about to spring at Bill and attack him so Tilly had no choice but to resume her authoritative position. "As the captain of this ship, if something has gone missing I'll be the one doing the finding," she started in her most confident voice. "Now hand me whatever it is of mine you've taken and Roger will put you in the brig until this matter is resolved."

"I'm not going to the brig," Bill started to protest as Roger grabbed his shoulders, in an attempt to force him through the cabin and out the door.

There was a bit of a struggle but eventually Bill was hauled out of the room and onto the deck. The crew all looked in awe as Roger dragged him to the stairs that led below deck. Tilly had grabbed the scrap of paper out of Bill's hand before he got to the door and so wasn't paying any attention to what was happening the other side of the open doorway. Unscrewing the tea stained paper, she saw it was the list of artefacts Bill had mentioned to them earlier. She stuffed it into her pocket and joined Jenny, who was already at the door.

"We need to find him," she said to Tilly as quietly as she could without the rest of the deck hearing her.

"Yes, but I don't think all of us can go, and it's not like either of us know how to fight," replied Tilly with a lopsided grin. Although judging by the mischievous glance in Jenny's eye she knew she was about to be proven wrong.

"Well actually I do. You know, Collective training." Her cheeky smile was accompanied by a wink and Tilly knew it was meant as a challenge but as no one was looking she didn't rise to the occasion. She gave Jenny a smile and then walked out onto the deck. A few of the crew stopped to look at her, she could see they wanted to challenge her. If she had time she would've tried to make them go for it, but she thought there had already been enough commotion for one day. As she took a few steps she heard some of the crew whispering.

"I can't believe she did that!"

"Harvey is going to be so mad."

"I'm not being the one to tell him," said Gerry as he stood up from the ropes he was tying up the last of the knots. Not wanting to get into another argument she passed them quickly.

Once she had reached the port side where Harvey had gotten off she tapped a member of the crew on the shoulder.

"Where did he go?" she asked firmly.

"Th-that way," the guy stuttered as he pointed forward with his arm. He then lowered his head and scurried over to the opposite side to clean.

With one look to Jenny, Tilly knew there was no way of leaving without her. Roger would have to stay in charge of the ship and Joseph would be coming with them. It wasn't even a decision to make, that's just how it would be. The ship was docked but not by any sort of anchorage. It was wedged up on shore and there was a trail of footprints in the sand. He should be easy to track for the most part.

Tilly didn't even think before she climbed down onto the beach to follow Harvey, but she was made to stop when she realised she had started the journey alone. Jenny and Joseph were only a few minutes behind her and they both had sacks with them, presumably carrying provisions for the journey. Tilly sighed with relief that at least one of them was thinking straight.

"Forgetting a few things?" Jenny chimed as she threw a small bread roll to her. "You also might want these, Captain," she said handing Tilly her sword, pistol and hat.

"I hardly need the hat, Jenny," laughed Tilly. "But thank you."

"Come on then girls, I need to catch a criminal," Joseph whined as he threw his hands up in the air. Very ungentlemanly.

They both looked at each other and then to Joseph, all three of them needed to find Harvey and all for different reasons, however, the girls couldn't help themselves and ended up in a fit of giggles. Joseph clearly didn't know how to handle two girls laughing uncontrollably so he just stood there staring at them. Tilly started to move forward along the beach, trying to focus on something else to stop herself from laughing, and it worked for the most part. Jenny stayed back with Joseph, still giggling to herself every now and again which made Tilly smile but left her in the lead.

They walked all along the beach, its golden sands glistening in the sunlight, until the trail of footprints they had seen ended when the sand got thinner and the forest started. The abrupt change in surroundings made them all stop and actually look around rather than at the ground. They could see the docked ship behind them in the distance still sitting on the shore, the crew just moving blurs in the distance. The beach ran alongside a slope, and now the mountain was towering above them, the grassy verges easy to spot now they looked close enough.

"Does anyone know A, where we are, and B, what we are looking for? Other than Harvey, of course," asked Joseph.

"We are in the middle of the Bermuda Triangle," Tilly started to say. "That's about all I know. Plus, I have this," she produced the crumpled bit of paper from her pocket to show them. "It's a list of things he needed. I don't know what for."

"A list of things he needed? Like random objects?" asked Jenny.

"No idea," Tilly shook her head. "He just has this list - see." Tilly handed the piece of paper from her pocket to Jenny and Joseph moved closer so he could read it too. The handwriting was messy and looked as if at some point liquid had been spilt over it but some of the words were still legible. Jenny looked away and took a few steps back with a confused look on her face.

"What are you thinking?" asked Tilly as she put the list back in her pocket.

"Just one of those items. I've heard of it before but it isn't supposed to exist anymore. I'm sure in our history lessons we were told of its destruction," she explained to them.

"Which one?"

"That one," Jenny pointed to the last one on the list. The ring.

"Okay, what is it supposed to do?" asked Tilly who didn't really want to know the answer because judging by Jenny's face, it wasn't good.

"The Ring of Deception changes your appearance to those who look at you while you wear it, and if he has it, well Fake Harvey has a lot of explaining to do. Does he have them all?"

"I-I don't know," replied Tilly, her voice catching as she realised Jenny had a look on her face that said she had just been given confirmation that Harvey is indeed a fake. "Okay, so what do we do now?"

"I guess we keep going," said Joseph, his face marked with concern. "I'm sure he's still by himself. What's one guy against a Kings Captain and… two ladies."

Tilly had to admit she wasn't exactly frightening, Jenny had the more bolshie demeanour. She looked at them both and smiled. If there was going to be any trouble this was going to be how it started. The three of them going into the jungle on a hidden island to find someone who was impersonating someone else. How hard could that be?

"Well let's go then," Tilly chimed as she tried to be brave. It was no use; she knew it would take more than her positive attitude to make Jenny and Joseph believe that this was a good idea.

How can chasing after a madman, no matter how necessary, ever be a good idea?

The three of them continued into the jungle along the path that seemed to have been made specifically for them. Tilly kept thinking that this was all far too easy and had this constant worry in the back of her mind that was picking away at her sanity. There were no animals in this jungle and the only sounds were the crunching beneath their feet, sometimes Jenny would grab hold of Tilly's shoulder, as if she had heard something, and they'd all stop but mostly it was just silent. Joseph was at the back, Tilly had started to notice how sometimes he would look behind and try to mark out the way they had come but there was honestly no way to tell. You could easily get lost and not find your way out.

Once through the jungle they came to a clearing with a cabin in the middle of it. Tilly looked at Jenny who just shrugged her shoulders and turned to Joseph who in turn did the same motion. Still thinking it was odd that they hadn't encountered anything, Tilly hesitantly stepped out into the clearing. As she did, she expected there to be a movie cliché of a bird flying from the trees and squawking but no sound was heard, except the crunching of leaves underneath her feet.

"Anyone else think this is too easy?" she asked.

"Oh yes. It's like a horror scene from a movie. We are totally getting killed," called Jenny from behind.

Tilly heard Joseph snigger from behind. *I guess comparing his real life to a movie is something he's never heard of.*

"You two talk such nonsense sometimes. I don't know why I even listen," he muttered.

"Because if you didn't, you'd step into that pit," said Jenny, pointing to the floor. "Looks like it's booby-trapped. Be careful where you step!" With an exaggeration on the last word she narrowly avoiding falling into one of the holes, badly covered by fallen foliage. Tilly couldn't help but laugh as she watched Jenny flail her arms around trying to regain her balance.

"I thought Collective training would prevent you from doing things like that?" she asked Jenny, who only returned her words with a scrunched-up face and a tongue waggle. After a few more near-misses the three of them crossed the clearing to the little cabin.

Jenny had gone off to walk the perimeter and see if she could spot anything lurking along the forest's edge, while Tilly and Joseph approached the front door.

"I'll stay outside in case you need back up," he told her. "He knows you so if he is in there probably best if you go in."

Taking his words with effect she opened the door and walked in. Although it was quite dark inside, there were cracks of light coming through the gaps in the wooden walls. Inside there were three rooms, a kitchen visible through the door in front of her, a large lounge where she currently stood, and one off to the left. Tilly entered the kitchen first.

The room was covered in newly settled dust. Fingerprints and handprints could be easily seen through the thick layer that covered everything. Someone, Tilly hoped it was Harvey, had clearly been looking for something. Leaving the kitchen, she tried the last room; if he wasn't in there, she would be out of options. Pushing the door open the first thing that became visible to Tilly was a small straw bed, followed by Harvey kneeling on the ground and surrounded by piles of dirt.

"Harvey?" asked Tilly quietly as she crept up behind him. He seemed to be digging in the ground.

"I've found it!" he proclaimed, lifting up the small square box. Tilly wasn't sure what to make of what was happening in front of her but she knew she should just go along with it.

"That's great but why did you come out here alone?"

"You were with your friends," he replied not taking his eyes from the box he was still holding up. "This was too important to wait."

Harvey now had the box on his lap and was trying to pry it open. Failing to do so he threw it at the wall and it bounced along the floor. Harvey didn't move so Tilly decided to pick it up, she was about to hand it to him when she saw an inscription on the side by the lock.

"Harvey, did you see this?" she said, moving her finger over the writing that was engraved into the side. "It's written in a different language."

"No, let me see," he replied, reaching out for the box. He basically snatched it back from her.

"Oh, there's a hidden button," he said like a child. Pushing the button into the box the lid popped open and he smiled at her. The box squeaked as it opened and Tilly only saw Harvey's face drop for a second before all hell broke loose.

"TILLY! TILLY HELP ME!" Jenny's shouts could be heard through the thin wooden walls.

"Gotta go!" Tilly yelled, grabbing the box out of Harvey's hands as she fled the room towards her screaming friend.

"Hey!" Harvey cried, chasing after her as she left the cabin. Outside Jenny was fighting with a man who clearly wasn't taking her no for an answer. She was kicking and punching but he just grabbed hold of her again before she got away. Joseph was unconscious, the man had obviously gotten to him first and thought Jenny was alone.

"You're insane! I'm not Jasmine!" Tilly heard Jenny shout.

Harvey launched for the box in Tilly's hand, knocking it to the floor. Tilly and Harvey rolled through the dirt as they fought over the box, and through the cloud of dust Tilly saw Jenny's attacker slam the hilt of his sword into her nose. Jenny sprawled to the ground, blood pouring as the attacker grabbed Jenny's collar and began dragging her away.

"No!" Tilly screamed, her anguish sapping energy from her arms; she couldn't go on much longer against Fake Harvey's stronger grip. Pushing Harvey off her, Tilly got up and stared into the distance.

"You can't help her," said Harvey.

"We either find her, or you don't get this box back. Who was that, anyway?"

"I don't know, but didn't he say something about her being someone's daughter?" asked Harvey. "Can I have my box back?"

"No, you can't and I think that was her shouting it," Tilly's eyes went to the floor. Spotting Joseph's feet in the corner of her vision she wandered over, bent down and placed a hand on his head. Gently she shook him until he came around.

"Where is Jenny?" was all he managed before falling back into his unconscious state.

"I don't know, but we will get her," is all she replied.

18
JENNY

JENNY AWOKE to an ache at the back of her head. Groggy, she rolled over and fell to the floor. She scrabbled to her feet as Jenny realised she was in strange surroundings. Looking around the room she now found herself scared for the first time in her career as part of The Collective.

It was a small, boxlike room, and in it was a bed (which she had managed to fall off) a chest of drawers and a window. It was all made of wood and from the look of it—and the painful condition of her back—the bed's mattress was made of leaves and straw.

Where the hell am I? she wondered, bringing her hand up to her head. It was throbbing badly. There wasn't many options for her but seeing as she was in an unknown location she felt that she had nothing to lose as she reached for the door handle and tried to open it. To her surprise, it was open. Creaking as she pulled it towards her she willed inside for the door to stop making such a loud noise in case her attacker came back.

The opening lead to a hallway that was all white and far too clean; it looked like something out of a horror movie. Jenny stuck her head out, looking down the hallway right and then to the left. It wasn't exactly silence that she encountered but there wasn't any known sound that she could hear. There were no voices but merely a distant humming, it was hard to tell which side it was coming from.

Another door opened and Jenny quickly pulled her head back in, leaving the door open a crack to listen. Loud footsteps started as someone stepped out onto the hard floor, from the sound she thought they must be wearing boots. For what seemed like forever, the footsteps finally stopped outside close by. Jenny peeked and saw that there was a man dressed in dirty work trousers, a grey t-shirt and boots. He carried a bow on his back and had the biggest knife she had ever seen strapped to his side.

She watched as he knocked on the door opposite hers and waited for it to open. As it did there was a rush of air and a stench that made Jenny want to vomit everything she had left in her stomach, however the guy seemed unfazed by it. He shook his head and the door closed again as the man turned towards her. Jenny slammed the door shut before she saw his face and took three steps back from the door.

Her heart pounded in her chest as she waited for the knock at her door to come. It was like her mind knew what was coming and within a few seconds of her stumbling back the noise from the door sounded like three deep drumbeats. When she didn't answer they only came again. Jenny, unsure what was going to happen, reached for the door handle with a shaking hand. Not wanting to feel the fear anymore Jenny quickly pulled open the door, the breeze it made making her hair fall back behind her shoulders.

"Come with me," demanded the man outside the door in a thick African accent. Although she couldn't explain it, Jenny somehow felt at ease, as if she knew this man. Without hesitation, she followed him out of the room and down the corridor.

When they finally stopped, they entered a small room with a circular table. Frowning, she sat down at the empty table when directed by her companion and waited. As he left the room a door on the opposite side opened and three people walked out. Two women and a man. They took a seat on the opposite side of the table before folding their hands in front of them.

Jenny looked between them all, but stayed silent. Unsure of what was going to come her emotions were heightened and her body tensed at the slightest movement from them. One of the women looked over her glasses at Jenny and made a disapproving noise.

"So, you're the operative they sent back to us?" she asked. Jenny responded by nodding her head, something about this woman was giving her the creeps but it may have just been the way she looked over her glasses. Reminded her of the old-school librarian who hated children.

"Obviously, you don't speak."

"I do speak," responded Jenny. The other two members of the table laughed at her.

"We have spent many years looking for you. How long have you been here?"

"I don't know, it's been a rush trying to find my friend and get back," replied Jenny.

"What?" asked the man sat to the mean librarian's right.

"I came back to find my friend who was kidnapped by one of our operatives and brought here. You took me from them," she explained.

"Yes, that wasn't our best extraction," admitted the second lady.

"If we're going to have a conversation could I at least get your names and an explanation? I'm assuming you know who I am."

"Of course, we do, Jennifer. Regents are fitted with identification software. I'm Ethel," she answered pushing her glasses back up her nose. *Typical librarian name,* thought Jenny.

"Vincent," said the man in a rough, deep voice.

"I'm Emily," said the younger of the two ladies. Emily wasn't exactly a whippersnapper, but she wasn't the old librarian type. To Jenny she was more of the warm-hearted type of girl.

"So why did you kidnap me?" asked Jenny bluntly. All three of them blinked as if she had asked a question they didn't know how to answer.

"Five years ago an operative was sent to us, the gate was

opened but no-one ever came to us. We waited and then when the gate was opened twice we knew someone must be coming to us. We found you and merely assumed you were the one who had evaded us all these years," explained Emily in a chipper manner.

"Yes, and we also wanted answers as to why no-one turned up five years ago." With a stern look on her face Ethel looked more aged than ever in the harsh light, her wrinkles casting dark shadows. "Seeing as we can't talk to anyone through time, merely only able to see what happens from the book."

Unsure what to say Jenny looked to the floor. She had no knowledge of anyone coming back, but then someone in her position wouldn't have been privy to that information to begin with. She was only supposed to read and report, and was only here on extreme circumstances.

"I'm afraid I don't know. I spend most of my time in the library," Jenny said.

Out of the corner of her eye she caught Vincent laugh at her and immediately felt embarrassed.

"You're not a collector? This is just brilliant. They sent us a Recruit," Ethel rolled her eyes and stood from her chair. "I'll have someone take you back to the boat you landed on. What were you even doing on our island?"

"*Your* island?" questioned Jenny.

"Yes, The Collective acquired this land almost four hundred years ago. The Bermuda Triangle is the best place to hide the main hub of Collective operations."

Jenny's eyes lit up. She wasn't supposed to know that information and now she had been to the control centre. She hoped it looked better in the future, with more colour.

With a nod from Ethel, she was again being manhandled out. Although Jenny assumed that she was being taken back, the man manoeuvring her took her back to the small bedroom she had awakened in.

"We need more answers so you'll have to get some rest," was all he said before taking his leave.

The door closed leaving Jenny in the small room alone with

more questions than answers. Who this mysterious collective agent from five years ago was at the top of her list to ask in the morning. Provided they let her ask the questions of course. Knowing she didn't have many options right now, Jenny laid down on the bed provided to her and contemplated how to get back to her friend.

※

Morning came far too quickly for Jenny and within minutes of opening her eyes there was a knock at her door. Today was another questioning day, time to get some answers and then get back to Tilly, who was probably searching for her now. *Or had she succumbed to whatever Harvey had planned next?* The thought was painful in her mind and not one she wanted to dwell on. The door swung open before she got up off the bed and Emily stood there with an all-too-large smile on her face.

"Morning, breakfast is ready," she practically sang as she spun on her heels and skipped down the hall.

Jenny changed out of the pyjamas they'd provided and began to follow her. It was still strange to her that everything in the hall was white. Pristine white with zero marks on anything, even the floor. Emily, who was still skipping ahead of her, came to a stop a few doors down from the room they had been in yesterday. Inside looked like a banquet hall. A long table down the middle laid out perfectly as if a scene from *Harry Potter*. Goblets and plates lined the edges but food was only visible down one end of the table, where Ethel was sitting.

Still skipping, Emily went down and took her seat next to Ethel, Vincent was on the other side and a spare place setting was left beside him. Feeling uncomfortable, Jenny took her seat and smiled.

"How did you sleep?" asked Emily. "Beds are comfier than they look, right?" Her happy demeanour was very off-putting to Jenny. She still didn't know if she felt comfortable around these people.

After a few seconds, before she had a chance to answer Emily, the food was brought out.

"Yes," she finally replied as she buttered up some toast. "They are nice beds to sleep on."

"I hate to stop the small talk but we really need to know some more information from you Jennifer," interjected Ethel. "I need to know why you're here."

"I've already told you. My friend was brought here by someone with access to a time portal, and I came to get her back home. That's all I know," Jenny stopped eating her food, feeling more uncomfortable for taking anything from these people.

"I'd like Vincent to go with you back to your friends, do you think that could be a possibility?"

"I suppose, although he might get threatened on arrival until I manage to explain the situation," informed Jenny in the hopes that they would just let her leave them with no other interactions. She would ask the Regents when she got back about all three of them. She knew she should distrust them but a voice in her mind kept telling her it was okay.

"That'll be fine, he is expendable."

Vincent didn't look shocked at Ethel's response to her statement. It was almost like she was planning on getting rid of him. "Corrupt" was the only word she could use to describe the head of The Collective. Well head of this small group of them anyway. If that was indeed who they were. Breakfast was finished off in silence and then Jenny and Vincent left the room. Jenny felt something sharp go into her neck and then the lights went out.

❧

Waking up after being knocked unconscious was becoming boring very quickly for Jenny, and it had only happened twice. As she looked around, Jenny saw that she was sprawled out on the beach, with Vincent sitting beside her on the sand sharpening a knife. They had made it back through the forest and were on the beach but it seemed the ship either had left or wasn't on this side.

"Where are we?" she asked him.

"Oh, you're awake?" he put the knife away and stood up, shaking the sand off his trousers. "I just wanted to wait while you woke up, you're not allowed to see how to enter or exit the control centre. Sorry about that." He seemed sweet.

"That still doesn't answer my question," she replied sternly.

"The ship is just around the corner, although I think your friends are back in the jungle searching for you."

"Well we better find them before we go back on the ship or you will definitely get killed."

"I am afraid my death is inevitable," he said looking at the ground. "Turn on your device."

She did as he asked and like he said his line was fading. "Oh," she said. "You knew this would happen?"

"All agents are told of their end date when they graduate to Head Collector," he replied. "It's just a shame my time in this position is so short." His time on earth was nearing an end and all Jenny could think of was finding a way to save him but she knew she couldn't tamper with the past. No more than she already had. She reached up and he helped her stand. Placing a hand on his shoulder, she smiled at him

Finding Tilly didn't take long, with Vincent's knowledge of the jungle they were easily able to manoeuvre themselves into her friends' path. They were still searching around the cabin Harvey had gone off to by himself.

"Jenny!" yelled Joseph as he started to run towards her. "Where the hell have you been? And who the hell is this?"

"I can explain everything but can we get back to the ship? I am bloody starving!" she shouted her words back at him, secretly hoping they would get her away from this island as soon as possible.

19

TILLY

TILLY ALMOST COULDN'T BELIEVE her eyes as she ran towards Jenny. Part of her had thought they would never find Jenny. She'd had a bit of trouble with Harvey trying to make him stay to find her, she even had to go as far as hiding that little box he coveted so much. Her hand instinctively went to her side where the box was as she thought about it. There wasn't even anything in it, just that cryptic little note. Tilly had loved taking control, even if there was doubt at the back of her mind telling her Harvey was allowing her the control. Becoming a pirate captain was like a game, except that she was in a real-life game and would be remembered through history. Stopping before she got to Jenny, Tilly noticed the man coming towards her.

"No, it's okay," replied Jenny waving her hands up at Joseph who was waving his sword in the air. Tilly furrowed her brow at him and continued towards Jenny. She pulled her into an embrace and breathed out.

"I'm glad you're okay," she whispered.

Jenny whispered back at her, "I'm glad you're still here! Now to the ship!"

"I won't be coming with you. This is where I leave," said Vincent.

"Are you sure?" asked Jenny.

"Yes, I need to get back. You have your friends." Vincent bowed and disappeared back into the jungle.

Back on the ship, Tilly was enjoying a small moment of silence in her quarters. She'd left everyone else to enjoy the finery and whatever food was left in the ship's kitchen so that she could attempt to decipher the cryptic note left in the box Harvey wanted her to have nothing to do with. How on earth she was going to figure out a different language by staring at it, she didn't know. It wasn't like it was easy to learn. It was all different images, some grouped together and some apart, which Tilly assumed meant they were words.

A cheer erupted outside her door. Hands started clapping and then feet stomping, everyone outside was obviously having a celebration. She wondered how long it would be until someone came and got her. Tilly was beginning to get bored of the constant noise from outside, it was like they were all having fun without her. None of them had decided to try and find her. Harvey had set them on a course to another stopping point so they could load up on more food and then the celebrations had begun.

The door to her cabin flung open and Roger fell to the floor with Bill on top of him. Arms were flailing as Roger blocked a punch from Bill who had one hand around his neck. Tilly stood up and slammed her fists against the table, effectively halting the fight. Both boys on the floor looked up at her and she crossed her arms. There was a crowd gathered behind them and Jenny was pushing herself to the front. All Tilly could make out was her hands squeezing through two sailor's shoulders.

"What in god's name is going on?" asked Tilly. Still, nobody moved an inch, unless you count Bill slowly turning his head to look at her. In one swift movement Tilly watched at Roger took advantage of Bill's distraction and pushed him off, allowing Roger to stand. He lowered his head in shame and opened his mouth to speak but stopped as Tilly's hand came up.

"Where is Harvey?" shouted Bill as he clambered to his feet.

"He will be able to sort this out for me." A coy smile played at the corners of his lips.

As if knowing he was going to be called Harvey appeared in the front of the crowd, it seemed none of the crew were going to do their jobs tonight. Not saying anything, he grabbed Bill by the back of the neck, nodded to Tilly and dragged him away from her table.

"Get back to work the lot of you, celebrations are over," Tilly commanded, waving her hand at them like they were servants. It was not her true personality at all, but it seemed to have the desired effect and sent them all packing back to their tasks. Jenny didn't leave like the other sailors; she merely sat down in Tilly's seat and picked up the paper. Tilly slammed the doors shut and turned to look at Jenny, who peered at the note from Fake Harvey's box with confusion. Without wanting to make a big deal of the fact Jenny was in her seat, and letting go of her pirate captain role, Tilly sat on the arm of the chair and stared at the paper with her.

"So, what do you think?" she asked.

"No idea, going to have to get a translation done. What language *is* this?" replied Jenny waving the paper around. "It's almost like a child was asked to draw the location in the messiest way possible. I mean, look at this; it's a sun!"

"I can't see anything with you wafting it around like that!"

They both ended in laughter as Jenny decided to dance around singing, waving the pictures around. Grabbing the paper off Jenny so she could see it, Tilly instantly thought of a child writing it out. The lines for the symbols were all broken as if the surface it was written on was rocky.

Tilly still had no idea how she was going to figure this out, but it didn't matter either because as she slammed the paper down on the desk in frustration, Harvey burst through the door. The doors almost came off their hinges swinging back from the force and crashing into the stairs. He swayed from side to side as he moved closer to the table; clearly, he had been enjoying the rum a little too much.

Walking into the table, Harvey didn't stop until his hand was on top of hers with the paper just underneath. Looking into his eyes, Tilly could clearly see that he was drunk. The whites of his eyes were duller and the edges were redder. She could also see his determination; taking a deep breath she geared herself up to have another argument about why he couldn't have the paper. *If I don't know what to do with it, how does he?* she wondered.

Behind him Joseph and Roger stood in the doorway with Bill in between them. Tilly laughed internally as she saw Roger shift himself away, an attempt not to punch him.

"Harvey, are you alright?" she asked him politely, not moving her hand from underneath his. He slightly turned his head and lifted his eyebrow, his lip lifted into a half smile and eyes turning dark.

"Of course, I am alright, it's a party, isn't it?" he flung his arms up and twirled. "Now, to business, there are things I need to tell you." When he turned to face her, he wasn't drunk anymore. His eyes were back to normal and he was standing perfectly still with his arms crossed, "I've chartered a course to America's West Coast, a port called Grouz, as I know someone who will be able to help us decipher that." Tilly's hand clenched over the paper as he pointed to it.

"Don't worry my dear; you can keep hold of it, for now. I *will* need it when we dock, though." that smile flashed across his face and on cue the hairs on the back of her neck stood up. With one final twirl, he skipped out of the cabin, taking Bill with him.

"I really hate that man," announced Joseph as he closed the door behind him. Roger had already made his way to Tilly's side and was looking at the map laid out on the table. It was going to be a long night.

Night went and morning came but Tilly hadn't managed to get an ounce of sleep. Joseph and Roger had both collapsed on the floor, allowing Jenny to have the bed though all she could do was pace the room. Fear had crept up on Tilly since Harvey's outburst and she was starting to agree with Joseph. She was starting to hate Harvey too. How she had managed to get herself into this position, she didn't know. What she did know is that she was here, but she wanted to be home and therefore needed this over as quickly as possible so Jenny could get her home.

※

They docked in Grouz early the next morning. Tilly and Jenny had avoided leaving the captain's quarters unless necessary, as Harvey's shadow Bill followed them wherever they went on the ship. Although it didn't scare Tilly to be followed, she knew she was doing nothing wrong; Jenny was trying to figure out something that didn't quite work with her. She had told Tilly her concerns as soon as Harvey had left; there was something familiar about the look in his eye he kept giving her and his character was all wrong. This wasn't her partner from The Collective; it was just an imposter wearing his face and they were going to prove it.

When Tilly finally exited the cabin, she was met with a wall of warmth as the heat from the Grouz coast hit her. She wasn't used to having so many layers on, but a pirate captain always had to look the part. On the deck, everyone was working promptly except for one man who was sitting on a barrel picking his teeth. It was disgusting. Harvey was navigating, back to his usual self, and as Tilly walked to the other side of the ship the crew stopped and nodded their heads to her before returning to their tasks of keeping the ship sailing.

Turning her head back round to the man on the barrel, she saw that he was now leant back against the mast dozing in the sun. What gave him the right to sit on his arse while the rest of the crew worked? Not knowing what overcame her she stormed over to the sleeping sailor and kicked his foot. It took a few moments before he lifted his handkerchief off his face and looked up at her. She scowled at him placing her hands on her hips.

"What exactly are you doing?" she asked loudly, the crew stopping their duties to stare. The gentleman in question didn't answer her, merely snorted and covered his eyes back up. Embarrassed by his actions towards her as the captain, she stood there pretending no one else was watching.

"I suggest you get your sorry excuse for a sailor's ass up from that barrel before I kick it out from under you and throw you off the ship."

Silence flooded the deck. The crew were still mid-task and now Harvey, Bill, and the navigator, Tilly could never remember his name, stood looking down at the commotion. The sleepy sailor still wasn't listening to her, so she decided to make herself known as the fearless captain she was supposed to be and make a spectacle of this defiant man.

"First Mate!" she called spinning around to Harvey. "Take this man to the brig and when we get back I'll have a little surprise for him."

Harvey nodded his head and gestured for someone to do as she had asked. Two of the crew came and grabbed the man who was clearly not shocked at her demand and took him below deck to lock him in the brig.

"What are you all staring at? Back to work!"

Jenny walked over to Tilly with a smile, as did Harvey and his shadow, Bill.

"Let's go then, Captain, as I am more interested to see what you'll do with Samuel when we get back. To the decipher." Harvey sang the last section of his sentence which made Jenny chuckle under her breath. Tilly gently slapped her arm, smiling at her.

Off the ship, it was very hard not to get distracted. Seeing Grouz transformed back to simplicity was something you weren't going to get from a history book. Grouz Town was beautiful in the sun, people were going about their daily business and not taking any notice of the newcomers strolling through. The small section of the town they walked through only had five buildings and they stopped outside the last one.

Grouz Town was not the picturesque place she thought it would be after the first few houses. Past the odd few fancy townhouses and town hall, the other buildings were smaller, although a few of them did have beautiful gardens. They came to the end of a row to a smaller building which was the size of a modern-day garage. Surely no-one lived in this little building. This shack-like building must belong to the owner of the townhouse which stood tall next to it. Tilly was in awe of the beautiful building, the only one on the whole row. It was hard to miss with its blinding white walls. Jenny wasn't looking her way, but instead back at the residents that they had passed. Not one of them had looked up as they walked through the streets, which both the girls found very odd.

Harvey stopped just outside the path that led to the door and waited. There was no way of knocking as the path was blocked by a gate and Harvey seemed to refuse to walk through it. Bill was pacing behind him like a shadow moving in the wind and the girls' companions were stood either side of them like bodyguards. The door opened by itself, and Harvey waltzed right on inside. Tilly wasn't going to follow but as Bill was only a step behind she decided it would be best if she listened in. After all she still had the paper with the writing on it. Inside was better than the outside.

The carpet was blood red and covered the whole room, three sofas made a square seating area in the corner and there was one other door at the back of the room. Although the room wasn't particularly large, it all fit in neatly and seemed bigger on the inside.

Harvey sat himself down at the table; there were only two chairs, so when Bill dropped down onto the sofa, the four of them did the same.

"He's going to wonder what all of you are doing here, only really needed Tilly and myself," Harvey said, Tilly couldn't understand his comment. Why would it matter if there were more people than the three of them?

"How did you know to come here, Harvey?" asked Jenny before Tilly could make any comment.

"I've been here a couple of times before, made some lovely friends," he responded with a wink. Tilly thought Jenny was going to puke from her facial reaction to his words. Joseph put a hand on her back and Tilly watched as her eyes lit up. She hoped Jenny wasn't falling for a 1700's soldier who had come to her aid. As nice as it was seeing her happy, Tilly didn't know much about The Collective and surely it must be against the rules to change history by falling in love.

The door at the back of the room opened as another man stepped into the room. His jacket was paired with a top hat and his grey trousers stood out against the dark colours. Tilly almost laughed at the man as his dress wasn't typical for this time period. Then again, from the looks of him he didn't get out much. Bill twisted in his seat to look back at Harvey, who he'd joined at the table, and then turned to Tilly and scowled. *If only there was a way to get rid of him.*

"I didn't realise we were going to have extra company today, Harvey," the new man said.

"You know me, Reginald. I like to keep things exciting," replied Harvey with a chuckle.

Reginald did not seem impressed. "So, Harvey, what have you brought me today? Another artefact?" his voice was slightly husky as he asked the question. Almost like he needed to clear his throat.

"No, no object today, just a riddle I need solving." Harvey motioned for Tilly to come closer, and reluctantly she went. She stopped closer to Reginald than Harvey, although neither of them felt safe to be around. She was unsure of what he wanted her to do, she didn't want to hand over the paper and it burned her inside as she waited for him to ask.

"What are we waiting for? Is she the object?" asked Reginald, a glint of a sparkle in his eye. There was something about him that wasn't right, he made her uncomfortable. Instinctively she took a step further back and delved into her pocket. She tossed the paper at the table and proceeded to turn on her heels and quickly walk back to Jenny, who was scowling at Harvey.

"This?"

"Yes, Reginald, that piece of paper needs deciphering and you are just the man to help me do it," explained Harvey. Bill was smiling as if something was funny, although for the life of her, Tilly couldn't understand what it was. They had only been after this for a few weeks, but how long had Bill been after it? The look he was giving the paper in Reginald's hand was not a look of excitement but of hunger.

"Right, not my usual work from you, let's see what we have," Reginald said, opening the paper and placing it flat on the table in front of him. "Now this is interesting."

Reginald got out a small magnifying glass and leant over the table until he was about five inches away from looking at the paper. Clearly the man's old age was catching up with him. He moved back and forth over the images and made a few grunting noises as he went. Tilly thought he didn't know what on earth he was doing, but then she wouldn't know where to begin with it either.

Tilly jumped from the noise of the chair when he stood up, and Jenny laid her hand protectively on Tilly's shoulder. It gave her a small amount of comfort but as she sat there she knew that this was a bad place to be; the feeling kept on growing inside of her. Looking away from Harvey and Reginald she noticed Roger was staring at Bill like a madman; she was going to have to sort that out as there was a look in Roger's eye that unsettled her. He looked like he was about to pounce on him.

Another noise alerted her attention back to Harvey. Reginald had gotten out a rather large book, almost as big as an old encyclopaedia. He was flicking through it so slowly that Tilly just wanted to take over. Harvey was also clearly getting agitated as he had started to fidget in his seat.

"Reginald. Surely you can tell me whether you know what it says or not; you know I hate it when you're silent," he said. His tone had an underlay of sarcasm but Tilly didn't think the old man noticed.

"Yes, yes, alright Harvey. I know most of these symbols but there is still one I have yet to figure out. 'Whatever you're looking for has been moved. Originally it was owned by a secret organisation but it was taken and placed, in an identical box, and hidden…'" Reginald paused as he looked back at the paper.

Harvey leant across the table to try and get a better look at what Reginald was doing. *Not*, Tilly thought, *that he would be able to see anything.* Reginald had his face right up against the magnifying glass and was stopped over a symbol. From the position she was in, she assumed it was the last symbol, the one that looked like it had been drawn by a child and was barely legible.

"I think it was hidden out of time," Reginald concluded.

"Out of time? What the hell does that mean?" demanded Harvey. Tilly stood up at his outburst and almost jumped as Jenny's hand grabbed hold of hers. Both Harvey and Reginald were now looking at her.

"I think you know exactly what that means Harvey," Jenny scowled at him. "Reginald, is there any more you can tell us?"

"It's definitely in Rochdale, England; it's just the time I'm having trouble figuring out. Possibly 1712," he replied. Harvey's eyes lit up, that was two years before the one they were currently in. Harvey's plan was coming together and Tilly wasn't sure she was going to last much longer before she broke down.

"Looks like we are setting sail then," Harvey announced. "Reginald, thank you for your time and help, as always. Payment will arrive this afternoon." Harvey was already at the door to leave as he spoke, Bill promptly on his heels. "Come along girls, we have some sailing to do." Joseph and Roger followed quickly behind Bill, they didn't trust him you could see it in their eyes. Jenny stayed by her side as she moved around the sofa. Reginald's hand reached out and grabbed her before she left the room.

"Make sure he doesn't find it, love," he said in a hush tone to her, placing a separate piece of paper in her pocket. "Terrible things will happen if he finds it."

Tilly didn't know what to do with that information, something about this situation screamed bad news. Yet, the sincere look in his eye made her want to believe Reginald. There was no time to ask questions as Jenny ushered her out, away from him.

"Tilly, we need to read what is on that paper before we get on the ship. If Harvey sees it," she gave Tilly a look. "It won't end well and you know it."

"It will be fine, we can do what we did for the last voyage, stay in the cabin," suggested Tilly. Although neither of the girls thought that Harvey would leave them alone. "Fine, lets read it now."

It's not in Rochdale, it's in Grouz. The Church of the Sun.

"Well now we have to tell him," said Tilly. "Or are we going to spend the next however long sailing to Rochdale? I want to go home."

20
JENNY

JENNY WASN'T SURPRISED by what was on the bit of paper Reginald handed them. There were symbols that were like an old language she was taught in The Collective's history classes. Although some of them were different to the ones she was shown. The language was used by the first Collective before it grew to the large size it is now. She was, however, surprised at the fact some man Harvey had found knew the language, as it was complete nonsense made up by the first members of The Collective.

"You're right, Tilly, we need to tell him," she announced to her friends as they got back to the dock. "I want to go home too and spending however long chasing after nothing is not going to get us there." Her friend's eyes lit up. "The only thing that concerns me is what happens when he gets hold of it? How do we stop him?"

"Let's deal with that when we get to that point," replied Tilly, eyes still lit up like the night sky. *Always so damn optimistic*, Jenny thought. Tilly took her arm and skipped down the dock. Jenny wasn't the skipping kind, and was basically being dragged along the dock until they reached the ship.

"Harvey, get our defiant sailor out of the brig and bring him here please," Tilly demanded. Jenny couldn't stop a confused look coming across her face. What on earth did Tilly have planned now? She was playing her part very well.

They waited on the dock until Harvey returned with two sailors dragging the other off the ship. Obviously, he had had some kind of beating before they removed him from the brig; his cheek was starting to bruise. Not wanting to upset her friend, who was clearly getting into the captain role, Jenny moved closer to Joseph who was behind Tilly and Roger.

Once they got him in front of Tilly they shoved him down onto his knees. Harvey had an evil grin on his face, almost like he was proud of what he thought was about to happen.

"See that post over there on the end of the dock?" asked Tilly, the two sailors holding the one on his knees nodded their heads. "Tie him up and leave him there. Harvey, meet us in my quarters in ten minutes. We have something to discuss."

Jenny was impressed with the way she had handled it, but something in Harvey's eyes concerned her. It was almost like he was expecting Tilly to dish out a harsher punishment, not that it was in her nature. Before he could protest Tilly walked straight past him and Jenny turned to look at Joseph before following Tilly onto the deck.

Back inside the cabin, Jenny felt slightly claustrophobic with the amount of people inside. The four of them had been joined by Harvey, Bill and the navigator. *I really should start to learn people's names*, Jenny thought. Not that it would matter; they needed to get home and this was taking far too long. Since Tilly had mentioned it an ache had formed in her heart for home. She wanted to be back in the security of the library looking for anomalies. *God*, thought Jenny, *I never thought I'd want to be back in that damned library*. Her first mission out was certainly not one she had dreamed of.

Jenny slumped down into one of the chairs and as everyone gathered round the feeling of being boxed in grew. Tilly, who stood next to her, leant over the desk and pointed at the map.

"Your friend wasn't very honest with you, Harvey," she started to explain. "He told me he lied to you and that he was going to send you on a wild goose chase to Rochdale, when actually it's here in Grouz."

"Don't be absurd; Reginald would never lie to me," he huffed back at her. Bill chuckled from his place behind Harvey like the evil sidekick he was.

"Unless he thought you were going to do something stupid, Harvey," spat back Jenny, slamming her hands on the table, her voice a little too venomous on his name. Tilly's hand had shot out in front of her as Jenny stood, and her stare made Jenny slink back down into her chair. Bill took a step forward so he was level with Harvey.

"What would you know about that, little dove?" asked Harvey.

Jenny's head snapped towards the henchman. There was only one person who called her that, and it wasn't Harvey.

"What did you just call me?" she asked. He smirked at her instead of replying. Tilly held her hand up and Jenny understood that this wasn't helping matters.

"Look, I want to go home; you won't let me leave until you've found your artefact so it wouldn't be in my best interest to lie to you, would it?" Tilly said.

Jenny touched her pocket and felt for her ticket home as Tilly spoke. It was still there and she let out a silent breath, soon she would be going home, she just needed to find a Regent with the other half of the teleportation device. "So, hear me out."

Harvey nodded and Bill took a step back.

The room was silent as Tilly prepared herself to speak. Jenny couldn't help but stare at Harvey; *why had he called her that?* He stood with his hands behind his back, a bored look on his face and a sparkle in his eyes. Roger had taken up his place by Tilly's side, although he did move away slightly when Tilly brushed his hand with hers by accident. Jenny had noted that Tilly pretended it didn't happen, and Roger, who was probably ten years her senior, stepped away from her. Jenny watched on as Tilly prepared herself to speak to them all again. Bill had begun tapping his foot and Harvey was about to lose all patience.

"It's in Grouz, it makes sense given the last symbol is a sun. I suggest that we," she pointed from herself to Jenny, "go back to Reginald and see if he can at least narrow down the area so that we can find it a lot easier and quicker. That makes everyone happy, doesn't it?"

"I agree with Tilly," Jenny stated, just to get her two pennies worth in.

"Yes, well, you would," replied Harvey as soon as she had finished speaking. Jenny scowled at him. "I suppose I can agree to that, but Reginald will have to pay for lying to me. I am your first mate after all, Captain." A sick feeling filled Jenny's stomach as he said the word "captain"; he had never sounded as creepy as he did in that moment.

"Well let's go then," Jenny jumped up from her chair and grabbed hold of Tilly pulling her along. "Seriously Jenny, what are you doing trying to pull my arm off?" Tilly said when they had landed on the dock again.

"No, I just need to be out of earshot!" she retorted back to her friend. She continued to pull Tilly along until they were on American soil and not the wooden dock. Jenny slowed her pace down as they walked towards Reginald's shack. "That's not Harvey."

"What do you mean?" Tilly looked confused. "How can that not be Harvey?"

"I work with Harvey, he would never call me 'little dove'. Only one person ever called me that and I need to find out if it's true, because if it is, this could be much bigger than we thought." Jenny could see in Tilly's reaction that she was scaring her. She didn't care, this needed to be over and they needed to be home as soon as possible.

"I know we both want to go home Jen, but we need to see this through or Harvey might leave us stranded here," fear laced Tilly's voice. "Unless you have another way home?"

"It'll be okay, T, I'll get you out of this place, that's what I'm here for. But you're right, we can't leave Harvey to do whatever he wants. He might ruin everything," replied Jenny.

"What are you talking about now?" Tilly whined. Jenny could see that Tilly was frustrated with her, but she was trying hard not to spill all her secrets about the society she belonged to. Something still told her if she didn't tell Tilly it would drive a wedge between their newly found friendship.

"I promise I will tell you everything but right now we need to get to Reginald."

Tilly nodded with a light in her eyes. *I hope that is trust I see in her eyes,* thought Jenny.

Back outside the shack Jenny waltzed right up to the gate, swung it open, and pounded on the door. After two knocks it opened and they crossed into the room. Tilly followed her in and seated herself in the chair Harvey had sat in. Reginald entered the room and smiled.

"I didn't expect you girls back so soon; did you manage to leave Harvey sailing for England?" he asked with a grin on his face. "I'll get us a drink." Reginald disappeared through the door and returned with a tray filled with three glasses and a bottle of wine.

"I don't think it's really the time for wine," Tilly said with a quiet voice, "we only came back for answers. Where do we need to look Reginald?"

"Straight to business I see. Well, I'm still pouring myself a drink," he replied ignoring her question. He poured two glasses of the red wine and sat himself down in the chair opposite Tilly. He licked his lips after taking almost the entire content of the glass into his mouth.

"Let's see, ah yes. The artefact Harvey is looking for, well I believe it's in the church." He paused and looked from Jenny to Tilly and back again. The second glass was now in his hand and he was trying his hardest not to consume it, Jenny could tell from the hunger in his eyes.

"Reginald, which church are you talking about?" asked Jenny not wanting to spend much longer in the room. Since there was only the three of them in the room, the smell wasn't masked by any of their scents. It smelled like a funeral home—the heavy stench of death, masked by several bouquets of flowers strewn about and gathering dust. "We need to get it before Harvey finds us gone." She was playing dumb. Reginald didn't need to know they had let Harvey in on his deception.

"You're just like him, you know. Always treasure hunting, after he found that ring there was no stopping him," mused Reginald. Jenny's attention heightened, *did Reginald know about the ring?*

"What ring Reginald?"

"The one on his left hand, have you not noticed? Evil thing that is, he always wears a different face," he paused again looking at the shock of Jenny's face. "Even so, he's not here so no need to conceal any more information. The church is in the next town, a day's ride north. However, I wouldn't know where inside the church it is."

It was all a little too much for her really, this entire situation was causing her stress when all she really wanted was to get home and to take Tilly with her. Of course, she actually had to find a Regent to activate the portal home, but that wouldn't take long. It would lead her to them when she eventually got the broach out and used it.

"This town Reginald," Tilly butted in before Jenny could fully lose it. "Where exactly is it? I mean can we have some more details? Directions? Name?"

"Oh yes of course, deary me," he replied standing up and going over to a nearby shelf, "I'm sure I have a map around here somewhere. Ah! Here it is, just follow this path." He traced their journey with his finger and smiled at her.

"Thank you," said Tilly before Jenny stood up to ask more questions.

"This ring," Jenny probed. "What does it look like?"

"Oh, it's like a black band wrapped in silver," he replied quite flippantly. Confirming her suspicions, Fake Harvey didn't just have the Ring of Deception, he was wearing it..Tilly gave her a stern look and stood up to leave. Jenny knew she wasn't going to be allowed any more questions and got herself together with a big sigh.

Tilly had them both out of the door before Jenny even had the chance to come up with more questions for Reginald. Jenny had a feeling that Reginald was keeping something back from her, but she couldn't put her finger on it.

Walking back to the ship, Jenny was still trying to compile in her mind everything that they had just been told. She thought this was going to be a lot easier than it turned out to be. Tilly was silent.

"Are you okay?" asked Jenny, unsure of where to start the next conversation.

"I think so, it's just all so crazy you know." Tilly started. "One moment I am sitting in a library thinking I'm making a new friend who likes history, next I'm being taken away by a guy I barely know."

Jenny was silent. She hadn't expected Tilly to start pouring her heart out when she asked her that question.

"Then," Tilly continued. "I'm actually back in the time period I am studying and part of his stupid plan to bring you here." Tilly was waving her arm around now, and pointing at Jenny.

"What do you mean he wanted me here?"

"Harvey, or whoever he is, said he wanted you here because of what you would bring," she answered.

"The only thing I brought here is a way home," Jenny said angry. She dug into her pocket and pulled out the half of broach she had and showed Tilly. "This, connected with one from another member of The Collective, will take us home. I'm here to get you."

"Then what does he want?"

"Apart from the telescope, I have no idea," answered Jenny, feeling mentally drained.

Tilly didn't stop before she got on the ship and as Jenny was following her it wasn't until they were right up to Harvey that Jenny realised what she was doing.

"Ah you're back!" he observed as he lifted his head from the map. "I was just charting our course to Rochdale so there would be no delay in setting sail, provided you didn't get any information of course," he bowed his head slightly which only made Jenny uncomfortable.

"I have information, but I'll need horses and two days to see if it is correct," Tilly wasted no time in telling him what she had learned.

He was obviously taking everything into consideration because it took him a while to respond. He walked over to the side of the ship and looked out onto the horizon.

"Okay," he said as he spun back around to face them, "I'll get you horses, I'll look after the ship and you bring me back that telescope."

Jenny was surprised by Harvey's reaction. She never thought Harvey would allow them to go, especially without him. He must have some kind of ulterior motive. She could see Tilly smiling, beaming. It was as if she was under some kind of spell and every time Harvey spoke she melted.

"I'll send Bill to fetch you five horses, I want him to go with you. You'll have forty-eight hours from the moment you ride off, if you're not back with what I want I will set sail for Rochdale."

Ah there it was, the ulterior motive of Fake Harvey. He didn't trust Tilly's explanation and Jenny knew he would probably set sail the second they left for the church. Although why he would leave Bill behind confused her.

21
TILLY

TILLY WASN'T sure if this was a good idea or a bad one, the five of them running off to some church to find a telescope. She didn't even understand what the telescope did, just that it was on the list of items Harvey wanted. Figuring out Harvey's intentions was still something of a mystery to her. Although being the captain of a pirate ship was fun, taking control like she had with that defiant sailor made her heart beat faster. It made her nervous to play a role out of her character.

Bill quickly disappeared after Harvey had given him his orders to find five horses and travel with Tilly and her group to get the telescope. Tilly knew this was going to go down entirely the wrong way. She could already picture the fights between Roger and Bill. They would be at each other's throats within the first ten minutes, but it didn't matter, some battles you won and some you lost. Harvey was not going to budge regarding Bill going with them and that was that.

They had forgotten to get the map so when Tilly had mentioned it was in the next town and they realised they needed Bill, as he supposedly had contacts in Grouz, much to the girls' amazement. They set off as soon as Bill was back with the horses

THE COLLECTIVE

and they'd stocked up on provisions for the journey. Although they were only going for forty-eight hours she knew something would go wrong.

By the time they made camp, no-one had spoken and it had been a silent few hours. Tilly was always uncomfortable with silence so the entire ride had been the worst experience for her. As soon as they stopped she hopped down off her steed and turned to Bill.

"Is this where we are stopping?" she asked Bill.

"Yes, there's camp stuff on the horses, you two are sharing a tent and so are they," he replied pointing at her and Jenny then at the boys. "You shouldn't need to bother me while I set up my own." He walked off to a nearby tree and sat down before getting out some bread and water.

Tilly shook her head and reached up to the pack on her horse. Opening it she found a folded-up tent, a couple of weapons, some food and water and some paper. Passing on the food for the moment, she grabbed the paper and opened it. The list that Harvey had been after somehow had ended up in her pack and she instantly knew that this was going to be a bad journey.

"What's that?" Jenny asked as she pulled the food pouch off the horse and dug in.

"Remember that list?" Tilly said trying to be quiet enough that Bill couldn't hear her, "I think someone is trying to get me in trouble." Her head flicked over to where Bill was still firmly sat under the tree and Jenny's eyes widened. She licked her fingers of the salt from the crackers she had been eating and stood closer to her. "He knows I have it."

"So, this is what he wants?" She asked as quietly as Tilly had. Tilly nodded and then stuffed the list into her pocket.

"We will have to get rid of this at some point!" Tilly tried to raise her voice as she whispered but ended up sounded a bit hoarse instead.

Roger and Joseph hadn't spoken the entire journey and were still silent as they pitched their tent. Tilly could tell something was weighing on them but with Bill around it wasn't like she could just come out and ask loads of questions. The best course of action would be to wait until the tents were built and Bill was asleep and then ask the boys what they thought of the whole situation. Night was coming in fast and while her mind was racing Bill sat against the tree and did nothing to help, he got up to build his tent and then went inside.

The boys built a fire as Jenny fetched some water and Tilly clung to the paper which felt like it was burning a hole in her pocket. The only thing she could do would be to ask Bill what this was doing in her pack, but she wasn't sure she wanted to do that.

Putting that thought at the back of her mind, Tilly walked over to Bill's tent. "Bill, you in there?"

"Yes, what do you want?" came his reply. His tone of voice implied he was definitely, not happy about her speaking to him.

"I was just wondering if I could ask you something."

The tent door flung open and she jumped back as he emerged. His facial expressions were not pleasant and Tilly was instantly regretting this decision.

"Yes, what do you want?" he snapped at her as he crossed his arms.

"What time should we be up in the morning? You never said," she changed her mind as soon as she spoke knowing that she had to keep the list to herself. "I didn't want to waste time so thought it would be better to ask you."

"Right, of course," his expression softened as he realised that what she was asking was logical. "Probably at first light, we have a way to go and I don't want to waste time. We need to get here and back before Harvey sets sail, if we actually want to work this out. I for one am not up for travelling to Rochdale either."

She nodded at him and he ducked back into his tent, conversation over. Tilly walked over to the fire and dropped the paper in there. She watched it burn and turn to ash before turning around and entering her and Jenny's tent. Once inside Tilly couldn't help but think that there was something weird about Bill now he was away from Harvey. Almost like he could actually, think for himself rather than just wanting whatever Harvey wanted.

"You seem a little lost in thought," said Jenny as she led down on her makeshift bed.

⁂

"Captain," said the voice that woke Tilly up. She got herself together, wrapping her coat around to protect her from the fresh morning air and opened the tent door; Roger was standing outside, waiting for her. Tilly rubbed her hands together, the friction warming her fingers.

"What is it?" she hissed at him, still half-asleep. Tilly had never been the best in the mornings and she was all too aware that they were the only ones awake as Jenny grunted in her sleep.

"I haven't been to sleep as I thought someone should keep watch. Bill's wandered off," he replied nodding his head in the opposite direction. "I followed him for a little while, as I just don't trust the guy, and I was right as he met up with someone." Now she was listening with her full attention. "I'm not sure who he was or what they were talking about, I didn't want to get too close in case they saw me, but it didn't look friendly. It ended with Bill being punched."

"That makes no sense at all. I'll get Jenny," Tilly didn't finish her sentence before she went back inside. "Jenny!" she whispered as she jabbed her side. A batting hand hit her away and Jenny rolled over. "Jenny, wake up!"

"What is wrong with you?" Jenny groaned. "I am trying to sleep here."

"Yes, and we have an emergency."

If she could have seen Jenny's face Tilly knew that there would have been eye-rolling. After wriggling around for a bit and getting herself out of the tent, Jenny finally joined them outside.

Neither Jenny nor Roger said anything as she walked up and down a mere eight steps before turning back and walking along.

She was still lost in thought when Jenny's hands reached for her shoulders and stopped her movement. "For god sake's, stop pacing before you tire us all out. What's happened? Why are you waking me up at the crack of dawn?"

"Roger saw Bill get punched," Tilly explained.

"That's what you woke me up for?" she laughed. "I'm going back to sleep." Jenny started to turn back towards the tent before Roger's words stopped her.

"There's no point in that, he'll be up to make us move in an hour so we might as well be ready," said Roger, his voice calm.

Tilly scowled at Jenny, who rolled her eyes at Roger and then moved away from him. They were acting like children and Tilly did not have time for it. She held her hands up to stop them from saying another word, and a rustling from one of the tents got their attention.

Bill emerged from his, and looked slightly shocked that they were all stood around outside. Tilly gave a weak smile as she locked eye contact but Bill just gave them an odd look, he obviously wasn't expecting to see anyone up before him.

"Didn't expect you lot to be up," he said, sounding somewhat nice for once. "I thought I'd have to wake you all up before we finally got moving." He smiled at them, but Tilly could tell it was forced. Jenny moved over to the men's tent to wake Joseph up and they all stood around awkwardly.

"Yes, well we want to make it back to the ship just as much as you do, Bill," said Tilly as Roger continued to scowl at him. She ignored the tension between all of them as she gestured for Jenny to move towards the tent. They both started to take theirs down but Tilly couldn't shake the feeling of eyes on her back. Something was very wrong and her gut was telling her this entire situation was a bad idea.

It didn't take them long to pack up their stuff and get back on their horses, but the sun had come up and was now rising steadily in the sky. The travel was again in silence as no one really knew what to say, Bill made it awkward for them. Tilly felt like she couldn't say anything that she wanted to, because if Bill turned on them he could use it against her. She wouldn't put it past him to try and leave them behind somehow.

When they arrived at the church Tilly didn't know what to think, it was a grand building and it looked like half the back was missing. Walls had crumbled leaving bare brown stone exposed to the elements, and the thick wooden door was kicked in at the bottom. It didn't paint the picture of safety. Bill pulled his horse around to the front and then tied it up to a random pole that, Tilly suspected, used to be a gate. Rust had started to gather on it and the paint was peeling off.

The sign for the church was hanging off one side and the weather had smudged the name. As far as churches go, this one was in pretty bad shape, and Tilly assumed that it was because it was so far out of town.

Behind Bill was Roger who was keeping a close watch on him, the look in Roger's eye told Tilly that he didn't believe Bill's nice act.

Bill didn't wait for Tilly before marching straight into the church, and she rushed behind him. She had to find it first or Harvey would get exactly what he wanted. Tilly needed it as a bargaining tool to keep herself, and her friends on the ship to find a way home. Inside it was cold; you could smell the dampness from the moss growing on the walls and the hole in the roof that was dripping water. She could feel the presence of Jenny and the boys behind her, Roger moved faster and pushed past her to get closer to Bill.

"I think we should split up and cover more ground," said Bill as he turned to everyone behind him. "Tilly if you look with Jenny in the back rooms, Roger if you look with Joseph that side and I'll do this side?" He said it like a question but he wasn't asking for permission.

"I actually prefer to work alone," piped up Joseph winking at the girls.

"Guess that leaves me with you then, Bill," Roger punched Bill on the shoulder, hard, but made it look like a friendly gesture. It left Bill scowling and rubbing his upper arm. Jenny grabbed hold of Tilly's hand and dragged her through the centre of the church and out the back towards the altar room. Inside there wasn't much to look at, the left wall was crumbling like some of the other walls of the church.

"Do you think it'll be like in the movies?" asked Jenny.

Tilly scrunched up her face, *what movies had Jenny been watching?* "What do you mean?"

"Well, that it'll be easy to find, in the most obvious place," Jenny jumped around the corner of the altar. "Like inside the bottom of the altar?"

Tilly smirked. "Thanks for traveling through time to come get me, Jen. I'm sorry I ever fell for that stupid Fake Harvey with his ocean-coloured eyes and flippy hair."

"Hey, don't worry about it," she replied placing a hand on Tilly's shoulder. "It's not your fault."

"I know but I just feel like I'm the reason we are in this mess."

"That is not true," Jenny's voice was stern, and she looked cross. "Don't ever think that okay."

Tilly nodded. It was nice to have a friend, even if they were both being made to search for something that was better left alone. Tilly moved away to the other side of the altar as Jenny got down on her knees.

"Do you think the boys will ever find out why Bill got punched in the face?" asked Jenny as she tried to pry the bottom of the altar apart.

"I don't think that is going to come apart, Jen," Tilly responded, trying to help. "And probably not, maybe they'll sort themselves out when we finish searching, or they would have ended up fighting." Both the girls were flung back as the wooden side of the altar fell away, forcing them both to land on their bums and start laughing.

Inside the altar was not what Tilly had expected to see. Jenny had joked about how in the movies it's always in the most obvious place and so Tilly expected the altar to be empty, to go along with the rest of their bad luck, instead it had a white cloth inside it. She looked at Jenny and shrugged her shoulders the laughter dispersing from both of them. They scrabbled together and Jenny pulled out the cloth. A metal clang sounded as the telescope fell from the cloth and onto the stone floor. Tilly reached for the golden tube and held it up. It was only half a telescope.

"Well you were half right," she chuckled.

"So, I was, where do you think the other half will be?" asked Jenny. Before either of them could think or say anything more shouting erupted from where the boys were supposedly searching.

Both the girls got up off the floor, Jenny with the half of the telescope, and ran towards the boys. As the girls reached them Tilly saw Roger on top of Bill who was clutching something gold and shiny. Joseph had grabbed hold of Roger and was trying to pull him off but neither of them were letting go of the object. Joseph fell back with an elbow to the face and that was when Tilly stepped in.

"What on earth are you doing?" she shouted making them stop attacking one another long enough to look at her. Bill took this as an opportunity to kick Roger where it hurts and make a run for it. It wasn't long before Roger had grabbed hold of him again and flung him around, causing the object to go flying down the middle of the church to land at Tilly's feet.

"Seriously? You guys are like children!" Tilly couldn't hide the frustration in her voice as she bent down to pick up the other half of the telescope. "Why were you fighting?"

"It doesn't matter," Bill said, folding his arms. "It's only half of what we need. We won't get back on the ship and we only have 24 hours left to find this god damn thing." Tilly looked out of a window to see that the sun was just passing its highest point in the sky.

"We can do a lot in twenty-four hours. What's really the issue?" she calmed her voice in an attempt to get him to speak to her. He scrunched up his face at her words and shrugged his shoulders. "I can't help if you don't tell me."

Joseph was still holding onto Roger, who was trying to get out of his grip, which Tilly only noticed by following Bill's glance towards him.

"Take him outside," she demanded pointing to the door. Bill switched his weight on his feet and put his eyes back to the ground. How on earth this got so complicated she didn't know. Jenny touched her shoulder in passing as she followed Joseph out of the church with Roger. Tilly didn't let her eyes move from Bill as she knew the second she turned from him he would make a run for it and she would never get the answers she needed. "So, what's the problem?"

"I can't tell you," he replied with a voice like a mouse, his eyes not moving off the floor. Fighting the urge to console him, she crossed her arms in an attempt to stay put.

"You need to tell me or we will leave you here. I'll let Roger tie you up somewhere and go back to the ship," she tried to make her voice seem stronger than it was. In honesty, she knew he would never believe that from her. "Why did Roger attack you?"

"Because he heard me say that this was only half of the telescope, and I don't know which half he needs," he explained. "Please don't make me say any more, if he finds out I told you anything..." Bill stopped talking as he gulped. On the ship, he was Harvey's shadow and biggest fighter, but stood here now in front of her Tilly saw that he wasn't as strong as he made himself out to be. There must be something else going on. His personality change must be the result of something,

Maybe Jenny would have more knowledge on it, or maybe Bill feared Harvey. Harvey might even have some information on him that he doesn't want shared, thought Tilly. There were loads of possibilities but there was only one way she was going to get answers.

"How did you meet Harvey?" Tilly asked.

"He found me on the docks and since then I've always been by his side," his voice was shaking. This was definitely not the Bill from the ship. "He has a way of keeping you there even if you don't want to be."

"Why did that man punch you?"

Bill's eyes flicked up from the floor to look at her. "What do you mean?"

"Roger saw you back at camp, you went off and met with someone who punched you. Although there is no mark on you, the look in your eyes tells me it happened."

"That was my brother," he replied, taking a step back from her, "there are many reasons I accepted Harvey's offer. My family needs money, my sister needs treatment and with my brother's injury he is unable to work. He said I haven't been sending money home, even though I am sure I did. My brother didn't believe me and so punched me."

Tilly put her hand up; she couldn't hear any more. If he thought he was sending his money to them and it wasn't getting there then something must be stopping it. *Maybe it's the same thing that happens when he is with Harvey?* thought Tilly. Bill was still standing in front of her with his head down. Her heart was bursting with sympathy for him however she knew that whatever leash Harvey had on him would return as soon as they got in his presence.

"Where do you think the money is going?" she asked him, hoping he would speak some more.

"I should speak to Harvey about it," he replied keeping his eyes on the floor.

"I understand," she said after a few moments of silence. She furrowed her brow, "but then why did Roger and you end up fighting?"

"He didn't believe me, I got mad and threw a punch. I guess it's my nature."

Tilly wasn't sure she believed anything he said to her but she supposed there wasn't really any other option.

"We should start our journey back, we don't want to be left behind," she smiled at him. "Can't let Harvey leave without us." *Or I might end up having to commandeer another ship, find a new crew, and take Harvey down.* She put her arm out to the door and Bill moved towards the exit.

Outside, Roger was still retained by Joseph and Jenny was

pacing. Clutching her half of the telescope, with a sour expression on her face, she only stopped walking when Tilly touched her shoulder. Smiling as she held up her half of the telescope Tilly nodded her head to the left and the girls walked off a little way from the boys.

"I guess we better make a plan then," said Tilly.

22
JENNY

JENNY COULD TELL Tilly knew she was uncomfortable from the way her hands tightened around the telescope, although she didn't quite know what words to use. Her fears were growing as the time to re-join the ship came closer, and there was a feeling she couldn't shake.

"A plan?" Jenny countered. "What kind of plan?" She twisted her lips still unsure of what they could do to get out of this mess.

"Something's bothering you, isn't it?" Tilly asked her. "Come on then, out with it!" Her arms went up and down in the air as she spoke. Jenny wasn't keen on her friends' tone of voice.

"I'm not sure we can trust them, Tilly, that's all," she replied to her friend. Not wanting to tell her everything.

"Who?"

"Bill and Harvey. We already know Harvey isn't actually Harvey, how do we know he doesn't do something to Bill. Tell me you've noticed the change since we've been away from him?" she asked.

"Yeah, he is different. I don't understand what you're getting at Jen," replied Tilly.

"That's all I know, and everything Reginald said makes sense in my head," Jenny explained. "I need to find out if what he said is true, because if it is, we might be in more trouble than we realise and I don't know what that means for us."

Tilly put her eyes to the ground. As if someone has turned on a light bulb inside Jenny's head, she had an idea. Well, part of an idea.

"We need to get the ring," Jenny announced. "We need to get that ring and rip it off his hand." Her hand was doing the actions as she spoke, the telescope under her arm. Tilly's eyes widened and she chuckled a little bit.

"Okay Morticia, you aren't ripping anything off. I'm sure we can find an easier way to get the ring," Tilly laughed.

"We need to do it before we get back to Harvey, and he cannot get this telescope," Jenny said twisting it in her hand.

Tilly nodded, and Jenny smiled knowing she was right. As much as she didn't need confirmation from her new-found friend, it made her feel all the more confident. Considering their situation, confidence was not exactly oozing out of any of them. They were in dangerous territory and they needed to get going before Bill turned on them. They had a day's ride before the time limit was up, which meant they weren't going to be sleeping before they arrived back at the ship.

"Jen," Tilly started, as if an idea suddenly popped into her head. "What if we hide it from him?"

"How exactly are we supposed to hide a telescope? It's not really inconspicuous, is it?"

"But what if it didn't look like a telescope? We could hide it in my sword sheath!" she was so impressed with her own idea her voice went up an octave as she said it. Jenny could tell that Tilly managed to suppress the hand clapping. Rushing to grab the telescope from Jenny she almost fell forward as the telescope was moved out of her grip.

"I'd prefer to keep it if that's okay?" Jenny asked, unsure if she could trust anyone else with this task.

"That's fine," Tilly replied instantly. Her face showed a little confusion into Jenny's request but Jenny was happy all the same. "You can hide it instead."

"How are we going to find the Regent to get us home?" Jenny moaned, connecting the telescope together. "That's all I came here to do, find you and go home, not gallivant around as a pirate crew member with you as my captain, no offence."

"None taken, I feel the same but it seems we have to play out this scene for that to happen," Tilly looked up at the two boys who were now on their own steeds, Bill was still closing some bags. Jenny did too and she could tell Roger was tense and clearly wanted to attack Bill again.

Jenny collapsed the telescope so it was small enough to hide under her jacket and that was when she noticed it. The telescope had started humming. She could feel it singing to her like it wanted her to use it. It was very seducing; she could see it easily lulling her into a false sense of security. Quickly, she covered up the top of it, mentally blocking the song in an attempt to not be swayed to use it. There are texts in The Collective's files where they speak of items with the call of power; they can take over one's mind if they are not strong enough to keep it at bay.

Instinctively, she touched behind her ear and started up the chip. Colours blinded her temporarily as it buzzed into action. With it running, the call from the telescope was quietened down as all she could focus on were the colours. She was surrounded by orange, at least she knew there wasn't much damage to clean up.

Not having a mess to clean up was a relief to Jenny as she knew how harshly the Regents reprimanded people who played with time too much. Although she supposed she didn't have any choice, given her current situation. Bill had already mounted his steed by the time the girls had finished talking and watering their horses. Knowing that Bill didn't want to stop on the journey back was a risk but they knew they didn't have a choice. Harvey's threat wasn't just words; he would leave them stuck in Grouz without a second thought.

Lifting herself up onto her horse's back, she made a silent wish that they would make it in time for the departure. A small nod from Tilly told her that they were ready to go; thankfully Roger had calmed down and was no longer attempting to punch Bill.

"Let's get back to the ship," called Tilly and they started making their way back.

※

Jenny ran down the dock as if she was being chased by a mad man. There was no way Harvey was leaving without them. She knew Tilly felt the same, as the further they got out to sea the longer they were going to be stuck there. Her feet faltered as she tried to push them further to make it before they let the last rope loose and began their voyage to England. Bill pushed past her as he gained speed towards the ship. Both girls stopped for a second as they watched Bill push past the sailor on the dock and jump up onto the ladder before it started to sail away. Cheers could be heard from deck and dread filled Jenny as the thought of them not getting on that ship filled her mind.

Tilly stood with her head back, facing the sky as she cursed under her breath.

Jenny couldn't help herself as she started to laugh.

"Why on earth are you laughing?" Tilly snapped. Her expression changed as they watched the ship, which was still slowly travelling away from the shore. "Why are they stopping?"

"They aren't," said Joseph before Jenny could respond. "They just haven't cast off properly yet and the current is taking them out to sea."

"We could still make it after that little rat," spat Roger. Tilly shot him a dirty look, she clearly didn't approve of his tone. "All we need to do is jump."

Without waiting to hear more of their deliberations Jenny ran and jumped onto the ship just like Bill had. "Well come on then, we don't have all day!" she waved her arm beckoning them to follow her. Emerging up on the deck she wasn't expecting the silence that she was met with. In front of her was the entire crew of the ship standing in a circle with Harvey and Bill in the middle. Harvey stood over Bill, who was crumpled on the floor clutching his face. His ear looked like it twitched as he turned to look at her. Tilly was now aboard behind her, and she looked furious.

"Well what's going on here then?" she asked.

Jenny smiled and moved out of her friend's way. If there was ever a time to play captain it was now, when the crew couldn't be given a choice as to whose side they were on.

"Harvey, let Bill go," Tilly said sternly. Bill gave a weak smile but Jenny could see from his eyes he was already under Harvey's control again.

"I didn't need your help," Bill said as he brushed himself off and disappeared below deck.

Harvey just turned to face them and gave a half-hearted smile. "Nothing is going on, I was just telling him that he shouldn't have come back without you, but clearly he didn't. I guess I owe him an apology." He started to walk away but the crew around them didn't move, most of them had sinister smiles on their faces.

"So, you just decided to what? Teach him a lesson? That's not your place," Tilly said as Harvey scowled at the crew, making them disperse. With the crew now back to their duties (while still eavesdropping), Jenny turned and watched as Tilly took a deep breath.

"Well obviously, I had to do something in your absence, of course," he bowed his head slightly. "Now that you're back, shall I show you the rest of the journey? Then you can show me your bounty."

"Are you sure you're okay going alone T?" she asked.

"Yes, I'll be fine," Tilly replied. "Plus, you'll be just outside, right?"

Jenny nodded, and watched as Tilly walked off with Fake Harvey. Jenny looked at Joseph and shrugged so he walked off and sat between two barrels, and leant his back against the mast. She watched as he pulled his hat over his eyes and made no attempt to interact with the crew members. Turning to Roger to say something, she closed her mouth before any words escaped as he was no longer there beside her.

Leaning back on the side, she scanned the deck to look for

him, while also trying to think of her next move. Her arm slipped as a wave of tiredness washed over her, the late night of riding taking its toll on her body. Turning to look at the horizon she held her head up with her hands. Her eyes turned heavy and after a few minutes of fighting the urge to sleep, she made the decision to go for a lie down in the captain's quarters.

Roger grabbed hold of her arm and dragged her beneath the stairs to the upper deck before she had a chance to open the door for her chance to sleep.

"I believe this is yours?" he asked her, holding the broach in front of her face.

"How did you get that?!" she snatched it from his hands without a second thought. The feeling of it back in her possession was almost like a weight lifted from her shoulders, although she also had a small inkling of fear for not noticing it was gone.

"Please, I might be a thief, a pirate and other things, but I am also a Regent. It's my job to be able to get things without other people noticing things." His smile made Jenny feel uncomfortable, and she shifted in her coat. "Now we need to talk because I want to get back."

"*You're* a Regent?" she asked her voice going up an octave, although she wasn't sure she could trust what he said. "I thought..." Her mind trailed off, she didn't know who she was supposed to find.

"Thought what? That finding a Regent would be easy?" he laughed at her. "Please, even the Bermuda HQ has trouble keeping track of their own. You'd be stuck here for years before you got home."

"I... Have you known this whole time?" asked Jenny.

"I became curious when you mentioned The Collective but then I saw you take the telescope. You heard it sing. I saw it in your face." Roger ducked lower into the shadows as a crew member walked down the stairs.

"You can get us out of here?"

"I can try, I haven't opened a portal in a while. We need to sort this mess out first," replied Roger. "Bermuda HQ won't get involved, there's not enough of them in this time period."

Now that caught Jenny's attention even more, he knew about Bermuda, that explained why he didn't show any emotion when Vincent died. He could already see it coming, just like she had, once she put her chip on. It was still odd that he had never mentioned his Regency before, especially as Tilly trusted him and Jenny had openly spoken about The Collective in front of him.

"Don't look so shocked, I can help. I'll get you out of here." Something caught his eye over her shoulder. "What on earth is she doing?" Jenny spun around and saw Tilly walking beside Harvey, they were coming towards them, and she kept reaching forward for his hand.

Jenny continued to watch in awe as her friend grabbed hold of Harvey's arm and then to his hand. As if time could be slowed Jenny watched everything play out in slow motion. Tilly's hand pulled at something on his hand, and a ring came off Harvey's hand. It slipped through Tilly's fingers and bounced three times on the floor until it came to a stop on the deck by someone's foot. Harvey slapped Tilly in the face, an action that made Jenny want to run forward to her friend but her feet were rooted to the spot. Her eyes darted from Tilly to the ring, which was now being picked up by Joseph, and then finally back to Harvey. His face was changing.

Slightly distorted, Jenny couldn't quite figure out who he was turning into. His hair turned just a shade darker and he shortened just an inch as a sinister smile crept across his face. A smile that she knew all too well.

Jenny couldn't move as a surge of emotions went through her. She didn't want to believe that it was happening, it didn't make sense, it couldn't make sense to her. She wouldn't allow her mind to accept it. After the conversation with Roger about him being the one able to take them home, she was not expecting to find out that Harvey was actually her ex-boyfriend. His expression didn't change as his face settled.

"Noah?!" Jenny exclaimed. "What the hell? How did...?" He

was there, standing in front of her, and she didn't know what to do, however her hands did. She walked over and punched him in the face.

Before she could think of another sentence she slammed her arms down by her sides and stormed off, Jenny didn't quite know how to handle what had happened in the past few minutes. As she was walking to the other side of the deck a thought popped into her mind. *The ring.* The only one she could think of was an illegal artefact that wasn't meant to exist outside of the vault. The secret Collective Vault was supposed to be guarded at all times and no-one except the Regents would know where it is. How did he get hold of it? Why had he turned up at her flat to then go running off with her new friend the day after? Nothing was making sense in her head and she started to feel light headed.

"I'm so confused," she heard Tilly say before she could get too far from them. "Who are you?"

"I'm her ex-boyfriend, I've been exiled from The Collective and I plan on getting back at them. Does that answer your question?" Noah replied sarcastically. "Jenny, please you know exactly how. Why do you think they kicked me out in the first place?"

"You were in the vault," her voice was barely a whisper as it all came together in her head and she turned to face him. Her eyes stung with tears that had yet to fall and she cursed herself internally for being so utterly stupid. All the signs were there, including her suspicions and yet she still didn't figure it out. When they were together he had always gone out on missions late at night, Jenny had never asked questions as she knew some missions were night time only, then he was kicked out. There was never an explanation given, he ran off to Australia as soon as he could and the Regents only made an announcement. They told everyone that Noah had broken the rules and was smuggling things from other timelines back here, which could've caused issues in both eras of time. That act was a breach of the rules and Noah had been removed from The Collective effective immediately. Now she knew exactly what he had been doing, but if the Regent's found out he had been in the vault, they would terminate his timeline. He would never have existed. Her heart had never felt so conflicted. "What the hell are you planning and why do you need the ring?" she said raising her voice.

"Is this all you're worried about Jen?" he rolled his eyes. "Still always fighting for them. You, stupid girl, can't you figure it out in that clever head of yours, little dove?" Noah waved his arm up pointing to her head, there was a spitefulness to his voice that made her heart hurt. "They took my parents from me, ruined my chance at becoming a Regent and now I am going to take their entire society from them."

"Revenge will get you nowhere," mumbled Roger just loud enough for Noah to hear.

"Your parents died on a mission for The Collective, no one could have foreseen that Noah, but that doesn't mean you should become the villain," Jenny shouted at him before he had a chance to retaliate to Roger's comment. "Is that why you left me?" Her voice caught. That wasn't supposed to come out and now she could feel her cheeks heating up. Trying and failing to contain her breathing, Noah only added to her heartbreak and anger as he smiled that cruel smile at her. If she had the strength she would have hit him again.

"Oh Jen, I love that you still love me," he wasn't going to be kind to her. "But that doesn't mean you are going to stop me from doing this. I deserve to be in The Collective and they deserve to pay for what they have done to me."

Her eyes filled with water as she blinked back the tears. She turned around and moved behind Joseph and Roger. One of them grabbed her arm in an attempt to stop her but she pushed past to conceal her face from Noah. She might be hurting but she wouldn't give him the satisfaction of showing it until the tears had passed.

"Anyway, now that's over can we get on with you giving me my telescope?" he said, taking no notice of the fact she had just walked off. Jenny felt like her heart might stop in her chest.

"No," Tilly said with determination and Jenny made a mental thank you for her friend speaking up when she could not. "I don't have it." This wasn't a lie Tilly didn't have the telescope, but this was just getting them borrowed time.

Jenny pulled herself together and wiped the tears from her eyes. If anything, she always had a good poker face and she would show that now. It was still singing to her, but she only picked up on it now she was focusing on it. The pull of the telescope called to her and she fought the urge to put her hand under her jacket.

"You wouldn't be lying to me would you," he whispered in her ear as he twirled a strand of Tilly's hair in his hands. Noah was staring at her, eyes slightly squinted. He moved closer to Jenny now, his fingers almost touched Jenny's face as her entire body went up in goose bumps. Stepping away from him she gathered up some courage and swatted his hand away from her.

"No, she would not be lying to you Noah, not that you would believe that being a compulsive liar yourself," she snarled at him. He smiled and it made her shiver.

"Why do you girls insist on lying to me? Bill's already told me you have it." Tilly shrugged as Noah turned his head to her. "Did you girls forget the part where I said I was part of The Collective? I can hear it calling out, so it's here." Jenny tried to keep her cool but she feared her gulp gave her away.

"Lock them in the brig," he shouted and grabbed hold of Jenny's arm. "You, I'll take personally," he whispered in her ear. For a few seconds, no-one moved and Jenny saw Tilly smile as if she had a plan but then Bill appeared out of nowhere and manhandled her to the stairs that led down to the brig. Noah led Jenny behind Tilly and Bill with some other crew members bringing Joseph and Roger behind.

As Noah threw them into the brig, Jenny felt the cool sensation of the telescope being removed from her back. Her hands were too slow to stop him as she realised what was happening and Joseph was thrusted in her way so she couldn't grab the telescope back from him. The door swung shut as her outstretched hands got close to him.

"Thanks, little dove," he said holding up the collapsed telescope on the other side of the bars. "I'll come back to you if I need to," Noah's all too familiar smile returned. "Watch them, I'm going up to my quarters."

Noah and Bill left the brig leaving two sailors, one by the brig door and one by the stairs that led back up to deck. How they were going to get out of this situation Jenny did not know. As she turned around to her friends that were locked up with her, she could see Tilly's face was etched with confusion and Roger was standing with his fists clenched.

"Well come on then, let us out," ordered Tilly, but the two crew members just stood there ignoring her.

"That's not going to work T," replied Jenny. "They're like Bill now. I really need to figure out how he's doing that." She'd taken to looking at the floor again, embarrassed that they were trapped here by her ex-boyfriend and she didn't realise it sooner. "We are just going to have to wait until he figures it out."

"Figures what out Jenny? That we are stuck here? That all we want is to go home? I think that is pretty obvious but he's more interested in getting back at you and your stupid organisation." Tilly was shouting now.

"Hey," said Roger. "You're insulting more than just your friend here. It's not our fault Noah is a maniac who thinks the world owes him something because he broke the rules." He crossed his arms and glared at her.

"He has a point you know T, if you get angry, Noah wins. We need to come up with a plan of action to get out of the brig," Jenny lowered her voice, "and I think I know just how to do it." She looked behind Tilly and saw Joseph lying on the floor. She moved closer to him and bent down to him, he was knocked out but there was something on his head. He had a small scratch which was bleeding but otherwise he seemed stable. However, this needed seeing too.

"He needs something to stop the bleeding, surely they could get us a cloth or something," Jenny said loudly, throwing a stare at the sailor by the door. He turned his head to the right in response to her words. Although his back was still turned towards them. "Are you listening to me? We need cloths and water, GO AND

GET ME SOME!" She was shouting now. The sailor turned to see them and she held up her bloody hands. In response, he cringed and backed away as if the blood would do something to him. *Guess that's how the squeamish are in the olden days,* her thoughts confirmed as he promptly threw up in a nearby barrel.

"T," Jenny whispered. "Go seduce him."

"What?!" Tilly mouthed, frowning at her friend.

"Oh, Jesus mate, watch where you spew that," said the sailor by the stairs. "Go up on deck, and Smitty," he called to the sailor who had been sick. "Send someone else down, I can't have you down here like this. May as well get them to bring the cloths the girl asked for."

Smitty clambered up the stairs trying hard not to vomit some more as when he looked over at Jenny she merely threw her hands up again. As Smitty's shoes disappeared up on deck, Tilly moved over to Jenny.

"I am not doing that," she said quietly to Jenny as she tried to take over.

"Why not? He's got the key to get us out" asked Jenny, "I'm covered in blood, hardly something that turns men on." She tried to suppress a laugh at her insane comment.

"Please," Tilly whined, "I was their captain, you really think it's going to work with me? Just rub most of it off in the hay." Jenny rolled her eyes at her friend, as she got up. She swung her hips from side to side as she walked up to the bars of their cell. Roger moved past her and gave her a look that merely asked *what are you thinking?* She returned his gaze with a small smile. Jenny could hear the ripping of cloth from behind her as Tilly tried to create a bandage for Joseph's head.

"Hey Sailor," she purred, linking her arms through the bars. "Why don't you come over here?" She beckoned him with her finger but all he seemed to do was look in her direction. "What's wrong? Not the shy type, are you?" The sailor still didn't move. "Is that why you won't come over here? Have you never been kissed before?" Her questions were clearly piquing his interest.

"You're wasting your time Jen, a pirate ain't got nothing on a lady like you. He'd be lucky to even get a kiss off you," Tilly called laughing to herself. Trying to provoke him clearly wasn't going as planned.

"Yeah, you're right, he probably couldn't handle me anyway," she replied walking away.

"Hey, I ain't never had no lady turn me down," he said taking a step forward towards them. "Why you interested?"

"A strapping young sailor like yourself?" replied Jenny, she fluttered her eyelashes. "Why wouldn't I? You're handsome, and strong. Something I been looking for in a man." Jenny could see the blush on the sailor's cheeks already, and she wasn't going to stop until he was by the bars. "Why don't cha come over here into the light?"

Jenny heard Roger talking to Tilly as he took over pressing the torn sections of the shirt onto Joseph's head. *God, I hope he's alright*, she wished before continuing her seduction. Turning her head back to the bars she could see that the sailor was now close enough to reach out and grab. A sick feeling started in her belly as she forced a smile and started moving her hands up his chest.

"It's such a shame," she started.

"What is," said the sailor, licking his lips in anticipation.

"That this is how it ends," Jenny smiled as she grabbed hold of the sailor's shirt and yanked him towards the bars. His head hit hard and he stumbled back, but not before Jenny reached for the keys. He fell to the floor like a sack of potatoes and Jenny turned triumphantly to her friends, holding the keys up smiling.

"Right, let's get out of here," said Jenny throwing the keys to Tilly.

23

TILLY

THE SOUND of footsteps turned her excitement into dread. Their time was running out and they needed to get out of there. Tilly ran to the cell's door and tried to unlock it as fast as she could, switching keys every time one of them didn't work. As the footsteps above drew closer Tilly's hands started to fumble. Before she managed to get another key up to the lock a hand enclosed over hers.

"How about I do this sweetheart, it'll be quicker and then we can fight the people coming to make sure we are still here," said Roger with a smile. Jenny nodded behind him and Tilly shrugged her shoulders before moving out of the way. She knew it would be the only way they could get out of there. Without any hesitation, Roger opened the door and gestured for them all to move.

As if, by some kind of miracle, Joseph was now waking up. Jenny was trying to get him to stand not realising.

"Jenny, he's waking up!" Tilly exclaimed.

"Oh, Joseph, are you okay?"

"Yeah, my head hurts. I think I can walk," he said in a few breaths. Tilly slung his arm over Jenny's neck and then started to move away.

"Are you sure you're alright to walk?" asked Tilly, looking at her friends.

"We've got no choice," responded Jenny who was only looking at Joseph. Tilly nodded and moved towards the stairs to see if anyone was visible near the top.

"I think we are going to have to move through the ship to get up on deck. There's a door just through there, but we need to move now before we get ourselves caught again."

Tilly nodded and hooked Joseph's other arm around her neck. Roger was best equipped to fight so it was probably better that her and Jenny helped him walk as his head was still bleeding.

They removed themselves from the brig and started towards the door that led to their safety. Tilly was not used to the weight of a man and seemed to get dragged behind as Jenny pushed forward with most of Joseph's body weight on her.

"Has the ship even been moving while we have been in the brig?" asked Jenny as she struggled to manoeuvre the dead weight of the injured.

"I think so, he's probably taking us to his next location, thankfully that won't be 1712 England," replied Tilly as she fumbled around behind, trying to help.

"Will you two shut up!" Roger hissed at them. "We are trying to make an escape and it's hardly like they won't notice we are missing when they find an empty cell with the door open and an unconscious sailor on the floor."

"Stop snapping at us, it's hardly like we wanted to be in this position," Jenny said mimicking his tone.

"It's your fault we are in this mess," Roger said jabbing his finger through the air at her. "Your crazy ex-boyfriend who really needs a reality check." He stopped himself from saying anything further.

"Well if you're so high and mighty why don't you do something 'Regenty' and make this all go away?"

"Okay stop!" shouted Tilly, she wasn't going to allow them to stop their escape and risk their chances of getting caught. "Right now, we need to keep moving you can bicker when we are safe."

She glared at him as they continued through the door. People started to come down the stairs and Tilly turned her head daring to see who was coming. As her eye caught sight of the first person she was met with Bill's angry face. She backed away and tried to shut the door but stumbled into Jenny, who was struggling to hold Joseph up. Tilly's hand slipped off the handle and Bill's grin got wider.

"What is wrong with you," Roger said as he grabbed her arm. "We need to move, not stare at him." He pulled open the other door to reveal Noah standing there with his arms crossed.

Jenny dropped to the ground with Joseph and cradled his head, looking up at Tilly. Jenny's eyes showed mixed emotions, and Tilly knew she had all but given up. Her heart twang with emotions that she did not know what to do with.

Even if they had gotten up on deck the ship was moving and jumping off wasn't an option when Noah had the telescope. They didn't know exactly what he had planned but Tilly knew it wasn't good and he should be stopped.

"Now where were you guys off to?" asked Noah as he stepped into the room. Tilly turned to see if Bill was coming through the back door, he was. Which meant they were now trapped. "We have cast off so you wouldn't have been able to get off the ship anyway."

Bill came up behind Roger and grabbed both of his arms, pulled them behind his back and tied them up. "Just a necessary precaution, wouldn't want you to try and attack me again," snarled Bill. His voice and face were slightly different than they had been when they were searching for the telescope. Whatever hold Noah had over Bill was back in full force. Tilly wanted to save everyone but right now, she didn't even know if she could save herself.

It wasn't long before they were all back up on deck. Joseph was carried to one of the other cabins which served as the infirmary and Tilly watched as Roger struggled against the sailors who were leading him back down into the brig. Jenny on the other hand, was slouched in a chair, opposite side of the table to Noah, with her arms crossed and a sour expression on her face. The telescope was laid out for all to see and Tilly sensed that Jenny wanted to grab it and run, because it was what she wanted to do too.

"Dear Jennifer, I'm impressed you managed to escape from the brig, but did you forget how good I was in The Collective?" asked Noah after a few moments of silence.

"Don't call me that," was all Jenny replied to his comment. Her eyes looking down at the telescope the entire time. Tilly wasn't sure how to respond or react, she felt helpless to save her friend from her ex-boyfriend's comments. She took a deep breath and waited for Noah to finish what he was saying, although she could feel Bill's eyes burning into the back of her head.

"Oh please, it's your name," Noah continued in response to Jenny. "Now let's see what we can do about you two. You'll both come with me back to the Ilsa de Rosa and then I'll show you exactly what I am capable of. In the meantime, your boys will continue to be locked up and you will only be allowed on deck and in here. Sound fair?" Noah was waving his arms about as he spoke but Tilly wasn't really paying much attention to him. Her focus was on the feeling she had in the back of her head.

"I think you're being absurd." Jenny's voice brought her attention back to the conversation. "What exactly do you expect us to do while you're showing off to everyone?"

"Stand and watch, there's no point in showing off if you won't be viewing it," a smile crept across Noah's face. He lifted a hand and pointed towards the door. A member of the crew Tilly had never seen before walked in with a tray of food and another with plates. The table was made up in silence until Noah told everyone to start eating. Hesitant at first, Tilly only started eating once Noah had. Jenny however, refused to eat anything at all except the bread. She ripped it apart and ate small pieces dunked into the gravy. Tilly couldn't hear exactly what Jenny was mumbling but from the few words she did pick up, if Noah was trying to provoke a reaction from Jenny it had worked.

"How did you get this?" asked Tilly pointing to the gravy.

"I had it brought here especially for us three, just because we are on a ship doesn't mean we should go without," replied Noah stuffing his face with chicken. She looked away from his animal-like eating habits and played with her food. Unsure of what to say Tilly stayed silent whilst she ate her food.

"Seriously, what the hell do you want Noah?" asked Jenny as she threw her bread onto the table. Tilly's eyes widened at her outburst but she stayed silent and allowed Jenny to carry on.

"I want justice, I want us to be the new head of The Collective, and I don't want any more questions about it."

"So you're not going to tell us anything," Jenny pouted. Tilly almost laughed but now was not the time to be amused. They were having a serious discussion and Tilly felt like a third wheel. "That's just great. We are expected to just go along with your plan and hope you don't ruin everything."

"Now just hold on a second little dove," Noah started before Jenny cut him off.

"Don't start with the little dove crap Noah. Finish your food and get out. I'm tired," Jenny held her head and closed her eyes. A wave of tiredness came over Tilly as she finished her drink. She couldn't explain it but something tasted wrong.

"Fine," Noah stood and stormed off, as the servers came and took the plates away. Tilly watched, barely able to move, as Jenny stumbled to the door to lock it.

"Jen," Tilly's voice cut off as she fell to the floor. The only thing she could do was crawl to the bed before the lights went out.

৫১৩

When Tilly awoke, she was cold. The blankets that had once been over her now lay on the floor and Jenny was entangled in them. As she sat up she realised the swaying of the ship had come to a stop, they were no longer moving. Her eyes were still blurry with sleep as she clutched her throbbing head. *What the hell has he done to us?* Trying to stand up, and avoid stepping on Jenny, she crept around her to the table. Something to steady her.

Reaching the table Tilly knew that there was something wrong. Outside was quiet, too quiet and there was warm air coming out from underneath the door. They had to have been asleep for more than one day. Her hand lifted to the handle but a sound made her turn around. Jenny had rolled into the table leg but was still asleep, much to Tilly's relief. Although why Jenny hadn't awoken after hitting her head she didn't know. Must be the fact that Tilly barely ate or drank from their meal.

Bringing her attention back to the door and the silence that lay behind it, Tilly couldn't help herself as her hand reached towards the handle. Pushing it she found the door was locked. She tried the door again but was met with the same outcome, Noah didn't trust them not to leave the cabin. She slammed both her hands on the door in rage. How dare he do this to them? Not only had he somehow managed to convince her that going on an adventure was something she should do, he also let her believe she could be a captain. Even if it was just a fleeting second before the need for home had set in. She'd played along with his game and now he had won.

Tears formed in her eyes as a wash of shame came over her. *How could I have fallen for this?* Wiping her eyes, she glanced behind her to see if Jenny was still sleeping, she was. At least for now she was, Tilly knew she wouldn't be after she started rifling through all the drawers in there again. She rushed over to the drawer where she had found the list of artefacts before. To her dismay inside the drawer was nothing but the odds and ends she had seen in there before. Slamming the drawer shut she took no care to avoid waking Jenny.

"What are you doing?" croaked Jenny from her curled up state on the floor. She flicked her blanket off her head revealing puffy eyes and messy hair. "Seriously, do you need to make all that noise?"

"Well we are locked in," replied Tilly turning to face her sleepy friend. "Good god, you need to look in a mirror or something. Do you always look like this in the mornings?"

Flashing Tilly a dirty look Jenny pulled the blanket back over her head.

"Oh, I'm kidding," pouted Tilly, trying to pull the blanket off

Jenny's head. "We are, however, locked inside the cabin and its completely silent outside." This caught Jenny's attention and Tilly successfully yanked the cover from her head. "We need to think of how to get out of here."

"Well we won't do anything like this," Jenny said, flinging her arms up in the air and smoothing her hair as she brought them down. "Good job I kept a few of these then." Jenny pulled a hair band off her wrist and held it up.

"Well let's hope no other ladies see you with one otherwise you might change the future, again," laughed Tilly.

"This whole escapade could change the future T," Jenny turned serious. Tilly wasn't sure what to say back and just stared at her friend. "The littlest things can make the biggest difference though. Especially if they haven't been invented yet."

Jenny tied up her hair, and Tilly ripped a bit of fabric off her shirt to tie over the hairband. Now that they were both awake, Tilly got them searching the cabin. For Harvey—or Noah, as he truly was—to lock them in there either he didn't want them to know or he wasn't ready for them to see what he was planning yet. His boasting had suggested to Tilly that all he wanted to do was show off his power.

Jenny was emptying the contents of the draws on the floor, rifling through them, and then replacing them back. Tilly had ransacked the two chests in the back by the windows but neither of them were having any luck finding anything that related to what Noah now planned to do, or a key to get them out of their prison, and she was becoming increasingly frustrated. The top of the chest slammed down which made Jenny jump. As Tilly turned to move onto the next section of the cabin a figure appeared in the glass of the door.

The figure moved closer to the door and the faint click could be heard as it was unlocked. Tilly felt frozen as she watched them open and Noah, followed closely by his shadow Bill, entered. They both instinctively took a step back as Noah and Bill walked closer towards them. Tilly swore she heard Jenny gulp.

Neither of them said anything, it was almost like a standoff and Tilly didn't like it. Confrontation had never been her strong suit, unless she was acting and that was now long over.

"Come along, we have arrived and now it's time to show you what I am doing," said Noah as he waved his arm up. Two of his other shadows moved into the room and grabbed both of them by the shoulder. Tilly tried to resist but was slapped firmly in the face. Pain radiated and she knew her cheek would be red from the mark.

"I'll deal with you later." Noah's face was dark and she couldn't tell if he was talking to her or the man that had hit her. Either way, something told her she didn't want to find out.

They were led outside the cabin and Tilly knew they were back at the island as soon as she saw her surroundings. A weird sensation came over her, as every step they took to finding out what Noah was planning was another step towards confusion. His actions didn't make any sense. Her cheek still burned from the slap her handler gave but she refused to let any emotion show in her face, even if it was difficult to hide it.

With their hands behind their back they were both marched off the ship and into the mountain.

24
JENNY

JENNY KNEW this didn't feel right. Coming in a different way on the island was easier than the last time she was here. There was no mist here so she didn't have to worry about anyone going missing. Whatever happened to the ones who disappeared? she thought.

"Hey," Tilly's voice pulled her from her thoughts. "Are you okay?"

Jenny nodded but stayed silent, she couldn't find words and she didn't want to talk about Noah. They had all walked together, or in her case got pushed forward every couple of steps, and it had taken some self-control for her to not turn around and scream at the sailor who kept prodding her in the back. Jenny could tell that Tilly wasn't looking forward to what was coming next. They were both scared and confused.

With both the boys left on the ship, guarded, a sense of feeling exposed had come over Jenny, as if Joseph and Roger were somehow their protectors. Her affections were small, and she knew there was no chance of anything growing between them. A silly crush was not going to change anything, plus, with the ever-changing emotions for Noah, things could get quite complicated. She still kicked herself for allowing him to control her like that.

They followed a path as they walked back to the hidden loot cave in the mountain. The trees swayed in the light Caribbean breeze as they walked. The guy prodding her back was getting on her last nerve and if he did it one more time she was going to cause a commotion and fall over. Just as she finished the thought his hand jabbed into her back and she cried out. Pretending to trip on something was easy, ending up on the floor was not and with her hands behind her back she hit her cheek on the ground.

"What the hell is going on?" Noah called from the front as he turned to see Jenny on the floor. "Get her up!"

"He kept pushing me and then I tripped," Jenny complained as she was pulled up, Tilly's face was a picture of shock and anger. Jenny's cheek burned and she knew it would be grazed, if not bleeding. Before she had a chance to do or say anything else Tilly interjected.

"Look at what he has done to her Noah," she exclaimed. Jenny could see she was trying to make this more dramatic than it needed to be. "I thought you weren't going to hurt us?!"

In response to Tilly's accusations he walked over to the brute that had been pushing Jenny and smacked him in the face. "Touch them again and I'll cut off your hands." Jenny shivered, he was definitely more scary than she had ever thought possible. It was strange seeing him like this, and she noticed that Tilly must be feeling the same way, as she was looking down playing with the dirt on the floor with her foot.

"Let's keep moving, we're nearly there. Then I can show my girls exactly what I needed this telescope for," he cackled like an evil villain in a movie, this didn't help Jenny's feelings towards him. She had started to feel quite sick.

Inside the villain's lair, as she liked to think of it, was more than she could have ever imagined. Everywhere was just filled with loot, gold and jewels. Jenny could see from Tilly's face that she was less than impressed, considering this was her second time in here Jenny assumed Tilly wasn't that surprised to see it all again. They didn't stop until they reached the stairs and started the ascent to the top. That's when things got interesting.

Up at the top, Jenny noted that they were on the cliff and that it wasn't a cliff at all but a volcano. One side was a curved edge, the other like a slant, almost as if it had been built, instead of being formed by nature. The view from the top was beautiful but that was overshadowed by the malevolent look on Noah's face. Jenny was still behind held by the brute that had pushed her to the floor, although he hadn't jabbed her in the back since Noah slapped him, and Tilly was being manhandled by another pirate but he seemed to be less forceful. He only had a grip on Tilly's hands. Their only saving grace was that they hadn't decided to tie their hands up, they were just being held, quite firmly, by the men manoeuvring them. Once they stopped Jenny tried to do some quick thinking on what their next moves should be, but as Noah pulled the telescope out from underneath his cloak her mind went blank.

All she could hear was the hum drawing her to it, and a nagging feeling in her gut to stay away from it. She watched as he split it in two and took out some of the cogs. Bill had retrieved some other objects and handed them to Noah as he went to work building a new artefact. Just out of her peripheral vision, Jenny heard a grunt and turned her head away from the draw of the telescope.

Tilly had used all of her weight and slammed her foot into the foot of her holder and smacked the back of her head into his as he bent over, causing him to let go. Jenny watched in awe as she then pulled out a sword and began swinging. As he didn't have his sword out most of his moves were just to avoid being cut by hers. Taking advantage of everyone staring at the spectacle Tilly had created, Jenny tried to pull away from "the jabber," a name she had taken to call Noah's henchman who seemed to enjoy stabbing her in the back with his hand to move her forward. Unfortunately, he had a tight grip and so she had to fling herself back causing their heads to collide and then, before the pain erupted, kicked her leg out behind her in the hopes that she would meet his groin. She did.

This caused him to let go of her hands and bend over. Jenny

glanced across at Noah who, although clearly wanting to focus all his attention on his objects, was averting his gaze from Tilly to her. His face scrunched into a confused expression and he took a step forward. Without thinking Jenny grabbed hold of the jabber's hair and smashed his face into her knee, just like Harvey had taught her to do, and then let him fall to the floor. She hoped that would keep him down long enough for her and Tilly to stop this madness. Spinning on her heels she was met with Bill, who was two steps away from her.

"I always knew you would be trouble, Jennifer," he said, his voice heavily accented. "How you didn't recognise me I'll never know. I guess Noah's magical charms work better than I ever anticipated."

"What are you talking about Bill?" she asked stepping away from him as he stepped closer, keeping him at a two step distance.

"Never were the bright one," he mocked. "Technically I didn't lie to you, before I start because you'll assume I have. That was my brother you saw hit me and I am sending him money, just not for the reasons I told you." *That's still a lie*, thought Jenny not wanting to interrupt him. "Let me take this ring off and then you'll see my face." Bill slipped off the ring and Jenny watched his face distort before returning to a face she recognised, and knew, but not for any of the right reasons. Standing before her was Charles Randall, a Collective Regent, one of the three who had sent her there. Before she knew it her hands were covering her mouth, "Oh my god."

"Wait, there's two rings?" Jenny heard Tilly mutter. The thought never even crossed Jenny's mind.

"I'm actually not from 2015, like you are, I simply reside there for my job. My brother lives here, with my family and they need money. Although he spends it all before they get anything. I questioned him and he punched me. He might be my little brother but as I'm the oldest I am the one who has to provide."

"How?" was all Jenny managed to squeak out, she was still in shock at seeing him here. By this time Tilly had her opponent on the floor with her sword against his throat. He was staring at Bill just as Tilly was, they both looked shocked.

"I'm not as old as they tell you I am," he said looking to the floor slightly annoyed that she didn't understand. How could she? Her mind was being full of all this information and none of it was making any sense.

"Why?" croaked Jenny. "What's your reason for doing this?"

"Chair Regent Matthews."

"What? Stop being so cryptic and just answer the question," demanded Jenny.

"He's my father, and because I wasn't wanted I was kicked out to be with my mother. Who happens to be from this era, so getting back at him is what I want to do most. Noah is just part of that plan," he explained.

It seemed there was nothing left to say and an awkward moment of silence hung in the air before Noah sliced it with the sound of metal breaking. He had successfully pulled apart the telescope and was attaching what could only be described as half a gasket to the front of it.

"What the hell is he doing?" demanded Tilly as she pulled the sword closer to her captive's throat. Jenny's eyes widened as her mind snapped back to what was happening. While Charles was distracted and looking in Tilly's direction, who was now clearly not opposed to hurting the man she had her sword against, Jenny ran at Noah and tackled him to the floor. They both landed with a grunt and a clatter of objects.

"No," Tilly said through gritted teeth as Bill went to move. "Stay where you are or this guy gets it."

"You're not really going to kill him are you dear?" he said in response, clearly not bothered by her threat. Jenny wrestled with Noah on the ground until he finally let go of the telescope. She kicked him before standing up and facing them.

"I don't think you want to find out what he's made her capable of, Regent." Jenny spat the last word as if it was poison on her lips. She knew she was lying, sure Tilly could fight with a sword now but she was still no killer.

THE COLLECTIVE

They all stood in silence and waited to see who would make the first move. With quick glances to each person Jenny launched the telescope in the air, aiming towards the centre of the volcano. She didn't know if it was active but at least no-one would be wanting to go down there. She received an elbow to the chest as Noah tried to stop her, hit her right where her heart was, and she fell back as Tilly launched forward drawing the sword across her captive's throat. A scream erupted from her mouth and Jenny and the sailor both hit the floor.

Jenny landed on her knees, her hand pressed against her chest, like it would relieve some of the pain. Before her was the sailor, eyes wide, laid on his side with blood pouring out of his neck. Tilly was whimpering now.

"See what he's done to her," said Jenny loud enough for the Regent to hear. "You allowed this. His blood is on your hands."

"No-one was meant to die, the colours, they're all wrong," the Regent clutched his head as he spoke, realisation washing over him. "What have you done?" The question wasn't directed at anyone in particular although Noah was the one who answered. Jenny switched on her implant and was shocked by what surrounded her.

"This isn't my doing. It's not my fault you couldn't resist the pull of the objects, not even Jenny can. How the hell am I supposed to get the telescope back?" Noah slapped Jenny across the face, and walked over to the corpse kicking him off of the edge. Jenny screamed at the hit, which snapped Tilly out of her sorrow, as she stood raising her sword. Fresh blood was still dripping from the tip.

"Touch her again and I'll cut off your hand," she said, her face red and puffy. Jenny didn't know what to do, she had to think of a plan.

"Now, now little lady, let's not do anything we might regret," Noah spoke slowly so to not provoke her anymore. Jenny knew it was all just for show, the second he could turn this around to be about him and his taking over The Collective he would. "How about this, you put down your sword, I don't touch Jenny again, and Charles goes down the volcano and fetches my telescope?"

"No," Tilly shouted, taking a step forward, sword still raised. Using her other arm, she pointed towards the Regent. "He isn't going anywhere and neither are you. Take us back to the ship and take us home. Then you can do whatever the hell you like." Jenny could see the desperation in Tilly's eyes. All that was on her mind now was home.

"I can't do that," said Noah. Jenny felt the coin shaped broach in her pocket. She wanted to go home too, and she wanted Harvey, the real Harvey. He'd know exactly how to calm the situation down and get exactly what he wanted. He always was a charmer. Returning her attention back to the silent standoff she decided to have twenty seconds of courage and be the one to take over.

"I have a solution," she announced. "Let's all calm down for starters. Tilly, lower your sword." Tilly did as she was asked, but kept it unsheathed by her side as Jenny continued. "You can't get your telescope from up here, so is there another way to get it back?"

"You're the one who threw it down there, and now you want me to tell you how to get it?" asked Noah. "Why so you can throw it into another bottomless pit?"

"Well you could not tell me, leave it there and we can all be stuck here?" she said sarcastically. "Is that what you really want?"

She didn't really know why she was helping Noah, she supposed in her own mind it was the easiest option to keep him thinking they were all on the same side. Everyone seemed to agree with her, although no one spoke, they all seemed to nod slightly and started to move towards the stairs that led back down into the volcano.

Jenny made Noah and Charles go first, for an older gentleman Charles seemed to be able to walk at a faster pace than expected. Once back inside the cave Jenny wondered if there would be a chance to get away. She could see Tilly was still distressed over what had just happened, her face was white as a ghost, and so

THE COLLECTIVE

tried to keep to herself. Her mind was filled with the image of the man's throat being cut and him lying there bleeding to death. How Noah could just roll him off the edge and walk away? It made her want to be sick. Noah and Charles walked to the far end of the treasure-filled lair and opened another door. From what Jenny could see, as she was standing quite far back from them, it looked like it was the inside of the volcano.

It wasn't quite what she was expecting, as it wasn't like a volcano at all, and from the look on Tilly's face she didn't either. Inside the volcano, there was nothing. Just a pit that spanned the whole of the mountain. It was like someone had just taken out the middle. Taking a step forward Jenny tried to look in further, but quickly turned away horrified at the sight. The body they had pushed over the edge had landed on top of the telescope which was now peaking out from under his side.

As quickly as she had stepped forward she took a step back, trying to avert her gaze from the body. Putting a comforting arm around Tilly, Jenny tried to move her away from the scene. She'd already cut his throat Tilly didn't need to see him lifeless too.

"We will get out of this soon. Then we will be home," whispered Jenny. Turning her gaze back to Noah and the Regent, she tried to concentrate on them. Noah obviously didn't want to touch the body lying on the ground and kept asking Charles to do it, although he refused as well.

"It's all starting to scare me now," said Tilly in a whisper quieter than Jenny had spoken. The boys were still inside the pit talking. "It was kind of fun when I was playing captain, it was like a game, but this is no game and I don't want to play anymore."

Jenny didn't look at Tilly as she was speaking. Instead her eyes were locked on Noah and Charles. They were whispering to each other and it unnerved her. Eventually Noah stepped forward and pulled the telescope free from the body.

"Brilliant," Noah muttered. "I had hoped this was all going to be a bit cleaner."

"I'm sorry, what?" Jenny was angry again. "You thought it was going to be cleaner? You thought kidnapping my friend to get me to come here and trying to take over The Collective was going to be cleaner? Why did you think you wouldn't get any obstruction from me?"

"Because you love me," Noah said instantly. "And they took your parents as well as mine." There was something familiar and cold about the look in Noah's eyes that made her skin crawl.

"You're insane," stated Tilly.

"You know, come to think of it Jenny, you're right," Noah crossed his arms, still holding the telescope. "This was a bad plan. Come on Charles, we better get going."

"Wait, you can't just leave us here," Jenny shouted as she followed them out to the beach. "Seriously Noah!" She could tell he wasn't having any of it and as soon as they hit the beach he turned to them.

"You two are staying here and we are leaving. I know you'll find a way home." He kicked up some sand so they shielded their eyes and once it had cleared he was on his way back to the ship.

"What did you ever see in him?" asked Tilly, folding her arms and slumping down into the sand.

"Don't just sit there, we have to catch them!" It was only then Jenny realised she only needed Roger. "Wait are the boys still on the ship?" Tilly nodded. "Crap. We have to go and get them or we are stuck here." Jenny started to make her way to the water. What had she seen in Noah that made her have a relationship with him for a year. Whatever it was made her feel special, and comfortable. It led her to invite him to stay for dinner and tell him about the girl in the library. This was all her fault.

25
TILLY

STANDING on the beach staring out at the ship they were supposed to be on was not how Tilly thought this would end. The ship wasn't too far out, they probably could swim to it if they tried, provided Noah didn't get there first and sail away. Jenny was already wading into the sea but Noah was in a row boat, obviously, he would get there first.

"Jenny get back here, you'll never make it before they do!" She called from the water's edge. To Tilly's relief, Jenny turned around. Noah's little boat was now at the side of the ship and Tilly could see them climbing on deck. Now it was anyone's guess what was happening but a wooden plank was pushed out from the deck.

"Oh, my god, is that a plank?" asked Jenny

"I think so, it's hard to tell from here," Tilly replied. Both girls had their eyes peeled on the scene that was unfolding in front of them. "Why would they need one?"

"Who else are they going to make walk a plank? Obviously, Joseph and Roger." Jenny's voice was sarcastic. Like Tilly should have known that.

"Wait, Jenny isn't that someone now?" asked Tilly pointing to the deck. All they could see was someone walking out onto the plank, their hands were folded in front of them. Two other people stood at the end of the plank and were refusing to let the person back on the ship. Eventually the first person walked to the end of the plank and jumped into the sea. Moments later they emerged close to shore. It was Roger and his hands were bound.

"Well now what are we going to do?" asked Tilly as she walked over to Roger and unbound his hands. Jenny now sat shivering from the cold breeze that had rolled in while Roger was just staring into the distance. Tilly could see from the look on Jenny's face that she was wounded by Noah's decision to leave them on shore, and even more so now that there was definitely no chance of getting back on the ship. "I guess we've probably changed so much of history we will have to come back and rescue ourselves, right?!"

"I think we will be just fine," replied Roger who was now smiling at the ship sailing away. He didn't seem phased by the cold breeze at all and was rooted to the ground. He didn't even look around to see if they were both listening to him. "He's doing a good job."

Neither of the girls had a bloody clue what this supposed Regent was going on about but as Tilly turned to the ship she saw the chaos that was happening on deck.

"What the hell is happening on there?" she asked not expecting an answer, because how could any of them know?

"It's okay, I think Joseph set up the gunpowder, it'll blow up the ship and then there will be no more problems. The Collective will have nothing to change and we won't be punished," said Roger smiling at Tilly.

"What?! You can't just blow up a ship Roger!" Jenny yelled.

"Why not?" he countered, "She did!" He was pointing at Tilly. He was right, she had blown up a ship but that one didn't have a crew. There was everything wrong about this. Tilly saw her friends face scrunch up, clearly showing her dislike for him.

"That does not mean you can do it too!" countered Jenny, crossing her arms. "I knew I didn't trust you for a reason. You don't even act like a Regent."

THE COLLECTIVE

"I still don't see why what I did was any different," he said raising his eyebrows.

"That's not the point. Tilly didn't blow up one with people still on it!" She was yelling louder now and had come closer to them both. "He needs to be taken back to The Collective and tried and put in prison and..."

Tilly placed a hand on her back, Jenny was sobbing now. Tilly could only imagine how emotionally conflicted she was. How on earth were you supposed to feel, after you had been tricked by your ex-boyfriend and then watched as the ship he was on blew up. Although Jenny hated him, Tilly knew that the feelings from their relationship never truly left her friend. Her eyes began to water. With a deep breath, she held in most of the tears and pulled herself together.

"They all know Jenny, we can't let that be in the history pages. Joseph agreed that if one of us was to stay behind they would try and blow the ship up. A small sacrifice for the good of the world."

"So, you're just going to change everything and screw up the future?! What if this causes a huge ripple through time? What if everything isn't the same when we go back? What if Joseph was meant for something more?" Although still sobbing she managed to yell through the tears.

"Turn your implant on and look."

Tilly watched as Jenny's hand moved up to her ear and pressed the button. Although she would never know what they saw, she imagined that once it was active Jenny would see what Roger was referring too and calm down. There was nothing Tilly could do, she felt like a spare limb being out of the loop.

"It's too late to stop it anyway isn't it?"

"Yes, I think so," replied Roger. Tilly dropped to the sand. There was no way to make her friend feel better about losing someone who decided to sacrifice themselves, but they had to stop a madman. A decision like that wasn't done lightly. Especially when Noah was looking for a way to fix the telescope. He had seemed rather sure of himself too. Jenny turned away from the beach just as the ship exploded. It wasn't that far away which made the sound almost deafening.

"Well what do we do now?" asked Tilly breaking the silence that had fallen between them after the ship was nothing more than a floating pile of burning wood. "I mean we are stuck on this island, it's not like we are going to find something to get us home here, are we?"

"You don't know that," said Jenny. "We just need to find a Regent, with the other half of this." Tilly furrowed her brow as her friend dug deep into her pocket. Jenny pulled out a broach and held it in the palm of her hand as she showed them.

"What does that do?" asked Tilly. *Seriously? How is this going to get us home?* She thought.

"Wait," Jenny said suddenly, closing her hand and pointing at Roger. "You're a Regent."

Tilly was even more confused now. "I don't understand," she said, realising unless she asked she wasn't going to get the answers she needed. "Can one of you please explain?"

"You already knew I was a Regent, what more do you need?" replied Roger trying to be humorous. This only caused Jenny to kick sand at him.

"It means," Jenny pulled herself up to standing with Rogers help. "We can use this to get home."

Roger took it from her hands and examined it. Flipping it over in his hands, he too got something out of his own pocket that looked similar. "I guess they didn't tell you this was only one half of the broach, right?"

"No, what do you mean one half?" Jenny answered with slight worry in her voice. "They told me to take this to a Regent and they would get us home. Did they not tell me everything?"

"I forgot I even had this on me," he said not looking up at her. "I guess I thought I must've traded it for a keg of rum or something stupid. I never was one for trinkets. I just need to figure out if ours will go together. Then I might be able to get us out of here." Tilly was watching this exchange almost like it was on TV. She felt so distant from the world of The Collective, yet she was already so far in it, wondering if she would ever become a part of it. *Or is there something they do to people who aren't supposed to know?*

"I just... need to find... got it," continued Roger as he clicked the two pieces together. "Two Regents are required to access a time tunnel as normally they wouldn't be without these." He held up the broaches that together made a complete emblem of The Collective compass symbol. "Time to go home?" Both the girls nodded in unison.

"It's definitely time to go home," replied Jenny. Tilly felt like she didn't have any words left to say. She was glad she was going home, but could she really forget what had happened here? They'd all changed, and done things Tilly never thought she would do in a million years.

"Well this is it," Jenny said as she took Tilly's hand.

Tilly looked to either side of her. She had always wanted an adventure but she didn't expect it to turn out like this. Being kidnapped and taken to the past, becoming a pirate captain, even if that part was all for show, being in a mutiny and stopping Noah from finding artefacts to take down The Collective with. Although they hadn't intended to blow the ship up with him on it, they didn't have any other choice. It was an adventure, but now she was to return home to 2015. Jenny, Roger, and herself.

It still amazed her that Roger had managed to keep his identity hidden from her. She had spent nearly all her time with him and he never once gave any clues as to who he was, that is until Jenny arrived. They would deal with any other incidences when they got back.

Tilly squeezed Jenny's hand. You didn't need to hold hands to travel through the time tunnel but it was a comfort to know it was over and they were going home. This whole ordeal had strengthened their friendship, and Tilly knew she wasn't going to let Jenny just leave her when she got back home. How do you start ignoring someone or not knowing them after you've commanded an entire crew of pirates and beaten a mutual enemy together?

"Let's go home," she said smiling at Jenny, "I have a dissertation to write and I think I know exactly what to put in it now. No more William Kidd, it's all about The Solitaire."

Tilly winked at her and they both laughed, even Roger joined in and chuckled with a cheeky grin. He threw the completed broach onto the ground and the light began to dim as the time tunnel started to open. The next few hours were surely not going to go well. Unsure of how these situations get sorted Tilly had a feeling she would be getting to meet the Regents while they deliberated on what to do with her.

As they walked through the time tunnel Tilly realised it was different than her original voyage through time. She couldn't quite put her finger on the reason why as they walked through, but coming out the other end she realised very quickly something was wrong. Tilly looked round at where they had come out. They were in 2015 but they were nowhere near Stawford. Worse still, Roger hadn't come out of the tunnel with them.

As panic started to set in, Tilly noticed Jenny was frantically trying to get her ring off her finger.

"Tilly, I need to get this off," Tilly could hear the panic in Jenny's voice.

"Suck your finger," Tilly blurted out.

"How is that remotely helpful Tilly?!" Jenny exclaimed.

"Trust me, suck your finger, if it's wet the ring will be easier to slide off," she said as she grabbed hold of a hopping Jenny. She did exactly as Tilly had told her to. As Tilly expected it slid off, however, Jenny did not look okay.

"What is it?" she asked.

"It's like a sort of communicator and tracking device all wrapped into one, but it wasn't working," Jenny looked up at Tilly. She raised her eyebrows at Jenny, indicating she needed more information. "All recruits wear them. I've had mine on for so long I forgot I was even wearing it. When they stop working they get hot, like burning hot."

"Is it alright now?" Although it wasn't much of an explanation, Tilly was hopeful that in time all the different things that go on in The Collective would be explained to her.

"I don't know," came Jenny's weak reply but as she finished speaking the ring buzzed to life.

"Maybe it just needed a little time to adjust to being back in 2015?" Tilly offered as some form of comfort. Jenny smiled in return but the fear was still in her eyes.

While Jenny was on her 'ringer', as Tilly was now going to call it, she looked around and tried to work out where they were. It wasn't too hot or too cold so the good thing was they hadn't been dumped in some kind of desolate land area. The sun was shining and Tilly noticed something glinting in the light. Closer inspection revealed it was the symbol that had created the tunnel. *Strange*, thought Tilly, *this is here but we are so disorientated and Roger is missing*.

"Hola Señora," called someone. "¿Estás perdido?"

"Ha-Habla usted Inglés?" she replied trying to think of how to say what she needed to. It had been years since she'd spoken Spanish.

"Si," replied the old lady, "I'm Isabella, what are you doing out here in my field?"

"Uh, we went for a walk and kind of got a little lost! Are we far from the town?"

"Tilly!" Jenny called. "Oh, hello. Nice to meet you," Jenny stuck her hand out to shake Isabella's. "We should get going, our lift will be here soon."

"Okay," Isabella didn't look convinced by Tilly's 'getting lost' story. "The path to the town is that way. You'd be surprised how many tourists get lost. Try not to wander from it again and you'll get back to the town."

"Thank you," Tilly said waving as Isabella walked back down the hill.

"Who was that?" asked Jenny.

"A lady called Isabella, she was speaking to me in Spanish to begin with," replied Tilly. "Are we actually in Spain?"

"Yeah, so they told me," Jenny nodded and held up her communicator ring. "I wonder where Roger went?" Jenny's voice trailed off as she kept her thoughts in her head and Tilly looked out at the horizon. *This is just the beginning.*

To Be Continued…

ACKNOWLEDGMENTS

This book would not be here today if it weren't for the people I surrounded myself with.

I'd like to thank my wonderful editor, Ashley Carlson. She showed me that although I thought my writing was rubbish at times, when someone else reads it with fresh eyes they can come to love every word. I need to thank Victoria, from Victoria Cooper Art. I had a hard time trying to find the perfect cover and yet she effortlessly portrayed the story perfectly.

To Rachael and Laura, who encouraged and stuck by me through all my tantrums, and moaning. Who picked me up when all I wanted to do was throw the book in the bin, we writers are stronger together & I will always support you as you supported me.

The beta's who gave me endless feedback to make this book the best it could be - thank you.

To my boyfriend, I can't thank you enough for being there for me. My brothers, who supported my love for writing and encouraged me to keep going.

My friends who gave me endless encouragement and told me to never give up my dreams. The ones who contended with my endless whining, and constant questions. And for reading my work numerous times to make sure I could publish something perfect for my readers.

I also need to thank, Mia and Aunty Dianne. Thank you for reading my book, helping take it to the next level. Remove Boat and make it Ship and allowing me to have the courage to publish!

This book is dedicated to my parents because they always allowed me to follow my dreams. When I wanted to be like Temperance Brennan they helped me get into university. It turned out uni wasn't for me and they encouraged me to do what I felt right, even if they meant coming home and ruining their peace. I know they are proud of me, and will always stand by me and for that, this first piece of work that I have created is for them. Thank you, for being the best parents a girl could ask for.

Finally, to you my reader, thank you for taking the time to read my labor of love. I hope you enjoyed it, and I'll be eagerly awaiting your reviews, tweets, or comments about it, while I write the sequel for you. Hopefully, this one won't take me quite as long to write, edit and publish.

ABOUT THE AUTHOR

Rhianne Williams, formally known as RS Williams, writes Fantasy and Adventure novels. She is the author of THE COLLECTIVE series and is currently working on books two and three, along with a fantasy trilogy, THE KANE SAGA. She lives in Southwest England, with her boyfriend and two cats.

As an avid reader Rhianne has always been in love with the written word and the emotions a good story can create. Her favourite genres are young adult, science fiction, fantasy and contemporary romance. Rhianne has a blog offering budding authors writing advice, inspiration, ways to live a balanced lifestyle, and book reviews of her most recent reads.

She is still employed full-time at her day job and writes in the mornings and on weekends. When she's not writing, you can find her catching plot bunnies, lost in the latest television programme or snuggled on the sofa with a good book.

For more information:
www.littlenovelist.com
littlenovelist@outlook.com

Printed in Poland
by Amazon Fulfillment
Poland Sp. z o.o., Wrocław